HERES

REBORN

EVENT SERIES

COLLECTION ONE

D0932999

HER○ES

REBORN

EVENT SERIES

COLLECTION ONE

DAVID BISHOP
TIMOTHY ZAHN
STEPHEN BLACKMOORE

Titan BOOKS

Heroes Reborn: Collection One
ISBN: 9781785652707

Published by Titan Books
A division of Titan Publishing Group Ltd
144 Southwark St, London SE1 0UP

First edition: March 2016
10 9 8 7 6 5 4 3 2

This edition published by arrangement with Bastei LLC,
Santa Monica, USA

TITANBOOKS.COM

HEROES

REBORN

EVENT SERIES

BOOK ONE
BRAVE NEW WORLD

DAVID BISHOP

PROLOGUE

*Are we defined by that which makes us great—our
ability to think, to hope, to love? Or are we doomed
to answer to our weaknesses—our tendency to fear,
to torment, to hate? In the end, perhaps it is both.
For what is mankind if not a host of contradictions?*
— extract from *Escalating Evolution* by
Mohinder Suresh (unpublished)

ODESSA, TEXAS — TWELVE MONTHS AGO

It was a beautiful summer day as the monarch butterfly
fluttered across the park, its orange and black wings a
majestic sight in the sunshine. It flew just above the lush
grass, flitting here and there before coming to rest on a
park bench. The butterfly paused to bend and flex its wings,
soaking up the mid-morning warmth.

Someone else was on the bench, close to where the butterfly
had landed. Noah Bennet looked every inch the company
man in his grey suit and tie, wearing an old-fashioned pair of
horn-rimmed glasses. He had an apple in one hand, uncertain
whether to start eating. People had been gathering for hours.
The summit was due to start at eleven. Once it was underway,
he'd get few chances to eat for a while.

Bennet sunk his teeth into the apple while checking his watch. 10:33—not long now. A shadow fell across him, prompting Bennet to look up. A tall, dark-skinned man loomed over him. Known simply as "the Haitian" within Primatech, many feared his rare ability. Bennet considered Rene an ally, a trusted friend within the company. But that didn't stop him from demanding answers as soon as Rene joined him on the bench.

"Is she here?"

Rene feigned hurt at his brusqueness. "What, no 'hello', no 'how have you been'? We've been friends for too long, Noah."

Bennet had little time for niceties. "Sorry, I'm just—"

"She's on her way. But she wanted me to talk to you first. To prepare you."

"For what?"

"This rift between you and Claire—it's not healthy," Rene replied. Father and daughter had not spoken in years, their relationship like a wound that never seemed to heal. Bennet knew the Haitian was holding something back about Claire, but didn't push it—yet. Instead he gestured toward the nearby Primatech facility.

"Why do you think I helped put this summit together? People have come here from all over the world—"

"Sure," Rene cut in, "to decide how people like me are supposed to live our lives. Where we can work, who we can marry."

"We all just want what's best," Bennet insisted, aware how weak that sounded.

Rene shook his head. "History is full of people who thought they knew what was best for others..." He rose from the bench, adjusting his jacket.

Bennet knew his friend was right, but he still had high

hopes. The summit was a fresh start for all of humanity—evolved or not. But it also had a bleaker potential, should those involved fail to grasp this opportunity to embrace the future. They had to make the summit work, for the sake of all those like Claire. Thinking about her brought Bennet back to Rene's unexplained remark. "What is it that she wanted you to prepare me for?"

The Haitian opened his mouth to reply, but again avoided giving a direct answer. "Like I said, she'll be here." He strolled off, heading away from Primatech, where a temporary stadium capable of holding thousands had been erected.

"Aren't you going in?" Bennet called after him.

"Never been much of a joiner."

Bennet smiled at that before taking a fresh bite of apple. He got up and strode toward Primatech headquarters, leaving his half-eaten snack on the bench.

The summit had attracted dignitaries and news media from around the world. Three days of discussions about evolved humans had also proven to be a magnet for spectators and protestors alike, forcing Primatech to double and then redouble its security detail. The whole event had blossomed in scale beyond all expectations, turning into a gathering unlike anything Odessa had ever seen.

Most people were kept outside the perimeter—especially any protestors—but those with powers and their families were allowed into the company grounds. Even with entry restricted, a temporary grandstand was still needed to accommodate everyone. Bennet moved through the throng, marvelling at how many had made the journey to be part of this unique moment. It was Woodstock for Evos.

A troop of dancers was performing for the crowd, shape-shifting as they twirled and spun, a rhythmic display of awe-inspiring abilities. Bennet admired their talents until his attention was attracted by a teenage girl dressed as a cheerleader. For a moment, until reality kicked in, he thought she was Claire. Nearly a decade had passed since his daughter last wore that uniform, cheering for other people's achievements from the side-lines. She was a grown woman now.

Bennet passed a father buying popcorn. Behind him, a giggling five-year-old boy was floating up into the air unaided. Bennet was about to call out a warning, but then realized that the boy was tethered by a cord. The father nonchalantly pulled his son back down to earth. Turning aside, Bennet almost bumped into someone invisible when a hipster with a goatee materialized out of thin air.

Ahead of Bennet a couple ambled by arm in arm, their young son skipping in front of them, a firecracker of excitement. Bennet watched the father, who was beaming with pride. Fifty years ago, the fact that this couple was interracial would have been remarkable. Now it was probably the most ordinary thing about them. Bennet pressed on, passing a row of TV reporters talking to cameras about the imminent summit, their different accents and languages proof that the whole world was watching.

"The eyes of the world have descended right here on little Odessa, Texas—"

"—headquarters of Primatech, the global leader in Evo research."

"—as thousands arrive to lay the groundwork for a new and lasting peace between human and Evo—"

"—a new dawn, a new beginning, and—one can only hope—a brave new world."

As Bennet cleared the media zone, a massive shadow fell across the compound. The air turned cold, almost as if an eclipse was blocking out the sun. Like everyone around him, Bennet looked up, searching for the cause. This was no naturally occurring phenomenon. It had to be the work of—

A sudden, blinding white flash exploded out of nowhere, followed by another and another. Bennet only had time for a single thought: the explosions were totally silent. Then all was oblivion.

When Bennet came to, all he could hear was a muted hum—like a distant doorbell, ringing nonstop. Acrid smoke filled his nostrils, threatening to choke him. He opened his eyes and saw a world cracked apart, flakes of ash falling from the sky like grey snow. Bennet pulled himself up to a sitting position on the ground, wincing at the sudden pain the movement caused. Everything was a blur—glasses, where were his glasses?

He reached out, feeling among the rubble and dust until his fingers closed round the familiar horn-rimmed frames. Clutching them, he rose groggily to his knees, then up to his feet. Finally, he put on his glasses. One lens was cracked, but that couldn't disguise the apocalyptic chaos around him. It looked like a war zone, like bombs had gone off everywhere. He grimaced. That's exactly what had happened, but who was responsible?

Bennet turned in a slow circle, bearing witness to the pitiless devastation surrounding him. Scattered everywhere were the bodies of those laid low by the blast. Some looked unconscious, but with others it was obvious that they would never wake again. Blood stained the rubble crimson in far too many places. As the persistent ringing in his ears eased,

Bennet could hear a growing chorus of pain and anguish from those still alive. So much suffering, so many people had lost someone they loved in the blink of—

Bennet's heart lurched. There, on the ground—the body of a cheerleader. No, not a body: a corpse. Bennet knew it wasn't his daughter, but she was still someone's child. The shock of seeing that poor girl snapped his thoughts into focus. He had to find his own child. He had to know where she was. He had to know if she was still alive.

"Claire!" Nobody replied. "Claire!!!"

SAINT-FELICIEN, QUEBEC—NINE MONTHS AGO

The man was running for his life. He raced along the road, breathless and desperate in the darkness. He could hear a utility truck behind him, powerful hunting lights mounted on top of it, their beams trained on him. He could hear the shouts of his pursuers, calling to each other in French.

As he ran, the man's head jerked from side to side, looking for anyone who might help him. But they were at the edge of town, heading into darkness, with only trees on either side. The streetlights were getting further apart. Soon it would be just scrubland.

The truck was catching up to him fast. He couldn't stay on the road. He would have to risk going into the woods and hope to lose his pursuers. Hope was all he had left.

The roar of a second vehicle joining the first made up his mind. He broke left and ran into the trees, weaving an erratic path between them, feet pounding the uneven ground. Bursting into a clearing, he stopped to get his bearings. But it was no use. He was lost.

The fugitive bent forward, hands on his hips—panting, gasping for air. His hair was carefully groomed most days and, with his sculpted goatee, usually gave him the look of a hipster—but not here, not now. Instead his body was covered head to foot in white talc, and a pair of tighty-whitey underpants was his only protection from the cold evening air. This was no midnight run to the coffee shop.

The roar of approaching engines meant the hunters had found a path through the woods. Shouted voices echoed in the darkness: "*Par ici! Ici!*" *This way*, they were calling. *Here! Here!* Summoning his strength, the man forced himself to move. He had to get away from them. He had to try. But no matter where he ran, escape seemed impossible. The search beams of the twin trucks stalking him were everywhere, angry French voices shouting over the roar of the engines. It was no good.

Then the clouds overhead parted for a moment and moonlight glinted off a wide, shallow pond up ahead. He dashed forward and dove into the dank water. It was ice cold, but that didn't matter. He scrubbed at his body, intent on washing off the talc. Suddenly, a voice close by was shouting: "*Ici! Sous l'arbre!*"

Here. Under the trees. They'd found him.

He was scrambling across the pond when both trucks roared up to the water's edge. Glancing back, he could see men in hunting gear leaping from both vehicles, armed with rifles, some with dogs. One of them was carrying a big cargo net. They would throw it over him, trap him underneath it like a wild animal. He was cornered. Helpless.

The hunted man saw faces in the searchlights. There was no pity here. No mercy.

He turned, running toward the far side of the pond—and disappeared!

The hunters gasped, spluttering curses at this impossibility.

Water was still splashing up from invisible legs.

But then their quarry got clear of the pond.

All trace of him vanished in the night.

YANQUING, CHINA—FOUR MONTHS AGO

Everything was blue and white and bright. The harsh winter sun gleamed on a landscape of ice stretching as far as the eye could see. The frozen lake looked smooth from a distance, but the surface was uneven and treacherous for anyone on foot. Wave crests had turned to ice, white hazards that hampered anyone trying to cross this wasteland. So clear and blue was the sky, it was hard to distinguish where it met the horizon.

Across the middle of this frozen wasteland lurched a single, solitary figure. His pale blue prison uniform marked him as a fugitive, while his shock of black hair was a stark contrast to the surrounding blue and white landscape. His progress was slow across the frozen lake. Exhaustion played a part in that, as well as malnutrition from a harsh prison diet.

But the major cause of his fatigue was a fifty-pound circle of rusted metal. It was a disc usually found on a weightlifting barbell, but someone had run a chain through the hole in its center. The other end of the chain was welded to a crude metal shackle clamped tight round the fugitive's right wrist. He dragged the weight behind him as he staggered forward, step after belligerent step. The edges of the shackle had rubbed against his wrist until it was raw and bloody, harsh metal slicing into the skin and flesh with each step he took. Finally, unable to carry on, the fugitive stopped.

His breath fogged the air, white steam rising into the

clear blue sky. How many miles had he trudged? How much further until he found sanctuary, someone who could remove this accursed millstone from his body? He sniffed the air, hoping for some scent that might offer a clue. But all he could smell was his own sweat and despair.

As his breathing settled from a rasp to a less strenuous effort, a sound reached him. Mechanical. Urgent. Getting nearer. The fugitive knew that noise: snowmobiles. They were coming for him. They were close. He looked round, searching for cover. But there was no hiding place, not for miles. Only two possible escapes were left to him, and both involved the crude blade shoved into his belt.

He had crafted it from a piece of sheared-off metal he found in the prison yard, binding bits of broken wood around it with scraps of cloth to create a handle. He could use the blade to cut his own throat and end this torment. Or he could use it to cut something else and set himself free. Ignoring the metal disc at his feet, he crouched down, face staring up into the sky. But when he snapped back upwards, his feet remained stuck on the icy surface, the accursed weight holding him down, keeping him prisoner.

The fugitive turned to face the onrushing noise. Two military snowmobiles and an armored vehicle with snow tracks were speeding across the white expanse, headed straight for him. Even from this distance, he could make out their green camouflage and the red star emblem. They would be on him in less than a minute. They would take him back to that hellhole.

He pulled the blade free from his belt, lifting it up in front of his face. He could see his exhausted features reflected in the metal, weary from having been a prison lifer. He had not asked to be like this, to be a freak, an outcast. How long could he go on fighting? But he had no time for self-pity now. The fugitive moved the blade's edge down to his right forearm, pressing against the skin. If he was going to do this, it meant hacking through bone. If he was going to do this, the pain would be excruciating. If he was going to do this, it had to be now. Because if he wanted to live, there was no other option...

The soldiers gunned their machines forward, accelerating across the frozen lake. Up ahead, the fugitive had stopped, as if giving up on his doomed escape attempt. But as they grew closer, a horrific scream sliced through the air-the sound of a wounded animal, so loud it could be heard over their engines, an anguished cry of loss and suffering. Ahead of them, something fell away from the solitary figure. Something red.

Free at last, the fugitive crouched down on blood-spattered ice as the soldiers stopped behind him. Before they got within range, he hurled himself into the sky! His body rocketed toward the heavens, moving faster and faster, a shriek of triumph and pain rising with him. Within moments, he smashed through the sound barrier. A circle of vapor billowed in the blue sky as he flew away, headed east—away from China, away from his captors. Away to find a new life for himself in a brave new world.

US–CANADIAN BORDER—SEVEN WEEKS AGO

Tommy Clark was doing his best to keep it together, but his best wasn't winning. It didn't help that Tommy wasn't his real name, no matter what it said in his passport. The photo—thin faced, wide-eyed, blessed with ears that stuck out too much—was him, alright. The stated age of sixteen was correct, too. But everything else in his passport was a lie, and it was stressing him out. This whole trip was stressing him out.

Then there was his mom, Anne. Driving here had taken hours, and she'd spent every minute making him rehearse their story, over and over. Now that there were only four cars between them and the Canadian border checkpoint, Tommy's mind had gone blank.

"Let's go through it again. Who are we visiting?"

"Cousins." Tommy wracked his brain for their names. "Ned and Tammy Cooper."

Anne drummed her fingers on the steering wheel. On edge, as usual. "Where?"

"Bram… ford?"

"Brampton!" She slammed a fist on the dash. Tommy watched her struggling not to yell at him. "Come on, Kevin, you've got to get the details right."

He held his passport open at the photo page. "This says 'Tommy'."

Anne peered at it. "Right, you're right. Tommy."

They weren't ready, not even close—and certainly not for this. Rain beat down on the windscreen, making it hard to see the way ahead. Tommy bit his bottom lip. Maybe he could persuade his mom to turn back. It was worth a try, anyway. "'Hero_Truther' says that in other countries they shoot people like me in the streets."

"It's Canada, not North Korea. You'll be safe. Canadians are nice."

Tommy grimaced. "That's what you said about people in Denver."

She ignored his comment, easing off the brake to roll

forward as their queue edged closer to the checkpoint. There were four lines waiting to get through, but only two lanes open in the opposite direction. Seemed everybody wanted to visit Canada today.

Tommy could feel panic rising inside him, like a fist trying to fight its way up to his mouth. They wouldn't have to run if it wasn't for him. Stupidest. Power. Ever. He swallowed hard, wiping sweaty palms on his jeans. "This is all my fault."

"No, it's not. We have a chance at a new life," his mom insisted. She reached out with her right hand to touch the side of his face, as if hoping to soothe his fears away. "If we can get to Saskatchewan—" She stopped, staring ahead. "What's happening up there?"

Tommy leaned forward, squinting to see through the rain. Armed guards were moving up and down the queues, glaring into the vehicles. One woman was standing beside her car near the front of the next queue over, mouth wide open as a border guard with latex gloves prepared a DNA swab.

"Oh, no," Tommy whispered. "They're swabbing."

Suddenly the woman bolted, abandoning her car and fleeing the surprised guard. She ran toward the border, but it was hopeless, the last act of a desperate person. Four guards came running over from the checkpoint, all of them armed. The woman only got a few yards before she was shot in the back with an orange dart. She crumpled to the wet road, her body twitching and convulsing as if she was having a fit. The guards surrounded her, weapons raised, ready to shoot her again—but she stayed down.

Tommy turned to his mom, terrified. "What do we do? What do we do?"

His mom was already putting the car in reverse.

Tommy twisted round, searching for a way out. There

were at least half a dozen cars behind them, the nearest one close to their bumper. They were stuck. Tommy heard his mother gasp, and faced front again. Two guards were marching toward them, faces grim and purposeful. Tommy sank down into his seat. This was it. This was the moment that the world found out who he was and what he was, what he could do—

His mom shoved the car back into drive and hit the gas. They slammed straight into the car ahead, shunting it several feet forward. That gave her enough room to swing left, escaping the queue. Tires squealed in protest as they veered round on the road. Tommy clung on for dear life as they made a wild U-turn. His box of *Ninth Wonder* comics spilled across the back seat.

Once they were facing south, his mom floored it, accelerating away from the guards, away from the checkpoint. Up ahead of them, a green and white RETURN TO U.S.A. sign directed them to bear left. Tommy risked a look back at the Canadian border. So much for a new life.

Special Agent Cole Cutler was making a routine visit to the border crossing when the Evo woman bolted. He corrected himself—Evolved Human was the preferred terminology at the Agency, though everybody still called them Evos. Made no difference to him. Finding and bringing them in, that was his job—plain and simple.

He watched guards bring down the fleeing woman with brisk efficiency. Border crossings were only one hotspot among many, but it was good to see the system working so well. Cutler pulled some pistachios from a coat pocket and popped one in his mouth.

Moments later, one of the queuing cars jumped out

of line. The driver was in such a hurry that they clipped another vehicle before accelerating away. Cutler suspected there was an Evolved Human inside, but decided against ordering a full-scale pursuit. He preferred to be sure. Besides, the Evolved Humans might run, but they couldn't hide forever.

Cutler savored the salty tang of pistachio before spitting out fragments of shell, his remorseless gaze following the car as it sped into the distance. *Catch you later.*

CHAPTER ONE

Before June thirteenth, Odessa was a thriving city in central Texas, a bright and sunny place full of prosperous businesses, busy high schools, and happy families going about their normal lives. But a cowardly act of Evo terrorism reduced the Primatech building and the area immediately around it to a desolate wasteland, killing 2,343 people. Even today—one year on from that atrocity—it's said that more than a thousand bodies are still entombed beneath the rubble. The rest of the city lives on, but its people have been left forever scarred by the terrible events of that day.

In this special report, we are looking back at a year of mourning and anguish—for some, a year of persecution; for others, a year of justice. No matter your political or spiritual beliefs, the Odessa tragedy has forced us all to look at ourselves, to question our shared humanity. We have been asking, what makes us human? What binds us together, and what tears us apart? This magazine's investigative team has spent the past three months asking a further question: why Odessa? We believe we've found the answer.

"Evolved Humans"—or Evos, as they're often called—have been living among us for decades,

staying in the shadows, hiding their abilities. But that all changed in 2010 when a young woman called Claire Bennet outed her kind on live television in New York's Central Park. Following that extraordinary moment, Primatech became the company most associated with Evos. Once steeped in secrecy, Primatech emerged to consult with governments around the world, training law enforcement agencies and helping to ease relations between human and Evos. That led to the company hosting a global summit on evolved humans, and the tragedy that followed.

On June thirteenth of last year, the company opened the doors to its Odessa HQ for what was to be a three-day summit. Some saw it as a symbolic gesture, but people gathered from around the world, hoping to build a better future—a future in which humans and Evos could live together in peace. That peace would prove short-lived.

—extract from The Odessa Files, *Enquiry magazine*, June 2015 edition

CHICAGO, ILLINOIS

The woman ran as if it was a matter of life and death. Joggers were common enough in this suburb after dark, but they didn't have her murderous hate in their eyes. They certainly didn't have shotguns slung over their backs like her, or pistols in their hands.

Joanne raced into a dead-end alley, her face full of the focused determination of a sprinter. She cut sideways to a fence and was over it in moments, slamming down hard on the other side. Pausing to catch her breath, she scanned the street ahead of her.

Someone else was out running tonight but, like Joanne, he was no jogger. For a start, he was wearing a mechanic's jumpsuit instead of athletic gear, and heavy work boots instead of running shoes. The crude Mohawk cut into his reddish hair gave him the look of a redneck, not a road racer. Sprinting as fast as he could, the man kept looking back over his shoulders, terror etched into his face. He was running scared. Literally.

Joanne stepped out of the fence's shadow so the streetlights caught her dark skin as he glanced back. She wanted him to see her coming. She wanted him to know terror.

Brandishing her gun, Joanne set off in pursuit of her target, a smile on her face.

Luke parked his station wagon across from a church. He watched as a few people hurried into the building, none of them arriving together, all looking round before they ventured in through a side door. Furtive, ashamed of why they were there.

Catching his own expression in the wing mirror, Luke realized it was much the same. Careworn creases were starting to collect at the corners of his brown eyes. He looked away, unable to meet his own gaze anymore. Not after all that had happened.

Luke got out of the station wagon and dug a scrap of paper from his pocket. One word was scrawled across it: COCKROACH. After a final look round to see if anyone was watching, he headed across the street.

Missing double math had been no sacrifice, but the trek from Carbondale had taken forever. Even when Tommy got to Chicago, he needed to change buses twice to reach the church. Tommy knew they couldn't exactly advertise, but did it have to be all the way out here? He gave a silent prayer of thanks for smartphone maps.

Stop putting it off, Tommy told himself—just go in. You came this far, man up and do this. But his feet refused to move, and his hands were trembling. It took another person's arrival to shake Tommy from his thoughts. The church exterior wasn't well lit, but that didn't prevent Tommy from recognizing the man who made his life miserable each and every week in gym class.

"Coach Lewis?"

The newcomer stopped, startled at hearing his own name. "Ah, jeez. You gotta be kidding me." Coach Lewis glared at Tommy before stalking toward the church.

Tommy shifted his backpack from one shoulder to the other and sighed. He never would have come if he'd known Coach was going to be here.

Caspar Abraham sat at a bus stop just up the road from the church. His appearance was quite incongruous, considering it was well after dark in this down-at-heel suburb. A light grey suit enveloped his generous frame, and a bowtie nestled beneath his greying goatee. He had a fresh red carnation in his jacket buttonhole and was sporting a brown trilby hat. Retro horn-rimmed glasses helped mask the fact that one of his eyes had an involuntary sideways twitch. Throw in the battered briefcase held tight on his lap, and he looked like a travelling salesman who had somehow wandered here from the 1950s.

Despite all of that, nobody paid him the slightest bit of attention. The young man who had gotten off the bus less than a minute before nodded to him, but that was typical. Caspar seemed to blend into the background, leaving little trace of his presence even as people walked right by him. It suited his purposes, and it never failed to make him smile.

Caspar watched the nervous young man hesitating outside the church. Finally, the teenager plucked up the courage to go in through the side entrance. Caspar remained at the bus stop, keeping his silent vigil.

Tommy approached a doorway in the church basement. He could still turn round and go home, it wasn't too—

An angry old man stepped out to confront him. "Password."

Startled, Tommy struggled to remember the word he had found online. "Cockroach?" The old guy glowered at him a moment before moving aside.

Tommy went into the meeting room, but what he found there didn't fill him with confidence. The walls and floor were various shades of green. That and the bleak overhead lighting gave the room a queasy, claustrophobic feel. A table against one wall was stacked with paper cups, and a filter coffeemaker was giving off an acrid smell. Eight folding chairs faced each other in a circle, but most people in the dingy room were gathered round a wall-mounted TV in one corner. Welcome to Evos Anonymous.

Tommy moved closer to the others, wanting to see what had them clustered round the TV. It didn't make for happy viewing. On screen were grainy images from the Odessa attack. Most of the footage came from cell phones, filmed by those who had survived June thirteenth. Tommy had seen it all before, far too many times: people running, sobbing. Smoke, chaos. And bodies. So many bodies.

"Within hours, an Evo-Supremacist named Mohinder Suresh had claimed full responsibility for the attacks," an authoritative voiceover announced. The Odessa film was replaced by a photo of an Indian man, his face calm with a certain professional detachment.

Coach Lewis shut off the TV with an angry sneer. "Lies, all of it."

People starting taking their seats. Tommy picked the chair two places down from Coach Lewis, not wanting a face full of gym teacher. He slipped his backpack underneath the hard plastic chair and sat down. Between Tommy and the coach was a man in his thirties, hunched forward, hands clenched together as if praying or deep in thought. He had brown hair and a close-cropped beard. Looked sad, like he'd rather be somewhere else, but then wouldn't they all? Tommy glanced round at the others, wondering what their powers were. Nobody offered to introduce themselves, so Tommy gave them nicknames in his head.

Past Coach Lewis was a lady in a flowery dress, a brown jacket, and brown boots. She reminded Tommy a little of his mom, but older and even more worn down. Next to her was the angry old man who'd been guarding the door. He glared at everyone with suspicion, which didn't make Tommy feel any more welcome, since they were sitting opposite each other. Beside the angry old man was an aging biker woman with a wild haircut and a face that had seen too many miles, then a Chinese guy with only one hand. His right arm ended in an ugly stump near where the wrist should have been. He didn't look happy about it—or anything else, come to that.

The last person, seated just to Tommy's right, was a soccer-mom type with a designer jacket and handbag. One man didn't sit down, a hipster dude with a goatee, checked shirt, and beanie hat. Instead he prowled the outside of the circle, nursing a cup of coffee, looking like he was ready to bolt for the door at any moment.

Biker Woman was first to break the silence. "This is pathetic. Nine of us? How the hell are we supposed to fight back if we can't even organize?"

Fight back? That was news to Tommy. He thought this was an anonymous support group for people with powers. What had he gotten himself into here?

"We gotta get creative," Soccer Mom insisted. "There's a guy in Los Angeles fighting back. Calls himself 'El Vengador'."

Coach Lewis snorted. "Seriously, the dude in the Mexican wrestler costume? That's a joke, right?"

"Least he's doing something."

Dress Lady leaned forward. "I hear he's got a whole underground railroad out there. Fake IDs, fake blood samples. A way to disappear—"

Beside her, Angry Old Man dismissed that with a sneer. "One guy! So what? Pretty soon they'll have drones coming after us!"

Biker Woman smirked. "Let 'em try." She flexed a hand in the air, making it spark and crackle with electricity. Tommy couldn't help envying her power.

Chinese Guy held up his stump. "Where I'm from, they shoot people like us, dump the bodies in a ditch. At least this is America. You still have rights."

Soccer Mom shook her head. "You reading the same papers I am?"

"June thirteenth changed everything," Dress Lady said. "We're third-class citizens now. The public's scared to death of us."

Tommy could sense his gym teacher bristling through all

of this. Sure enough, Coach Lewis couldn't keep quiet any longer. "Most of these incidents have been isolated. Tulsa, Cedar Rapids—vigilantes, a few bad apples, that's all."

"If the problem was just vigilantes," Angry Old Man snapped, "the government wouldn't be forcing us to register every time we move."

Hipster Dude slammed down his coffee on a folding table, anger bringing out the French in his accent. "You people don't get it. It's not the government or vigilantes we should be worried about. The ones really hurting us are in the shadows. They read our emails, track our cell phones—they know every click on our computers. There's something else going on. They're everywhere!"

A long silence followed as he turned away from them, rant over. Tommy could feel his heart sinking. Things were even worse than he'd thought. Terrific.

"So what are we supposed to do with that?" Coach Lewis hissed. "Chase ghosts?"

Dress Lady had a suggestion. "My daughter and me, we heard about a place in North Saskatchewan where Evos can walk around in the open."

"My mom and I tried to get there, but they were swabbing people at the border." Everyone turned to look at Tommy, waiting for him to continue. He'd spent so long keeping secrets, not talking to anyone but his mom about this. Now he was in a room full of people like him. They all knew how it felt to be different, to be an outsider. If he couldn't talk here, where else could he go? Tommy swallowed hard before continuing.

"We're wanted in three states because I can't really control my... power. We move a lot. Mom sleeps with a gun under her pillow, when she sleeps at all." Words were tumbling out of him now. "We use fake IDs most of the time. I'm calling myself Tommy now."

"No names," Angry Old Man snarled.

Tommy stopped a moment, stung by the rebuke, but he had to finish this. "I came here because I thought someone could give me a few tips, maybe help me out a little?" He looked round the circle, desperate for someone, anyone, to respond. But all he got was silence. Nobody would meet his gaze, not even Coach Lewis, who knew him.

It was Hipster Dude who finally spoke up. "Came to the wrong place, my friend."

As the others resumed arguing, Tommy felt a vibration in his pocket. Pulling out his cell, he swiped the screen. *Rent check on the counter. Let landlord in.*

Crap. Unless he got home in time, his mom would figure out he'd gone AWOL. "Sorry, I gotta—" Tommy snatched at his backpack under the chair and half its contents spilled out: school books, pencils, papers. Blushing crimson, he rammed his stuff back into the bag before scurrying away through the double doors.

Tommy burst out of the church. His pace quickened when he saw a bus idling at the stop, ready to leave at any moment. Some old man in a suit was already there, maybe he—

Tommy ran straight into the delivery guy, knocking him and his bicycle over. Cartons of Chinese food went flying, noodles spilling across the pavement.

"I'm so sorry," Tommy stammered, all too aware of the waiting bus. "Really sorry." The engine began to rev as the vehicle prepared to leave. Tommy sprinted for the bus, banging on the side as it started pulling away. To his relief, the bus slowed down and opened its doors. He threw himself inside and clattered up the steps, gasping for breath.

* * *

Caspar watched the bus depart, a quiet smile of satisfaction on his pudgy features. But dark muttering from the other direction soon demanded his attention. The delivery guy was picking lo mein out of his slacker hairstyle, grumbling about stupid brats who didn't look where they were going. Caspar's eyes narrowed.

In the basement, any semblance of meaningful debate had degenerated into shouting.

"Suresh? That terrorist! Hell, he's the reason we're in this basement!"

"You can't have a revolution without casualties! Resistance is our only answer!"

"Exactly. We have to stop acting like victims. We're the ones with powers!"

"Face it, people, Suresh was right. We are the future of the human race."

Luke laughed out loud at that last comment. The others stopped to look at him.

"The future? That's a good one," he said. "My wife and I brought our nine-year-old son Dennis to Odessa on June thirteenth to watch history being made. Sun was out, summer heat just rising. I'm watching my boy play outside on a sunny day, feeling free for the first time in his life." Luke paused. Tears were running down his cheeks, but he didn't wipe them away. "And I'm thinking about how he's gonna be able to live a life without hate, without persecution. Just like any normal kid."

The pretty woman on his right leaned over to touch his arm, to comfort him.

Luke bent forward, staring at the shabby floor. His hands squeezed into fists, knuckles whitening. "And then you people—you freaks—you ruined it for everyone."

Silence. His accusation soured the air, hardening the faces of those gathered. The old guy who'd been at the door spoke first. "Who the hell are you?"

Before Luke could reply, the doors behind him flew open. A newcomer burst in, mechanic's overalls drenched in sweat. "It's a trap! They found us!"

Joanne stalked in and shot the mechanic through the chest, his blood spattering those nearest. Luke rose from his chair to stand beside her, pulling out a concealed weapon, an eerie calm on his face. The couple opened fire, executing those nearest to them with brutal, merciless efficiency.

Luke took aim at Coach Lewis, but the muscle-bound gym teacher slammed his hands together, creating a concussion wave that threw Luke and Joanne back toward the double doors. Coach Lewis pulled his hands apart, and a hot ball of living flame grew in the space between them, swirling and crackling with malevolent energy. Luke grabbed a fire extinguisher from a bracket on the wall and sprayed the contents at Coach Lewis. Having doused the fireball, he executed the coach with a shot to the head.

Luke heard gunfire over his shoulder and saw Joanne shooting at thin air. But her bullets still found a target, blood spraying from where they hit. The Canadian hipster materialized as he fell to the floor, dying or already dead. Joanne nodded to Luke, then her eyes widened in surprise. He spun round to find the pretty woman who'd tried to comfort him now transforming into an ugly mass of craggy vines. One vine sprouted across the room, reaching for a window. Luke unfolded a portable hatchet from a sheath hidden behind his back. He swung the blade down into the nearest vine, hacking straight through the limb. The dismemberment shocked the woman back into human form. She writhed on the floor, blood spurting from her severed arm. Luke put his gun to her ear.

"You were talking about El Vengador. Where do I find him?"

Her face was pain and anguish and terror. "I don't know. I swear." Her denial sounded credible, but another vine grabbed a coffee urn, launching it at his head. Joanne deflected the urn with a chair. Luke pulled the trigger and all the vines fell to the floor.

Then there was silence. After a minute of mayhem and bloodshed, the sudden quiet was unnerving. Luke wrinkled his nose at the stench of gunpowder. He looked over at Joanne. "What took you so long?"

She shrugged, swiping blood from one of her shoes. Luke spied a white rectangle of paper on the floor, underneath the chair where the kid had been. He picked it up, turning the card over. There were ten squares on it, with holes punched through nine of them. Someone had drawn a red smiley face in the final space.

"What's that?" Joanne asked.

"One of them got away. He dropped this."

She took the card and smiled. "'Moe's Ice Cream Parlor, Carbondale, Illinois.' Hmm, one more and we get a free ice cream."

Blood from the man Luke had extinguished was flowing across the floor toward them. Luke pulled matches from a pocket and lit one. "This is for Dennis." He dropped his match into the blood. It caught fire like gasoline as Luke and Joanne marched out.

* * *

SAN PEDRO HARBOR, CALIFORNIA

Charlie could see fog rolling in across the docks from his vantage point in the warehouse, but most of his energy was focused on not drowning. Two armed thugs had wrapped heavy chains around his ankles, tied rope around his wrists, and were using a pulley to dunk him in and out of a large tank of rusty water. They dropped him feet first into the liquid for several seconds before slowly, laboriously lifting him out again. Charlie choked, gasping for air.

"Give up the Evos and we cut you down," one thug snarled.

"I told you," Charlie spluttered between breaths, "I don't know anything."

"Come on," the other thug urged. "Where does the railroad lead?"

"They just paid me to drive the truck, that's all. I swear." Charlie saw his captors exchange a look. Maybe they were finally starting to believe him.

"Alright. We're done here," the second thug announced.

The duo let go of the rope. Charlie plunged toward the water, but this time there was no way for his captors to pull him back out. He screamed and got a mouthful of water as he sank to the bottom of the tank.

Bubbles rose around him, his frantic efforts to shake loose the chains or escape the ropes worse than useless. He was going to drown here, inside a forgotten warehouse on an abandoned pier, and all because he agreed to help some—

A muffled scream reverberated through the tank, then another.

Charlie looked up at the surface, hoping against hope for a miracle—and then it happened! A muscular arm plunged into the water, grabbed hold of the chains, and lifted him out of the tank.

He tumbled to the warehouse floor like a wet fish, coughing water and bile. As he recovered, Charlie dared to look round. The thugs' broken bodies were close by, but there was somebody else standing closer, casting a mighty shadow over all of them.

Charlie rolled over to see his savior. He was tall, with a muscular frame clad in dark body armor and chiselled features hidden by a wrestling mask. Strong hands reached down, freeing Charlie from his chains.

"Thank you, thank you!" Struggling to his feet, Charlie stumbled out of the warehouse. He expected his savior to follow, but instead the powerful figure stayed with the thugs. Charlie stopped by the doorway to watch.

One thug was reaching for his discarded gun. A heavy boot smashed down on the weapon, crushing it underfoot. "Tell your bosses I know where they live."

The thug managed a croak. "Who… who are you?"

"I'm El Vengador."

CHAPTER TWO

We pride ourselves in providing students with an outstanding academic and athletic experience. The faculty and staff work collaboratively to provide an education that will prepare students for continued success throughout life. We truly believe this is the best high school in southern Illinois, and one of the best in the entire state. That's why our motto is "Dedicated to Excellence".

—text from the Pinehearst High School homepage

CARBONDALE, ILLINOIS

It was dawn by the time Tommy got back from Chicago. His trek home had taken even longer, made worse by the lack of answers or hope at the meeting. Plus now he had the problem of facing Coach Lewis at school, both of them knowing the other's secret. Like gym class wasn't bad enough already.

Tommy snuck in through his bedroom window. As he put his backpack down, he heard a noise in the hall. He threw himself into bed, grabbing a comic from the floor. Moments later, his mom burst in, a 9mm Glock in one hand. But by the time she'd turned on the light, Tommy was reading the latest issue of *Ninth Wonders*.

"Dammit, Kevin! I thought you were a—"

"It's Tommy," he reminded her for the millionth time. His mom let go of the trigger, her fingers white from gripping it so hard. "I know you're stressed out, Mom, but maybe don't bring the gun to your interview."

She smiled at the mention of her positive job prospect. Moving so often and using fake IDs meant getting paid under the counter most of the time, working two jobs to pay for things they used to afford on one salary. But an old friend had gotten her an interview and was helping smooth over the gaps in her resume.

"I've got a good feeling about this," she said. "Neonatal nurse, just like the old days. So I need you up in twenty. No, make it ten."

A wry smile crossed Tommy's face as his mom started to leave the room. He was already dressed, so that should speed things up. But something was nagging at him. "That text you sent about the landlord. Sorry I didn't—"

"The what?" His mom paused in the hall, distracted.

Tommy stopped himself from answering. Explaining would likely only lead to more questions, and that always spelled trouble. "Nothing. Never mind."

Nodding, she headed for the kitchen. So, if his mom hadn't sent it, who had?

AUSTIN, TEXAS

Ted Barnes was waxing lyrical in the front passenger seat. "Memories are funny things. The good ones fill your life with meaning, with context, with clarity… while other memories can deceive." Ted Barnes wasn't his real name, but few people knew that.

"They're the dangerous ones that can hold you hostage. When you look back on the decisions you've made in life, the thing you don't want to feel is regret, am I right?" He patted the dashboard. "That's why this car makes so much sense."

The woman behind the steering wheel had no idea Ted's real name was Noah Bennet. She couldn't know he'd been part of extraordinary events involving people with incredible powers. Ted was just a guy with a charming—if hokey—sales pitch.

Bennet smiled at her. "Gas mileage, safety, style, this one has it all... not to mention that new-car smell." He turned to the bored child slurping from a juice box in the back seat. "What do you think?"

Bennet noted a blue sedan outside the showroom. It had been lurking there all morning, a driver visible behind the tinted windows. Bennet reached to adjust his glasses so he could see the car better, a gesture borne of habit. But Ted Barnes didn't wear glasses. He sat back in the passenger seat. "So, shall we start the paperwork?"

The woman hesitated. "I'd like to check those safety stats first. You understand, don't you, Mr Barnes? You probably have kids of your own."

Ted Barnes didn't have kids, not yet. And Noah Bennet tried not to think too much about his daughter Claire, not after what had happened to her. It still hurt too much.

LOS ANGELES, CALIFORNIA

Lisa Carpenter had made plenty of jackass moves in her twenty-seven years, but this was Hall of Shame stuff. Sure, Carlos Gutierrez was charming, and a war hero—not to mention the fact he had a smokin' hot bod. But getting busy with him in the broom closet at Linderman Junior High—during a school day, no less—was definitely not her finest hour.

Carlos kept pulling her closer, his body hard against her, his kisses urgent and wanting. She wanted him too, despite the warning bell ringing loud and clear in her head. What he said next didn't help matters. "Linda, you're amazing."

"It's Lisa."

"Lisa, right. Sorry."

Then a real bell replaced the one in her thoughts—in fact, it was the school bell! Lisa pushed Carlos away, but he was eager to finish what they'd started.

"We gotta stop."

"What? Why? What's wrong?"

"It's lunchtime. You're on in five." Lisa was still rearranging her clothes when the closet door swung open. The school janitor stood outside. Now everyone would know she'd let the guest speaker jump her bones less than an hour after he'd arrived. Great.

Carlos stood by the podium in the school auditorium, gazing out at his audience. "Being a hero is not something you're born with—it's how you react to a life-or-death situation." The words sounded noble, but he'd said them too many times. Could probably say the whole speech backwards by now.

In front of him was a hall full of seventh graders, their body language ranging from boredom to awe. A twelve-year-old boy in a red-and-white striped t-shirt was soaking up every word from an aisle seat, enraptured and proud. Carlos took a sip from a Coke can atop the podium before continuing.

"If you told me back when I was your age that I was gonna get a Medal of Valor for saving three soldiers from an ambush in Afghanistan…" Carlos paused, shaking his head for effect. "I'd have said you were nuts. But—here I am. So, I'd like to thank Principal Marks and Miss…" He glanced over at the woman by the wall. He'd been with her in that closet only twenty minutes earlier. What was her name again?

"Carpenter," she prompted, giving him a look that could freeze the sun.

"Carpenter, right. I'd like to thank them for giving me such a warm welcome today." Carlos smiled. "I'll leave you with this last thought. It doesn't matter how ordinary you think you are, or what kind of screw-up you think you've been." Unseen by the audience, he emptied an airline booze bottle into his Coke. "We all have the potential to be heroes. It's about what you do when the opportunity presents itself. Thank you."

Carlos raised his can in salutation and drank it dry during the half-hearted applause. The boy in the striped t-shirt clapped the loudest and longest by far. Carlos gave the boy a sly wink. Least he could do for his nephew Jose.

CARBONDALE, ILLINOIS

Tommy believed there were four rules for surviving any given day at Pinehearst. Don't raise your hand in class. Don't do anything that might get you noticed. Don't make eye contact. And whatever else you do, don't get on the wrong side of the school superstar.

Brad was Pinehearst's hero of the hallways—or an all-American asshole, depending on whom you asked. Half jock and half jerk, he probably had more athletic ability in one finger than Tommy possessed in his whole body. A professional sports star in the making—if you believed the hype—Brad already had an entourage of buddies hanging on his every word, laughing out loud at every lame joke. Tommy could've ignored all of that if Brad hadn't been going out with Emily.

Okay, sure, it was a cliché, but looking at her really did make Tommy's heart skip a beat. Emily was cute, she was pretty, and she was kind to boot. She was always first to volunteer for any charity event or to talk other students into helping out with a bake sale or car wash for a good cause. So why on earth was she dating Brad?

The question nagged at Tommy as he dawdled along a crowded hallway between classes. Three cheerleaders bounced past, all of them giggling about what a hunk Brad was. Banners for the Pinehearst Lions hung from the ceiling in between signs displaying the school's proud motto, Dedicated to Excellence. Tommy had been through too many schools to pay much attention anymore. But he couldn't help notice Emily further along the corridor, talking with Brad. The cronies were there in attendance, as usual. Brad leaned over Emily, whispering in her ear while he grabbed a handful of her ass.

She slapped his hand away and jabbed an angry finger in his face. But the jerk just laughed at her, his buddies all joining in. Emily stalked off, angry and upset. Tommy watched her go, wishing he could help somehow. Then he noticed Brad staring at him. Oh, crap. Tommy turned away, angry at himself for having broken rules two, three, and four all at once. Brad marched over, his buddies close behind.

"Like my girlfriend, do you?" Brad shoved Tommy's face into a locker. "Think you can stare at my girlfriend?"

"What? No, I wasn't staring—" Brad slammed a fist into Tommy's gut, doubling him over. He crumpled to the floor, all too aware of everyone in the hallway watching his humiliation. Instinct kicked in, and Tommy thrust out a hand, fingers stretching, power surging. He felt the world distorting, bending, as if time and space were being undone. Brad loomed over Tommy, the air rippling around him—

No, he couldn't, he mustn't. He had to keep control.

Tommy pulled the power back into himself, letting his body go limp. He even threw in a pathetic whimper of pain, knowing how much bullies liked to hear that. Sure enough, Brad gave a sneer of satisfaction. "Wuss." He strolled away with his buddies, all of them laughing. Denied a spectacle, the crowd that had gathered to watch drifted off.

Still cursing his own stupidity, Tommy got back to his feet and stumbled away, making sure to go in the opposite direction from Brad. Rounding the next corner, he found students crying and hugging each other. Tommy saw Chantelle, a smart girl who sat near him in biology, huddled with her friends.

"—didn't even know he was in Chicago."

Tommy saw Chantelle's eyes were red. "Did something happen?"

"Coach Lewis died in a fire last night. Him and six other people, all of them in a church basement."

Tommy stumbled backward, reeling at this—a church basement? But that meant…

The bell rang and everyone headed for class, but he didn't follow them. The last thing Tommy could face right now was algebra. Instead he bolted for the nearest door.

* * *

CHIGACO, ILLINOIS

Caspar strolled into the police precinct as if he owned the place, one hand gripping the handle of his battered briefcase. Nodding to the desk sergeant on his way past, he ambled onwards to an internal hallway. He straightened his bowtie and adjusted his hat before opening a door marked "Interview One".

The room was basic, even utilitarian, with scuffed walls, a plain table and two chairs—nothing more. Slouching in a seat by the table was the delivery guy Caspar had noticed outside the church the previous night. All the Chinese food Tommy had spilled over him was gone, but the sour attitude remained—no sweetness here. Caspar sat opposite the surly witness, hefting his briefcase up onto the table. It landed with a heavy thump.

"Been here an hour," the delivery guy complained. "Other guy told me to wait."

"Ah, waiting, yes." Caspar smiled, one of his pupils twitching. "'Too many people go through life waiting for things to happen instead of making them happen.'"

"I don't know what the hell that means."

Caspar sighed, weary of such ignorance. Pushing back both locks, he released the catches to open his briefcase. Inside were pennies, thousands of them—some dull and worn, others bright beneath the stark ceiling lights in the interview room. Caspar sifted through the coins, eventually selecting a shiny penny from among the multitude. He lifted it out and shut the briefcase, smiling at the surly slacker across the table.

"Okay, so let's talk about what you saw."

The guy leaned forward. "I'm riding down 'H' street with my delivery, and this little prick runs right into me! Twenty-eight bucks worth of food, all of it on the ground. Next thing

I know, the brat's jumping on a bus and taking off like his worthless little life depended on it." He paused, licking his lips. "He came outta that church right before it caught fire. So I'm guessing he's the one who killed all those people."

Caspar rolled the penny back and forth across his chubby fingers, considering the witness's words. "And could you identify this 'prick' if you saw him again?"

The delivery guy slid back in his seat, a sly smile playing about his lips. "Depends. Is there a reward if I can?"

Casper slammed the penny down on its edge. With his other hand he flicked the coin so that it went spinning across the table. The delivery guy stared at it, mesmerized. Eventually the penny came to a stop in front of him, finishing heads up. The guy looked from the coin to Caspar, as if asking permission.

"Go ahead."

The delivery guy picked up the penny, studying it, uncertainty in his face. "I don't understand. What's this for?"

Casper couldn't help smiling. "Penny for your thoughts."

Detective Griffin was not having a good day. He'd been dragged out of bed after a late shift when firefighters found seven bodies in the basement meeting room of a burnt-out suburban church. Any hope it might be a freak accident—an electrical blaze trapping the local AA meeting, for instance—was abandoned as more and more evidence emerged from the embers. Bullet casings at the scene and bullet holes in the bodies suggested a shoot-out, but no guns were found in the smouldering rubble.

Several of the bodies had been killed at point-blank range, execution style. One victim—most likely female, though an autopsy would be needed to confirm that—had lost an arm, apparently hacked off with an axe or similar weapon, suggesting the incident had involved torture. The number of bodies implied multiple shooters, but there was no CCTV in or around the church to confirm that. Fire investigators had ruled out an electrical source for the blaze, but had been unable to find any trace of accelerants or an incendiary device, so the actual cause remained a mystery.

As for motive? Detective Griffin knew he was striking out there, too. The ruthless nature of the slayings suggested organized crime, but the disparate characteristics of those killed contradicted that. So far they had identified a Chinese immigrant missing part of an arm, a guy from Canada, a couple of suburban moms, and a Carbondale gym teacher.

If Griffin could find out what the hell they were all doing in the church basement, that would go a long way to unlocking the puzzle. His gut was saying hate crime of some sort—the attack had been so fierce, so brutal, what else could it be? But who had reason or cause to hate such a diverse group of people?

Going house to house had gotten the investigators nowhere, with the locals unable or unwilling to remember seeing anyone or anything unusual until the fire had already engulfed the church. Then, finally, a witness had walked into the police precinct claiming to have collided with a teenager fleeing the scene minutes before the blaze. Griffin was still at the church when he got word, and it took him an hour to return to the precinct, his clothes rumpled and stinking of smoke. No matter, this was a breakthrough—he could feel it.

The detective paused to grab a coffee and splash water on his face before heading for the interview room; he didn't want to be yawning in front of an eyewitness. Rounding a corner, Griffin noticed an odd figure coming in the opposite direction—a heavy-set man in a suit with a red carnation in the buttonhole and a bowtie beneath his greying goatee. The stranger was carrying an old briefcase and raised his trilby hat to the detective as they passed each other. Griffin kept walking, trying to remember whether he'd ever seen the man inside the precinct before. But by the time he reached the door to the interview room, Griffin couldn't seem to remember what the guy looked like. Didn't matter, anyways. Griffin bustled inside and sat down opposite the witness.

"Alright, so let's see if we can get a description of this kid."

The witness stared at him as if waking up from a dream. "Kid? Sorry, I don't remember any kid." He blinked twice. "What were we talking about again?"

Detective Griffin breathed out, exasperated. Yep, this was turning into a very bad day indeed.

AUSTIN, TEXAS

Bennet was finishing up paperwork at his desk. It had taken some time to work through all the safety statistics, but Bennet was a patient man and he had won the mom over in the end, even with two kids in tow. Too many of his colleagues wanted a quick sale, the easy bucks. Bennet knew better— anything worth having needed a little more effort.

He completed the final document, remembering at the last moment to sign himself as Ted Barnes. It was a nondescript name for an everyday guy, the kind of guy who blended in, someone everybody trusted and nobody doubted. You could depend on him.

"Making us look bad, Ted."

One of the other salesmen was leaning over the cubicle,

shaking his head at Bennet. Errol Rivera had been top dog at the dealership before Ted arrived, but he didn't seem to mind being usurped by such a stand-up guy, at least not anymore. There'd been some tension at first, but Bennet had smoothed that out by keeping well away from Errol's best clients and even throwing a few juicy opportunities his way. They even went for the occasional beer and ribs sometimes after a big sales day.

"Friedkin says you're a lock for Employee of the Month again," Rivera grumbled, but with a good-natured smile on his face.

"No trick," Bennet insisted. "Bag and tag, that's all."

"There's a trick. I'll figure it out." Rivera jerked a thumb at the main doors. "Oh, and your favorite customer's here to see you." He ambled away, smirking.

Bennet stood up, smoothing his tie. A beautiful redhead in her late thirties was coming into the showroom. Seeing Bennet, she sashayed over, a flirty smile on her lips.

"Can I help you, Miss?"

She leaned against the edge of his desk, eyes sparkling with mischief. "I was hoping you could take me out for a little test drive."

Bennet let his gaze savor the new arrival's lithe body, responding to her flirting with a twinkle of his own. "Depends on how fast and how far you're willing to go."

She moved round the desk, placing her left hand on his chest as she whispered in his ear with a husky voice. "Pretty far... pretty fast."

Bennet couldn't help noticing the prominent engagement ring on her finger. "Sure your fiancé won't mind?"

"I won't tell if you won't," she promised. Julia kissed him, her arms pulling Bennet close, her body pressing itself into his embrace.

"Hey, you two—get a room!" Rivera called from across the showroom.

Smiling, Julia broke away from Bennet to pull a stack of brochures from her purse. She spread them out on the desk. Each one was for different aspects of an elaborate wedding. "So: if we can knock off the cake tasting, the band audition, and the gift registrations this week, we're way ahead of schedule."

Bennet nodded and smiled. It wouldn't be the first marriage for either of them, but Julia still had regrets about a Las Vegas special with husband number one. This time was going to be different. This time was going to be perfect—come hell or high water.

Bennet loved everything about Julia, from the way her eyes sparkled when she was excited to the freckles on her shoulders from too many summers spent outdoors as a kid. But the level of planning she had devoted to their wedding day was more than some armies managed before invading another country. So he'd become adept at listening to half of what she was saying while letting his mind work on other things. Like why that blue sedan was parked across the street from the dealership…

The stack of files was threatening to spill off the front passenger seat of the blue sedan. Each one had a photo clipped to its front, names alongside the pictures— Mohinder Suresh, Angela Petrelli, Matt Parkman—and a corporate stamp: PRIMATECH—Evolved Human Research Program. The corners of every file were dog-eared, evidence they had been examined again and again.

The driver was re-reading another file. Like the others, the subject's name was beside his photo: Noah Bennet. He looked just like the salesman in the showroom across the road, but for two differences. The man in the photo was younger by at least half a decade, and he wore horn-rimmed glasses. They suited him. Almost looked like a part of him. Those details aside, Noah Bennet and Ted Barnes could be identical twins—or the same man.

As Bennet watched the blue sedan drive away, Julia was still outlining the wedding masterplan. "For the registry, I thought we should start with china. I think I just want to go white. All white." Bennet realized she had paused. "Are you even listening to me, Ted?"

He smiled. "Of course I am. White china it is."

CHAPTER THREE

#Evernow = impossible! Cannot beat Bandit Leader.
Some1 tell me how 2! Is there a cheat/hack 2 reach
#finalbossbattle? Pls x infinity!!!!!
　　　　　—online message written by @gamergirl1999x

TOKYO, JAPAN

You are surrounded, evil bandits closing in from every side.
You are exhausted, spent from battling the armies of your
sworn enemy—the evil shogun. You clasp both hands to the
handle of your blade, lowering your head. It is over, you can
fight no more—or so you want it to seem. The bandits surge
forward, eager to please their unseen master. Suddenly you
leap into the air, eluding their deadly advance!

As you come back down, you spin round in a circle,
your weapon now a whirling blade of death, cutting
through bandit after bandit, devastating their ranks. Within
moments, they are all dead or dying, writhing on the
cobbled path—all but one. Only the bandit leader remains,
a warrior so malevolent he has never been beaten.

You advance on your foe and bow to him. This show of
respect seems to surprise the bandit leader. No combatant
has ever done him the honor of bowing first. It is a sign of

49

mutual respect and civility that cannot go unacknowledged. The bandit leader returns the bow, a reflexive action that leaves him vulnerable. In that instant, you see an opening and take it, hurling your weapon at the bandit. It is an act of madness, leaving you with no blade and no defense against this impossible foe. For an agonizing moment, nothing happens. Then the bandit leader's head topples off and his body falls over!

Ren Shimosawa stared at his TV in disbelief. He had played through the videogame again and again since downloading it, each time coming undone when face to face with the bandit leader. Every attack, every strategy had failed. Having his samurai bow was meant as a delaying tactic after forty-five—no, forty-six—hours of non-stop playing. Had he stumbled across a way to defeat the unbeatable foe?

The whole screen lit up, filled with a blaze of color and graphics.

He'd done it. He'd actually done it.

Dropping the controller, Ren leapt to his feet.

"*Yata!*"

The young Japanese gamer bounced round his apartment, crushing abandoned food boxes under his feet, hands punching the air in triumph. So elaborate was Ren's victory dance, he almost missed the words scrolling across his TV screen. But the kanji characters flashed off and on, catching the corner of his eye. Ren lunged for a pen and paper, scribbling down the message before it disappeared.

Having defeated the bandit leader, Ren was eager to continue playing. Gamers around the world were racing one another to complete Evernow, but Ren was the first to get this far. Everyone online agreed that killing the bandit leader was so hard, it must be the precursor to an epic final boss battle. Ren cracked his knuckles one by one, licking his lips at the prospect of facing the evil shogun in digital combat.

There was one problem: the game had shut down. The controller was working fine, the console was fully functional, the TV remained unaffected—but the game wouldn't play. Ren tried switching all his devices off and on again, jiggling all the connections, even downloading a fresh copy of the game to start again from scratch—still nothing. It was as if the game had a mind of its own, as if it refused to let Ren continue until he had performed the task stated in the on-screen message. And that meant going outside.

Ren sniffed his armpits. Maybe take a shower first.

Forty-nine minutes later, Ren was in an elevator heading up to the seventh floor of an apartment building. He had followed the message's explicit instructions, not talking to anyone else and staying off all social media. For someone who lived and died by the page views on his video channel, this was close to torture. But when he told his subscribers about beating the bandit leader and revealed what came next, those numbers would go crazy.

Ren used the elevator doors as a mirror to check his thick black hair, pulling it forward over his ears and forehead. The shower had taken three minutes, getting his hair right much longer. He had no idea what was waiting at his destination, but Ren wanted to look his best for it. The doors opened and he ventured out, cautious. A few steps down the hallway was a door marked #732. Ren double-checked his instructions—this was it.

He knocked at the door, firm and resolute, not noticing

it was already ajar. The force of his knock pushed it open, revealing a silent apartment beyond. Ren frowned. Who leaves their front door unlocked, let alone open? He leaned close, calling out in Japanese: "Hello? Anyone here?" No reply. He stepped across the threshold, nerves jangling.

The apartment was quiet, almost eerie in its stillness. The interior was cluttered yet neat, hundreds of empty food boxes stacked along one wall. Dozens of origami dragons were organized in rows along a countertop, their intricate folds mute evidence of a focused mind and precise, delicate fingers. Ren wondered if whoever lived here had a cleaner, and whether they might be willing to tackle his garbage dump of an apartment.

A scream burst from behind a doorway in the apartment, followed by a powerful guitar riff—there was somebody here! Ren strode toward the source, eager for answers. Instead he found himself entering a young woman's bedroom with pink-patterned walls. Pride of place in the room was given to a music center that was booming out shrieking chords and piercing vocals. Sitting facing the sound system was a young woman dressed all in red, a hoodie hiding most of her face. All her focus was bent on achieving the perfect final fold for another origami dragon.

Ren shouted to be heard over the music. "Hello!? 'Scuse me."

The young woman spun round, her surprise turning to anger. "Who are you?"

Ren stumbled over his response, struck by her beauty and the fire in her gaze. She had jet-black hair with neatly trimmed bangs, but the rest was long and straight, spilling out from inside her hoodie. He had marched into her bedroom uninvited. How on earth could he explain this behavior? "I am Ren Shimosawa... and I think I'm supposed to be here."

Oh yeah, that should definitely impress her. Watch out, genius at work. Despite his feeble opening, her expression softened. Maybe there was still hope…

"I'm sure you're not."

Guess again. But he pressed on regardless. "I'm a gamer."

"A what?"

"I play… games." Ren almost blushed with embarrassment. Saying that out loud, it sounded childish, even ridiculous. He almost never met people who didn't already know his achievements. Having to explain himself like this wasn't what he had expected, but there was no point backing out now. "I'm actually quite famous—well, internet famous. Anyway, I've been playing a game called Evernow for four straight days. No one has beaten this game. But I have gotten the farthest."

"Evernow?" She said the word as if it had meaning, something distant and elusive.

Encouraged, Ren pressed on. "I finally reached the second-to-last level and unlocked a secret message—it was this address!" He showed her the piece of paper on which he had scrawled the apartment number. But after reading it, she backed away.

"No. That's impossible."

As she retreated, light caught her face at a particular angle that set Ren's mind racing. There was something familiar about this young woman. "Wait, do I know you?"

She shook her head.

Ren persisted with his questions. "What school do you go to?"

"I don't know."

"How can you not know what—"

"You have to go," she insisted, pushing him out of her room. "Now. I'm not supposed to let anyone inside."

"I swear I've seen you—" Ren's protests died in his mouth as he spied an ornate Shoji door down the hall. It felt as if the screen was calling out to be pushed aside. But before he could respond, the young woman was standing in front of him, propelling him back to the front door. She pulled it open and shoved him out into the hall.

"Please, don't come back."

The apartment door slammed in Ren's face, but he didn't move. His mind was still racing, searching every scrap of recent experience, desperate to remember where he had seen the young woman before. Her look, he recognized it from somewhere—

Of course! That's how he knew her face!

Ren sprinted to the elevator, stabbing a finger at the call button. He needed to reach his apartment as soon as possible. To get back into apartment #732, he needed proof.

CARBONDALE, ILLINOIS

Tommy shoved the textbooks into his locker and shut the door, glad another school day was nearly over. He'd been exhausted before it began, thanks to that fruitless round trip to Chicago. Throw in a close encounter with Brad's fist, not to mention hearing about what had happened to the people from the meeting—it hadn't exactly been one for the yearbook. He closed his locker and secured it with a combination padlock. Better safe than—

"Hey, you're the ice-cream junkie, right?"

Tommy actually jumped, startled by the warm voice close behind him. He spun round to find Emily smiling at him, no doubt amused by his reaction. "What?"

"You're at Moe's all the time."

"Oh. Yeah, I guess I like ice cream." Tommy winced

inwardly. Had he really just said that? What a dork. But it sounded better than the truth: *I've got the hots for you, Emily, and my ice-cream addiction is a cover story so I can see you outside school.*

"So it's not because of me," she teased.

Tommy laughed, struggling to keep the panic off his face.

"Just messing with you." Emily play-punched him in the arm. "I'm the one who drew the happy face on your punch card."

He nodded, not trusting himself to reply out loud.

"Hey, you know what? We need a new scooper. You should come in to the parlor. They're letting me do the interviews." She gave him a conspiratorial wink.

"Okay. Yeah. Maybe."

Emily looked round to see if anyone was watching before moving a step closer, her face more serious. "Look, I heard what Brad did to you during the break. I'm sorry."

"Why? You didn't do it."

"I know. Brad acts like a tough guy but he's not. He's just…"

Tommy finished the thought for her. "A total narcissistic jerk?"

She smiled. "Sometimes. Yeah." But worry furrowed her brow again. "Did you hear what they're saying about Coach Lewis? He might have been an Evo."

Play dumb. Play dumb. "An Evo?"

"You know—evolved. Had powers."

"Really?"

Emily scrunched up her nose as if smelling something bad. "He always seemed a little bit pervy to me." Tommy shrugged, not sure why she was sharing so much with him. "Well, I gotta take off—French Club meeting."

Emily brushed past him as she left, and Tommy caught a

hint of her scent—warm and lush, like a hot summer's day. She called back to him as she walked down the corridor. "Seriously, you should come by for that job."

Tommy was going to say something back, something witty and intelligent, guaranteed to impress. But while he was still thinking up a suitable reply, Emily ran into Brad at the far end of the hall. The jock slid a possessive arm round her, pulling Emily close as they walked away.

A bleep from his pocket saved Tommy from having to watch any more of that. He pulled out his cell phone and swiped the screen. It revealed a text message from an unknown number: *Don't trust anyone*. Tommy looked round, but he was all alone.

EAST L.A., CALIFORNIA

The neighborhood had gotten worse since Carlos last paid a visit, if that was possible. Street after street, all he saw were run-down bodegas and payday loan centers. The few moments of beauty came from elaborate graffiti murals spray-painted on cement block walls and abandoned storefronts. As Carlos strolled beside his nephew, one particular mural caught his eye. Elaborate lettering asked: "Where are the Heroes?" Good question.

Jose had badgered Carlos into walking him home after school. The boy was proud to be associated with his war hero uncle, but that didn't stop him from giving Carlos the third degree. "How come you don't ever stay with us?"

"They cover my hotels when I do these speaking tours, so—"

"But my Dad wouldn't mind if you did," Jose persisted.

"I don't know. Think he's still pretty sore at me."

"Maybe he's over it—now that you're a hero."

They were within sight of an auto repair shop. A careworn sign hanging over the entrance proclaimed the premises as those of Gutierrez and Sons. Past the sign, Carlos could see the neon emblem of a dive bar. That felt more like home these days. He slipped into Spanish as they ambled closer to the garage. "Yeah, well, sometimes heroes aren't as heroic as you think they are."

Jose wouldn't hear of it. "But you are! You're like El Vengador!"

Carlos had a blurry memory of seeing a guy in a luchador's mask on the news—Vigilante Troubles City, something like that. "He's one of those Evos, right?"

"They're not all bad. El Vengador's the only one taking care of this neighborhood—the only one the gangbangers are scared of."

Carlos saw his brother emerge from the garage, wiping oily hands on a rag, grease stains covering much of the mechanic's overalls. Oscar was only a few years older, but he resembled Pop more and more every day—rugged, diligent, steady. Carlos had gotten their mom's good looks and her tendency to flee commitment.

Oscar pointed a finger at his son. "I've heard enough about El Vengador—I've seen enough, too." He gestured at the garage wall, where someone had painted a crude version of a luchador's mask. "That yours, Jose?"

"Yes, but people need to know he's not in hiding like the rest of them—"

"No," Oscar snapped. "People need to come to a garage without graffiti on the wall." He nodded to a bucket of paint and roller brush under the tag. "Now clean it up."

Carlos almost laughed at the sight of his nephew trudging toward the paint, sulky reluctance obvious in every step. He recognized so much of himself from way back when in Jose. "So, the kid's got a hero, someone to look up to—what's the problem?"

"El Vengador isn't everyone's hero. The tag is bad for business. Besides—" Carlos felt the full force of his brother's glare "—why does Jose need some caped crusader to idolize when he's got *Tio* Carlos, Uncle Carlos the war hero?" Oscar stalked back into the garage, where a mini-van was waiting with its hood up. Carlos followed, glancing at the engine.

"Think she's a lost cause," Oscar admitted. "Transmission's shot."

Carlos leaned in for a closer look. Oscar was a decent mechanic, good on routine jobs, but Carlos was the one with the gift. Sure enough, he spotted the real problem in moments. "You just need to replace the vacuum lines to the modulator valve."

His brother slipped into Spanish, like he always did when angry. "You telling me my job? 'Cause unless you're ready to pick up a wrench…"

Carlos backed off, hands held up in surrender, shaking his head. "Hey, I told Pop to paint over the 's' in the word 'Sons' years ago."

Oscar jabbed a finger at him. "War hero or not, you broke his heart."

A black Charger with tinted windows rumbled to a halt outside the garage door, blasting music so loud the brothers' argument couldn't escalate any further. After idling for a few moments, the cacophony died and a skinhead gangbanger got out from behind the wheel, his brown arms adorned with plenty of ink that announced his affiliations. Sauntering a few steps toward Oscar, the newcomer tossed his keys to the mechanic.

"Oye, need me some new rims," he announced in Spanish. "Pronto."

Oscar nodded. "You got it, Pelon. One car before you—"

"Bump me up, bitch," the gangbanger scowled. "Ain't no one going before me."

Carlos mentally prepared himself for violence. Nobody spoke to Oscar like that and got away with it—nobody. But instead of bristling for a fight, his brother was giving in to this punk.

"You're right," Oscar smiled, all meek and mild. "No problem."

Nodding, Pelon strutted away to a low-rider that was waiting for him at the curb. Once he was inside, it rolled away, music blasting out at ear-splitting volume. Carlos waited for the din to die down before taking his older brother to task.

"Look who's breaking Pop's heart now. He would've stood up to those guys." Carlos could see the muscles in his brother's jaw rippling, anger close to boiling over.

"Things are more complicated than when Pop was around. All I know is one of us is still here, trying to keep the family business open. The other one's not."

They glared at each other, but Carlos had no interest in playing Prodigal Son while Oscar claimed the moral high ground. Neither of them was any kind of hero—maybe they never had been. Carlos strode away from the garage. "Like it was ever gonna be fifty-fifty."

"That's it, walk away!" Oscar shouted. "You're real good at that, 'hero-man'!"

AUSTIN, TEXAS

Bennet washed dishes at the sink of his tract home while Julia sifted paperwork at the dining table. He didn't recall wedding planning being such an all-consuming effort the last time he got married, but Julia was devoting an hour to the task most nights. What made her happy made him happy, although Julia wasn't sounding happy tonight. "I don't know. If this thing gets to be over seventy-five guests, we might have to rent a tent," she sighed.

"Sure it's not too late for us to elope?"

She padded over to the sink and slipped her arms around Bennet, pulling him into a hug. "Sorry, my friend, you've already been roped and tied."

Much as he enjoyed her attention, Bennet's focus was torn away by movement outside. That same damn blue sedan was parked across the street, but this time the driver was getting out from behind the tinted windows. He scuttled toward the house, doing his best to stay hidden as rain lashed the street.

Julia wanted a kiss, but Bennet laid a finger on her sweet lips. "Hold that thought."

"Why? What is it?"

He didn't answer, heading for the outside door instead.

After watching Bennet from a safe distance all day, Quentin Frady finally mustered the courage to move in for a closer look. Locking his sedan, he pulled his blue hoodie up over his head as protection against the rain and to keep his face hidden. Quentin had seen Bennet going into the tract house with a beautiful redhead and bags full of groceries. Did she even know that Noah Bennet was his real name, or was she in love with friendly car salesman Ted Barnes?

That didn't matter now. Quentin had plenty of evidence, but he needed a witness, someone who had been there during the events of June thirteenth. What better person to spill what really had happened that day than Primatech's own Evo control guy?

Quentin patted the messenger bag slung over his shoulder, checking that he'd brought the evidence with him. Judging by the files, Noah Bennet was not an easy man to pin down, let alone turn against his masters. But Quentin had the truth on his side, and that was more powerful than lies and corruption and cover-ups.

He took a deep breath, preparing to edge even closer, when suddenly Bennet came out of the house. He strolled down the pavement as if going for an evening walk in the rain, a man without a care in the world. Quentin followed, careful to keep his footsteps in time with those of Bennet. He didn't see the garbage bag until he tripped over it, sending him sprawling onto the ground. By the time he had scrambled back up again, Bennet was gone. Vanished, disappeared—but that was impossible. Where had he—?

"First rule of tailing someone," Bennet snarled as he advanced on the shadowy male figure, "is know how to tail someone!" He grabbed hold of the man's blue sweatshirt and shoved his stalker back against a lamppost. The guy was a mess—short, overweight, unkempt, and twitchy, with ginger hair and a beard. His breath stank of coffee, and his eyes were wide as saucers. A frayed messenger bag hung heavily from one shoulder. This was no elite operative. This was an amateur. "Who are you? What do you want?"

"Answers," Quentin said. "To know what really happened on June thirteenth."

"What's that got to do with me?"

"You're Noah Bennet. You knew all of those people."

So, an amateur with some knowledge. Bennet shoved

a forearm against the guy's throat, pushing in hard to emphasize his control. "Who do you work for?"

"I worked at Renautas," was the gasped reply, "but not for them. And I know you worked for Primatech."

"I sold paper."

"Sure, along with bagging and tagging and keeping 'powers' under wraps."

"And you know about this how?"

"Because Renautas secretly owned Primatech."

Bennet shook his head. "Primatech's dead. Nothing but a hole in the ground."

"Unless it's not," Quentin replied, between gasps for air. "That's what I'm trying to tell you. I've found things I wasn't supposed to find."

Bennet eased off a little, let his captive get enough air to explain. "I'm listening."

"There's something coming. Something huge heading this way—and Renautas is at the wheel. June thirteenth was the beginning, I just don't know of what."

Bennet stared into his captive's eyes. The guy believed what he was selling, but it might as well have been Greek for all the sense it made. After June thirteenth, Bennet had searched long and hard for answers to explain what had happened. But all he'd found were crazy conspiracy theorists. They even had a self-aggrandizing name for themselves.

"Lemme guess," Bennet sneered. "You're a Truther."

"That has nothing to do with it," his stalker insisted. "But come on, man, you really think Mohinder Suresh was behind that attack?" Quentin laughed, as if the answer should be obvious to a five-year-old, let alone a grown man. "He's a patsy."

"I saw what everyone else saw. I know what everyone else knows." Bennet let go of his stalker. The man fumbled in his messenger bag for a ragged paper document, at least three hundred pages long. Bennet recognized the title: *Escalating Evolution*.

"This is Suresh's manuscript," the stalker said, full of pride. "Never published."

"How did you find—"

"It's all in here. The Evos, these powers… he says their numbers are increasing. Escalating! But he doesn't say why. Are they here to take over, like the government and the media keep telling us? No." Quentin leaned close, his ragged voice dropping to a whisper. "I think they're here to save us!"

Bennet almost laughed. "Then where are they? Look around." He gestured at the rest of the empty street. "You see any people with powers around here? They're gone. Hiding. Dead. If they were here to save us, trust me, I'd know." Bennet shoved his stalker into the road. The guy struggled a little, but it was no contest. Suddenly sirens filled the air and flashing red lights illuminated the street. A police car squealed to a halt, and two cops jumped out of it, drawing their weapons.

"You called the cops?"

Bennet shook his head, bemused. Julia ran out of the house, pointing at Quentin. "That's him! That's the guy!"

The nearest cop waved his gun. "On the ground, hands over your head!"

Quentin dropped to his knees in the street, hands raised as the cops approached. "June thirteenth didn't happen like they say it did!"

"I've been over that day a thousand times," Bennet replied. "It's the day my daughter died. You don't forget a day like that."

"You do if someone didn't want you to remember it!"

The cops snapped handcuffs round Quentin's wrists before pulling him back to his feet. As they led him to their squad car, he called back over his shoulder. "That's what I'm trying to tell you!"

Bennet's mind was spinning as he watched the police car drive away. What if this crazy story was the truth? What if his memories about June thirteenth were wrong? The implications were staggering and terrifying in equal measure.

CHAPTER FOUR

Speed traps on I-57 have proven effective in cutting motorized fatalities for the county, according to Highway Patrolman Vincent Mortimer. "We've seen a big drop in deaths due to folks driving too fast," he said yesterday. "Most locals know better than to speed along this stretch of interstate now. There's still a few tourists who come through thinking the law don't apply to them, but we show them the error of their ways."

—*Marion County Sentinel*, Illinois

INTERSTATE 57, ILLINOIS

Luke stared at the ice cream parlor punch card in his hands, the one he'd found on the church basement floor. His fingers caressed the holes perforating the creased card, while his gaze fixed on the red-ink happy face drawn in the tenth and final box. It looked so friendly, so affectionate. What did it say about the kid who dropped the card, if he inspired such a response from the person serving him at Moe's? And what did it say about Luke and Joanne, driving through the night to find and kill him?

"You've been pretty quiet since we left Chicago. Something wrong?" Joanne was behind the steering wheel, her eyes fixed on the long, straight, empty road ahead.

Luke shrugged. "Nothing. Just… This kid we're looking for… I was just…"

"Just what?" She turned to stare at him, disapproval obvious in her eyes.

"Thinking, that's all…"

"Well do me a favor and don't. The mission's pure. We're on the side of the angels here, remember that. We don't need to 'think'." But her calm insistence was shaken moments later by a siren and flashing red light behind them. "Dammit."

Luke glanced in the wing mirror. A highway patrol vehicle was catching up to them fast. Trying to outrace it was not an option in their suburban station wagon. For better or worse, they would have to try and talk their way out of this.

Patrolman Vincent Mortimer was about ready to sign off for the night when the station wagon blew past him on I-57, hitting ninety-three on the radar. Didn't these people pay any attention to all the warning signs about speed traps in the area? Instead of heading home to Avril and a warm bed, now he had to beat the devil chasing down these fools. Well, at least it gave him a chance to test the acceleration on his new patrol car. Let's see how long it took to catch up to them.

The answer was not long at all. The station wagon had been going flat out when it passed, but his car had more than enough gun to overtake it within a few miles. Mortimer let them know he was coming by hitting the lights and music, intrigued to see how they would react. But this was no hot pursuit, no high-speed chase. In less than a minute, the station wagon pulled over to the side of the interstate, the driver and passenger meek as church mice.

Mortimer called in the registration, checking to see if there were any outstanding warrants or warnings about the vehicle. If it were local, he might have thought it was teenagers stealing their folks' car. But it had New York plates, so either the driver was a long way from home or the car had been stolen. Family station wagon wasn't exactly the ride of first choice for carjackers and thieves.

The radio crackled into life. "Car is registered to a Luke Collins of Buffalo, New York. No outstanding warrants, no theft reported."

"Thanks, Maisie."

Mortimer got out of his vehicle and ambled along the gravel toward the station wagon, one hand resting on the gun holstered at his hip. He pulled a small flashlight from his belt, clicking it on as he reached the driver's side. The window rolled down to reveal an African-American woman behind the wheel, a white male in the passenger seat. They both seemed a little tense, but that was normal in the circumstances—Mortimer would be more worried if they were too relaxed. That always spelled trouble with a capital T.

"You folks know why I pulled you over?"

The woman nodded. "Speeding. My sister's having a baby in Carbondale, her first. You know how it is, Officer."

Mortimer focused his attention on the license and registration she was holding out: Joanne Collins, also from Buffalo, New York. Looked like these two were husband and wife. "Carbondale, huh? Must be in a pretty big hurry to get there."

"Yes, sir, I suppose we are."

Mortimer returned her documents, still puzzling these

two out. He used his flashlight to illuminate the station wagon's interior. The couple seemed regular enough, but there was something *off* about the pair of them. He let his flashlight beam slide back behind them, checking if they had any kids or—

What. The. Heck?

The back seat was stacked with half the stock of a small hardware store—coils of rope, rolls of duct tape, two gas cans and a hatchet. The hairs on Mortimer's neck were standing up. Something was very wrong with this picture. He moved back to the driver's window, pointing his flashlight beam full in Joanne's face.

"This stuff you got back here—someone might get the wrong impression. Unless you got an explanation for it." Mortimer waited, letting silence do its work. Back at the academy, his instructors had once said that if you asked a question, the average person could last about seven seconds before they felt compelled to answer. Sure enough, this couple were no different. After exchanging a look with his partner, the passenger leaned across to answer, smiling up at Mortimer.

"Yes, sir, we do indeed. I guess you could say we're on kind of a killing spree." The guy looked at his partner. "Right, sweetheart?" He turned back to Mortimer. "Evos. Powered people. We track 'em down, one at a time— although we prefer to find a nest. Then we shoot 'em in the head and burn all the evidence." He sat back.

Joanne gave a shrug, her face a picture of innocence. "It's just how we roll."

Mortimer stared at them, counting Mississippis in his head, but this time the couple didn't crack, holding his gaze without blinking. After ten Mississippis, Mortimer lowered his flashlight and smiled at these two odd fish. "Of course it is." He forced a laugh, as if joining in with their joke. "You two just watch your speed from now on, you hear?" Mortimer edged a hand toward his gun, aware that Joanne was staring at him.

"You betcha, Officer."

Then everything was a blur—the sound of a gunshot, the shriek of protesting metal, and something smashing one of Mortimer's legs out from under him. He hit the gravel hard, sidearm bouncing out of his reach. Pain exploded through his body, forcing a scream of anguish. It got worse when he looked down at the bloody mess where his knee had been. He could see clear through the joint, splinters of stark white bone jutting from the gaping hole, crimson spurting out across the gravel. He would never walk unaided again, assuming he survived the next few minutes.

Instinct took over as adrenalin pumped through him, willing him into action. The sidearm, he needed his sidearm. Twisting round, he spied it a few feet away. Mortimer stretched out an arm, clawing with his fingers, desperate to reach the—

"You have a nice day," Joanne said.

The last things Mortimer heard were another gunshot and tires squealing as the station wagon sped away. Then the darkness claimed him.

TOKYO, JAPAN

Ren's quest was destroying his apartment. Shelving units had been emptied across the floor, games and books spilling across every available surface. A thief ransacking the apartment would have been tidier, but Ren didn't care. He had to find it, he had to—

"Of course!" Abandoning his fruitless search under the

bed, he clambered across to his desk, feet slipping and sliding on unstable piles of debris. By comparison with the rest of his apartment, the desk was an oasis of calm, if still not exactly tidy. Ren shoved his state-of-the-art computer to one side, groping behind it with both hands. He couldn't see what was back there, but a jangling memory told him he should find—

"Aha!" His fingers closed around a video game manual, pulling it free of the nest of writhing cables where it had fallen and lain forgotten. He stared at the cover, a broad smile of triumph spreading across his face. "I knew it!"

Miko did her best to ignore all the banging and shouting coming from the front door of her apartment. But when the building supervisor rang to say that her neighbors were planning to lodge a formal complaint, she had no choice. Bracing herself, Miko opened the door.

Standing outside was the stranger—Ren something?—who had invaded her apartment before. Despite her frustration with him, Miko had to admit he was kind of cute. He was almost bouncing up and down on the spot with excitement, like an anime character with ants in their pants. "You're the Katana Girl!" he shouted. "I can prove it!"

"Katana Girl?"

Ren thrust a computer game manual at her, the word Evernow emblazoned across it in English. She took the manual and studied the cover—it was like looking in a mirror. A female warrior was posing in the center, a long red ribbon tied in her black hair, brandishing a fearsome sword in one hand. The character resembled Miko in almost every detail. The likeness was uncanny.

"No player has ever figured out how to unlock her," Ren

babbled, coming into the apartment and closing the front door behind him. But Miko's attention was still fixed on the manual. She swept back her hoodie, revealing the long red ribbon tied in her black hair. "You have the same eyes, the same mouth—even the red bow!"

Miko shook her head, dismissing the coincidence. "I always wear this. My father gave it to me—"

"Katana Girl's father gave her a red bow, too!"

She turned away, hiding her feelings. "I'm nothing like your Katana Girl." But this stranger wouldn't give up. He followed her across the room, flipping through the manual to show page after page of concept art from the game— Katana Girl kicking ass, Katana Girl in a parallel future Tokyo, Katana Girl fighting in a world reclaimed by nature.

"You see? She swore vengeance on those who kidnapped her father."

That forced Miko to pay attention. How did he know about that, how could he?

Ren kept babbling on. "Her sword is the key—hidden under the floor of her father's study! It transforms her into a deadly warrior." He pointed to a page in the manual showing a close-up of Katana Girl's sword. A glyph was apparent on the hilt, etched in a narrow S shape. Two short horizontal bars jutted out to the left from the bottom curve of the S, while a single horizontal bar stuck out to the right from the upper curve. The glyph resembled a broken strand of DNA helix, but different from any found in most normal humans.

Seeing that shook Miko to the core. "Leave. Now!"

Her anger stopped Ren in his tracks. All the boyish enthusiasm drained from his face, replaced by disappointment. "But… what did I—?"

"I said GO!"

Ren retreated from her, bowing in meek obedience. Pausing only to leave the game manual on a nearby shelf, he strode out of the apartment. She closed the front door after him, locking and bolting it. Her breath was coming in short gasps, spots dancing in front of her eyes. How could this be possible? How could—

Miko snatched up the manual, flicking through the pages, searching, searching. She found it on the back page—a photo of a man smiling, his name and significance defined in a single line underneath: *HACHIRO OTOMO, game designer of Evernow*. On a desk behind him were various origami shapes. Many of them were dragons.

AUSTIN, TEXAS

Bennet lay in bed, awake even though midnight was a memory now. Beside him Julia was sound asleep, her slumber undisturbed by the events of a few hours earlier. But Bennet could find no rest. His mind was racing, still troubled by the stalker's wild claim.

Few people could forget where they were or what they were doing the previous June thirteenth. For those who had been in Odessa that fateful day, the terrible events were liable to haunt them to the grave. Bennet had been near the epicenter of it all, so his memory of what had happened couldn't be false—could it?

But he knew how easy it was to erase people's fragile grasp of the past, to tear away the most shocking scenes they had ever witnessed and turn them into smoke, gone forever in a moment. Bennet had made that happen to others with the help of an old ally. Could he have been subjected to the same treatment? And, if so, who had ordered it? There was no use staying in bed any longer; he wouldn't sleep tonight.

He had to know. If there was the slightest chance his memory of June thirteenth had been altered or rewritten, he had to find out. He needed the truth—whatever it might be.

Bennet slipped out of bed, careful not to disturb Julia. He crept through the house to the dining room, where a painting of the stars and stripes was prominently displayed beneath a wall light. Lifting the painting away revealed a large hole in the drywall. Bennet paused a moment, knowing that reaching inside the hole was liable to undo nearly a year of hard work establishing himself as Ted Barnes, friendly car salesman. But if he wanted answers—and he did—that was a necessary risk. He stretched a hand into the blackness and pulled out a dusty, neglected duffel bag.

Unzipping it, Bennet lifted out the contents one by one and placed them on the dining table. This was his go-bag, with all the trappings from that former life at Primatech: five bundles of cash, each containing a thousand dollars, two handguns, and a pair of passports in different names. Also in the bag was a tattered leather datebook. Bennet flipped through it, looking for clues in his meticulous handwritten entries. Each day was an hour-by-hour observation log—"No vehicles parked in driveway, subject spotted through kitchen window".

But the page marked June thirteenth was blank, untouched. The datebook had been packed with information for the preceding days, weeks and months, but June thirteenth was empty, a void offering no information and no answers. Bennet skimmed the remaining pages—nothing. His entries stopped the day before Odessa happened. But as he flipped back to that date, something fell from the page for June fourteenth—a business card. It settled on the table face up, two words on it: Lumiere Ophthalmology.

Bennet picked it up for a closer look. For a business card, it was lacking in any useful contact details. Turning it over, he found a short message handwritten across the back: See More Clearly. This didn't ring any bells at all, certainly stirred no memories.

He repacked the duffel bag and took it with him to the study. A quick web search on his laptop got a match. It seemed Lumiere Ophthalmology specialized in Lasik eye surgery. But something didn't add up. The business was listed on Yelp, but it had no comments, no reviews of its services—and not even a phone number, just an address. There was one further piece of information at the end of the listing: Lumiere had relocated from Odessa to Dallas in the last twelve months.

Bennet had seen too much in his time to believe in coincidences. He jotted down the Dallas address on a slip of paper. Out of habit, he destroyed the three pages below it on the pad and also deleted his search history from the laptop. "Better safe than sorry" was his philosophy. It had kept him alive this long, so why stop now? Dallas was about three hours' drive from Austin, especially at this early hour. He could be at the office of Lumiere Ophthalmology by the time it opened.

EAST L.A., CALIFORNIA

Carlos could never sleep the first night in a strange bed. The second night wasn't much better—or the third. Fact was, he didn't sleep much at all these days. It wasn't getting to sleep that troubled him, but the dreams that came when he did. Nightmares, if he was honest with himself, which was something Carlos did his best to avoid.

One time he tried describing his nightmares to the

counsellor provided by a local veterans' association, but she hadn't been there, hadn't seen what he'd seen. Really talking about what it was like in Afghanistan—not the prepared speech he performed for impressionable, willing audiences on demand, but really talking about it—well, that was impossible unless the other person had been there. It didn't make the talking any easier, but at least the silences were understood.

When sleep wouldn't come, or when he couldn't face what was lurking in his subconscious, Carlos turned to an old friend: drink. After the argument with Oscar he had gone back to the hotel room, prowling around there for a few hours. Eventually he went for a walk round the old neighborhood. It took a while to find, but there was a liquor store still open on one street. He exchanged two crumpled bills for a bottle in a brown bag with a screwtop lid. As soon as he was outside, Carlos opened the bottle and took a long pull. The familiar burning at the back of his throat felt good.

He ambled along the street, nursing his bottle, avoiding the gaze of other pedestrians. Anyone out at this time of night was either trouble or troubled, and Carlos had had more than enough of both. He stopped outside an electronics store, the windows covered by thin mesh screens to protect them. Peering through gaps in the wire, he could make out a local news channel playing on one of the TV screens.

Some guy was ranting into a microphone with what looked like his wife and two young daughters beside him. In the background was a flock of protestors brandishing signs with religious symbols on them. "God Hates Powers" read one, "God is the Only Power" another. A headline across the bottom of the screen provided context for the images: EL VENGADOR VICTIM SPEAKS. The interview footage was replaced with a fearsome and brutal artist's impression of what El Vengador looked like.

Carlos took another long pull from his bottle, fascinated by the spectacle. Jose hero-worshipped El Vengador, but the news made him look like a menace. Which one of them was closest to the truth? It didn't matter to Carlos, but he wouldn't want to be the guy in the luchador's mask when the police finally caught up to El Vengador.

A woman's scream in the distance snapped his attention away from the news. Yes, the neighborhood had definitely gotten worse. Carlos took another drink from his bottle, hoping that the woman found some refuge from whatever was troubling her.

El Vengador stood on the rooftop, watching over the streets he called home. Police patrols were few and far between in this part of East L.A., what with the war on drugs, gang conflicts, and Homeland Security consuming most of law enforcement's time and resources. The concerns of ordinary citizens, the people who did the living and the dying round here, didn't get the attention they deserved— and they certainly didn't get any protection. If someone had to wear a mask to reclaim a few blocks for the good, decent people of this area, so be it.

He had heard screaming and the sounds of pursuit, coming closer. He had chosen this rooftop for the overview it gave of local streets and alleyways. His keen eyes spied movement—a young woman running, two men in hoodies pursuing her. She darted down the alleyway below El Vengador, dashing through puddles and dodging round piles of garbage. But those hunting her were closing in fast. It was only a matter of time before she became another crime statistic.

El Vengador leapt from the rooftop, plummeting to the alley below. He dropped into a crouch as he hit the roof of an abandoned car, its chassis and his body armor absorbing most of the impact. The car's windows exploded outward, showering the men with glass. They spun round, their original target forgotten for now. Good. He wanted the scum to see his mask, to know that this neighborhood was under his protection.

One of the predators reached for a gun, but El Vengador was on him in a flash. Powerful hands grabbed the thug and hurled him forty feet! He flew face-first into a wall, hitting it with a wet smack. His body slid to the ground, leaving a bloody smear on the bricks.

The second predator refused to back down, slashing a blade through the air—a foolish decision. El Vengador grabbed the assailant and flung him into a nearby dumpster. The thug slammed into the heavy metalwork so hard it crumpled, like a fist punching aluminium foil. He twitched once but did not move again. The fight was over within moments.

El Vengador nodded in satisfaction. But where was the woman he had sought to protect? Before he could turn to look for her, gunfire lit up the alleyway. El Vengador felt two bullets slamming into his armor, but it was strong enough to withstand them. As he twisted round to confront the shooter, another bullet struck him. This one found a narrow gap in his armor, piercing a joint to plunge deep into his side.

El Vengador crumpled to one knee, pain searing through him. His shooter emerged from the shadows, smirking—it was the woman he'd been fighting to protect! The whole thing had been staged, a lure for the local hero, and El Vengador had fallen for it. His assassin came closer, not wanting to botch her kill shot.

Gritting his teeth against the pain, El Vengador snapped one hand forward, sliding a concealed knife into his palm. Before the assassin realized what was happening, the blade had buried itself in her throat. She fell backwards, choking on her own blood.

El Vengador winced as he got back to his feet. Fingertips reached between the plates of body armor, feeling for the gunshot wound. They came away bloody. He had to get off the streets, had to get home—before it was too late.

The distant wail of a police siren approached, as if mocking him. El Vengador clenched his jaw beneath the luchador's mask, strength seeping from his body with each step as he staggered away into the darkness.

CHAPTER FIVE

Few people visit the site of last year's atrocity. State authorities have positioned heavy barriers across approach roads to discourage catastrophe sightseers, the curious and the ghoulish. Forbidding signs on chain-link fences warn of the dangers still lurking in the rubble. Like the disasters at Chernobyl and Fukushima, what happened at Primatech seems to have a half-life that extends well beyond the original tragedy.

Our investigative team felt obliged to visit the blast site, to see for ourselves what remained. We had no wish to dishonor the memory of those lost on June thirteenth, nor to desecrate what has become the final resting place for so many lost that day. But a trip to the center of the atrocity seemed necessary, even essential.

We never reached Primatech. Like many others, we were turned back short of our destination. Federal agencies say they are still working to understand what happened and to make the site safe. All we could see of Primatech were ruins. Massive remnants of broken cement on the horizon resembled a child's broken toys. Beyond that—nothing.

The perimeter of the blast site is now empty and eerie, the hinterland of a terrible desolation. If we needed proof that the aftermath of June thirteenth still resonates in this place, we found it on the roadside. Dozens of dead pigeons litter the landscape, their bodies left untouched by other animals. No living creature goes near Primatech now. Even birds will not fly over what is left of that unfortunate site.

—extract from The Odessa Files, *Enquiry magazine*, June 2015 edition

INTERSTATE 35, TEXAS

Bennet watched the sun come up as he drove north toward Dallas. He should have been tired—in fact, he should have been exhausted. No sleep to speak of, leaving his home in Austin before dawn to trek hundreds of miles on what was most likely a wild goose chase. It was foolhardy behavior at best, but at the same time it made him feel alive.

Ever since that day in Odessa, he seemed to have been sleepwalking through life, his thoughts a quiet fog. Falling for Julia was the one shining light in the last twelve months, a beacon to help him get past the grief and trauma of what had happened on June thirteenth. Bennet had attributed his numbness to loss, similar to the way scar tissue over a wound leaves an area that is never quite as responsive as it used to be. That was how he had felt, numb all over and missing something vital. But what if Claire's passing was not the only loss he had suffered as a result of the events in Odessa?

He had been back there only once, and that day he'd vowed never to return. The hurt was too strong, the loss too raw. Now, as he passed a sign announcing fifty-seven miles to Dallas, Bennet wondered what he might learn about that day. One year on from June thirteenth, it was time to push past the pain and discover the truth. He pressed his foot to the gas, eager for answers.

EAST L.A., CALIFORNIA

Carlos stared up at the Gutierrez and Sons sign, his fingers failing to massage away the hangover lurking behind both eyes. A long night of thinking and drinking had done him little good, so he had come back to the place that had been his home for so many childhood years. The garage had been a kind of playground for him and Oscar, with Pop a constant presence in the background. Maybe here Carlos could feel useful again—assuming Oscar forgave all his misdeeds and misdemeanors. It was a big ask.

He lurched toward the garage door, fumbling with the many keys on his chain. Eventually his fingers settled on the right one, and he reached out to the lock—but the door was already open. Carlos frowned. His brother never, ever left the garage unlocked overnight. The Gutierrez family still commanded respect from most people round here, but that didn't make them invulnerable. Petty thefts and break-ins by junkies looking to score anything they could sell or exchange for a hit were the price of doing business.

Carlos pushed the door open and went inside. "Oscar?!"

No reply. The place looked empty, nobody around. So much for starting over.

He turned to go and his boot slipped on the cement. But it wasn't spilled grease or oil—it was red. It was blood. Carlos crouched for a closer look—the blood was still wet. He had seen enough of it in Afghanistan to know that it was fresh. A trail of drops led from the door to a hydraulic lift, where a muscle car was raised up in the air.

As Carlos got closer, he saw a metal staircase hidden in the access well beneath the lift, descending into darkness beneath the garage. *Madre de Dios*, how long had that been there? He crept nearer, wary of what he might find but curious, too. The blood drops continued down the steps, increasing in frequency. Someone had lost a lot of blood getting down these steps. Careful not to slip, Carlos clambered down the metal staircase.

As he descended, the space around him opened out into an underground chamber with circular brick tunnels leading away from it in different directions. Judging by the smell, they probably ran into the city sewers. There was a workbench with a police scanner on it and strange gadgetry he didn't recognize. Mounted on one wall was a collection of weapons and blades. Close by was a battered championship wrestling belt, its familiarity nagging at Carlos—he'd seen it before, but where? On another wall, a cat's cradle of red yarn was strung between dozens of different names and pictures. Shafts of light streamed down through glass bricks overhead. The torso of a mannequin hung on chains from the ceiling, a dark jacket covered in body armor draped over it. The chamber had the look of a secret lair.

A moan of pain from the gloom around the workbench made Carlos realize that someone was slumped over it. No, not someone—his brother! Oscar struggled to his feet, clutching a hand to his side, blood staining his fingers. He managed a weak smile.

"I don't understand…" Carlos whispered.

"World's gone mad since June thirteenth. I'm just trying to make a difference."

On the floor between them was a discarded luchador's

mask, the same one Carlos had seen depicted on the news. "Are you… Are you telling me that you—"

"We all have secrets." Sweat was pouring down Oscar's face, and his breath came in short gasps. He moved a hand aside, revealing a bullet wound. Carlos saw his brother's knees buckle and he lunged forward, catching Oscar as he fell to the dusty floor. Carlos forced a hand against the wound, applying pressure, but it was no good. Blood spilled through his fingers, warm and red and all too familiar.

"It was a trap," Oscar whispered between breaths. "They knew I was coming."

"Who?"

"It's all there." A trembling finger pointed at the string map and a nearby computer. "Carlos, listen to me. Jose really looks up to you. He's gonna need a strong hand, so you gotta—"

"The hell you talking about? We're getting you an ambulance."

Oscar clutched at Carlos, coughing blood. "It's not just Jose. There are others."

"Others? What others?"

"Someone like you… You can put on the mask—"

"I can't do anything! I'm… everything they say about me, the medal, all of it—" But Oscar went into a seizure, and Carlos never got to finish his confession. Oscar's grip on him tightened, eyes widening, face twitching in agony and anguish.

And then he was gone.

"No! Oscar, no!" Carlos shook his brother, willing his sibling to live, to survive, but to no avail. He had arrived too late, just like in Afghanistan. Then he had been called a hero. Now he was the brother who had abandoned his family, and nobody gave out medals for that. Carlos buried his face in Oscar's hair, clutching his dead brother closer. His gaze slid over to the abandoned mask, the emblem of the mighty El Vengador. He could never put that on. He couldn't.

CARBONDALE, ILLINOIS

Tommy couldn't remember the last time he had sweated this much. His first job interview was nerve-wracking enough, but being with Emily in the tiny back office at Moe's Ice Cream Parlor, the two of them sandwiched so close together that their knees were touching? That was stress on top of stress. Like a big old stress sandwich, with extra slices of stress in it and maybe a little more stress on the side. *Stop babbling in your head, just concentrate and smile.* But don't smile too much. Wouldn't want to freak her out.

"You feeling okay?" Emily asked.

"Yes, fine. Great. Terrific, in fact. Couldn't be better," Tommy stammered.

She laughed, but it was sympathetic, not mocking. "It's okay to be nervous. I remember when I was sitting where you are. My heart was pounding something awful."

Tommy nodded, not trusting himself to answer.

Emily scanned through the long, long list of previous addresses on his job application. "Wow. What are you, like, from some weird nomadic tribe?"

"I am, as a matter of fact." Tommy loved the fact that she had a sense of humor. Almost as much as he loved her cute-as-a-button nose. "Is that a problem?"

She shook her head, smiling. "Okay, enough joking around. Let's start this interview for real." Emily's face got very serious. "Can you scoop ice cream?"

Spooked by her sudden change in demeanor, Tommy paused before answering. Was this a trick question? No, that didn't make any sense. Maybe it was a test. *Of course it's a test, idiot, you're at a job interview. Just tell the truth!* "Um… yes?"

Emily beamed with delight. "Congratulations! You're hired. Welcome to Moe's."

"Wow, thanks so much. My mom's going to be really excited." Good grief. Who talks about their mom at a moment like this? Yeesh! But somehow, despite everything, Emily was still smiling—almost as if she liked him.

"Great. I'll get you a uniform, you can start tomorrow." She stood up, reaching for the closet door, but Tommy's chair was in the way. "How about you wait for me out by the counter, and I'll bring some uniforms out for you to try on?"

Joanne sipped her Coke through a straw while her husband stared off at nothing, his coffee going cold on the laminated red table between them. The silences were getting longer, his thoughts elsewhere more often these days. Losing her son had been the worst day of Joanne's life, but at least that had been quick. Luke seemed to be drifting away from her, piece by piece, little by little. She put down her glass.

"You alright?"

Luke looked up at her, but he still seemed detached and distant, despite being only an arm's length away from her. "Yeah, it's just… This kid we're looking for…" He twisted his coffee cup round on its saucer. "Maybe he didn't even notice us the other night. Maybe we're wasting—"

"The kid has powers," Joanne snapped, anger surging deep inside her, the same burning rage that had fuelled their crusade since Odessa. "He can identify us. He can certainly identify you. So we're gonna finish what we came here to do."

Luke was chewing on his bottom lip. Never a good sign. Joanne softened her tone, determined to win him round, to get her husband back by her side. "Then we can head to Los Angeles, see if we can find this Mexican wrestler. You've always wanted to visit L.A.—well, this'll be our chance, okay?" Luke nodded. Not much of an endorsement.

Joanne looked away from him, her attention caught by a newspaper folded on the table. The headline did nothing for her blood pressure: EVOS BEHIND CHURCH FIRE—Suresh Claims Responsibility. A wild-eyed photo of Mohinder Suresh flanked the article, making him look every bit a brown-skinned evil Evo terrorist.

"Unbelievable. We do all the hard work and that son of a bitch gets all the credit," she fumed. But Luke showed little annoyance, looking more curious than anything else.

"That's the second time. One time might be a mistake, but not two."

Joanne checked her watch. They'd been in this 1950s-themed place for an hour, and there were only so many times she could hear *Rock Around the Clock* before putting a bullet through the jukebox. The place was clean and seemed popular enough with the locals, but its green walls and red leather seats were gonna give her a migraine, and soon. "When's this little prick gonna show up?"

Luke shrugged. It took all her strength not to reach across and slap some sense into him. She stood up instead, eyes searching for the bathroom. "Gotta pee." Joanne stalked away from the booth, not noticing the slender teenage boy emerging from the Staff Only doorway. The sooner they got this done and moved on, the better.

Tommy waited by the ice-cream counter, beaming at having gotten the job. For the first time in a long while, he was doing something normal, something ordinary. He peered over the counter, trying to imagine himself on the other side, serving a customer. But a punch card on the counter caught his eye. All ten squares had holes in them, so the card was complete. But in the last square, the hole had been punched through and a happy face drawn in red ink. That was his card, and somebody had redeemed it! But he had lost it when he went to—

"I got three sizes." Emily bustled in through the Staff Only door, carrying a selection of uniforms. All were bright white and green, with more white and green in the candy stripes running up the sides. "You can try them on in the men's room."

"Okay, sure," Tommy said. "Just give me a second. I'll be right back." He scanned the parlor, searching the faces of all the customers. There, at that booth. It couldn't be, but it was—the guy who'd been sitting next to him at the Evo meeting. Tommy strode over and the man looked it up, surprise all over his face. Surprise, and something else. He glanced sideways, as though he'd been expecting someone else.

"Can't believe you got out alive," Tommy whispered, slipping into the bench seat on the opposite side of the booth. "So, what happened? All I know is the place burned down. Did you get the same text I did?"

The guy shook his head. "What do you think happened?"

Good question. Tommy had been going over it ever since and still didn't have a good explanation. But he knew one thing for sure. "I think we shouldn't talk about it in public."

"Good idea," interjected a woman's voice. An African-

American woman was heading for them, sly satisfaction on her face. As she reached the booth, the woman parted her leather jacket, revealing a pistol tucked into black jeans. "Let's go. Move."

Emily sorted through the uniforms while she waited for Tommy. He certainly wouldn't need a large, those were closer to tents than shirts. Even the medium might be big on him. He was a good height, but she wouldn't exactly call him muscle-bound. Emily kind of liked the fact that Tommy wasn't obsessed with working out and proving his manliness, unlike some people she could name. In fact, she almost wished—

Then the strangest thing happened. Tommy marched right past her with two customers, a white guy in front and an African-American woman behind. He didn't even look at Emily, let alone explain where he was going. Stranger still, all three of them went out the back door of the parlor, which led into the alley behind it. Emily abandoned the uniforms and hurried round the counter after them.

By the time she reached the alley, the three of them were headed toward a station wagon. Emily ran after Tommy, calling out to him. "Hey, you forgot to try on—"

The words died in her throat when she saw the gun. The man had a pistol in one hand, his other keeping a tight grip on Tommy's left arm. Tommy was as white as a ghost, pure terror in his eyes. The woman swivelled round, aiming her pistol at Emily.

"Looks like both of you are going for a little ride," the man muttered.

Then things really got strange. Tommy grabbed hold of the woman, his face all fierce like he was concentrating on something really hard. The gun pointing at Emily vibrated in the woman's hand, then sort of vanished into itself, like it was being sucked through a tiny hole in reality. A moment later it was just… gone.

The woman swung round to Tommy and the same thing happened to her. One second she was standing there, reality vibrating and warping all around her—then she was gone, too. Tommy turned to the man, staring at him. Emily blinked. When she opened her eyes again, the guy was nowhere to be seen. In the space of a few seconds, two people had disappeared in front of her eyes. It was like a terrifying kind of magic—and Tommy was the magician!

No, there was no such thing as magic. But that meant Tommy was—

Emily found herself staring at him, at the spaces where those people had been. And then he was running away from her, going flat out. Before she could react, he was round the corner and gone. Only then did the pieces slot together. Tommy Clark had powers. He was one of them. The boy she had a crush on… was an Evo!

By the time Emily got her breath back, Tommy had gone. But she had an advantage over him—she had her own car. Sure, it was just a beat-up, seen-better-days VW Beetle, but it had four wheels and got her around Carbondale. Emily ran back into Moe's, got her friend Monica to cover her shift, and grabbed her car keys from the staff room.

As she drove up and down the streets around Moe's, Emily thought back over what she had just witnessed. Tommy had a power, but he wasn't dangerous like the people they were always talking about on the news. He could have done what he did at any time, but instead he used his power to protect her—to save her. Tommy was an Evo, but he was no terrorist. She had to find him. She had to thank him.

She spied Tommy a few minutes later, hurrying down the sidewalk as if the whole world was weighing down on his shoulders. She'd seen him like that in the hallway at school. It was one of the things that caught her eye. Brad seemed so sure of himself, so arrogant. That was attractive at first, but acting like he owned her got old real quick. She'd never seen that from Tommy. He wasn't a doormat, but he wasn't a jerk either.

Emily pulled over in front of him and jumped out of the car. Tommy kept walking, not making eye contact. "Hey!" Finally he stopped. Looked at her. She could see tears in his eyes, and it broke her heart a little. "Where are you going?"

"Where do you think? Home. To pack up and leave, like we always do." Tommy shook his head. "I am such an idiot. Thinking I could actually have a normal life here." He stared at her, and his eyes seemed to dig into her soul. Was that part of his powers, making her care for him? "I'm just... I'm sorry."

And then he was walking away from her again. Emily ran after him to catch up. "Those people—where did they go?"

"I don't know. I don't know where any of it goes. Oblivion, for all I know. How's that for the worst power ever? I can make things disappear, but I can't find them again."

Emily stopped, determined to talk some sense into Tommy. "It was self-defense. She had a gun, they both did. They were going to hurt you." But he kept walking, getting yards ahead of her. "You saved my life." Still no response. "Tommy!"

Finally, he stopped, turning to face her. Emily smiled at him.

"Your secret—it's safe with me."

EAST L.A., CALIFORNIA

Something Carlos read for school long ago kept nagging at him as he clambered up to the roof of Oscar's apartment: Neighbors bring *food* with death and flowers with sickness and little things in between. True, very true. All the relatives and neighbors were down in the kitchen, mourning the murder of his brother with bowls and dishes full of food. It was the way of things, but it didn't make the loss any easier to bear.

Jose had gone missing an hour earlier, but Carlos knew where to find him. It was the same place he had always hidden as a boy—up on the roof of the apartment building. The view across the East L.A. skyline wasn't anything special, but it was a good place to think, to rage—or to mourn. Sure enough, Jose was sitting on the edge, legs hanging over the side. Carlos sunk down beside him, putting a plate of food between them.

"Your Aunt Carmen made tamales."

The boy glared at him, anger burning in those eyes, burning through the pain. Carlos knew better than to say anything more. That much rage needed something to attack, to accuse, to blame. Jose would vent when he was ready.

"Why didn't El Vengador stop them from killing my dad?" Jose snarled at last.

Carlos knew what Jose must never know, that Oscar *was* El Vengador. For his nephew's safety, that had to remain a secret. "Maybe he tried."

"Not hard enough."

"Who knows what really happened."

Jose shook his head, full of fury and righteous anger. "What good is a hero if he's not gonna help people when they need him most? You would have!"

Carlos wished that were true—oh, how he wished it were true.

His nephew stood up, hands balled into fists, knuckles turning white. "They killed my dad, and El Vengador's not even gonna do anything about it." He stalked away, thudding down the steps, leaving Carlos to stare out over the neighborhood. These were the streets his brother had fought to protect, and look where that had led.

Jose was right about one thing: Oscar's murder had to be avenged, somehow. But Carlos didn't know if he had what it took to be that avenger—to become El Vengador.

CHAPTER SIX

At Lumiere, our board-certified ophthalmologists are among the most respected Lasik surgeons in Texas. We use advanced technology lens implants to correct complex issues such as astigmatism and near-vision focusing problems. Laser Eye Surgery for vision correction is performed right in the comfort and convenience of our office. The friendly and professional team of surgical care specialists and administrative staff will give you top-notch eye care. If you want to see clearly, come and see us!

—text from the Lumiere Ophthalmology homepage

DALLAS, TEXAS

Bennet arrived early in the city, his eagerness for answers getting the better of him. He had phoned home to smooth things over with Julia, reassuring her that yes, he'd be back later in the day, or that night at the latest. Truth be told, Bennet had no idea when—or even if—he would return to Austin. It would hinge on what he found at Lumiere Ophthalmology.

The Lasik surgery clinic was at the end of a long corridor, its name etched into a clear glass door panel beneath a pair-of-spectacles logo. Bennet looked through the door before entering, his old instincts kicking in. It was a drab, innocuous waiting room with a receptionist in a red-and-white sleeveless gingham top behind the counter. Bennet stepped inside, still cautious, still careful.

"Can I help you?" the receptionist asked, concern in her face.

"Yes, I…" Bennet realized he hadn't thought through how to play this, but bumbling middle-aged guy usually did the trick. "I'm sorry, I know this is an odd question, but… have I been here before?"

"I don't believe so, no."

The receptionist seemed uncertain how to deal with visitors. That might give him an opening. He threw in the name on her staff badge for good measure. "Dahlia, could you do me a favor and check your records? The name is—" Bennet stopped himself from saying Ted Barnes just in time. Boy, was he rusty. "Bennet. Noah Bennet."

Dahlia nodded, opening a file cabinet beside her knees to look inside. While she was distracted, Bennet glanced at the patient registry form attached to the clipboard on her desk—it was empty. He studied the rest of the waiting room. There were magazines on a coffee table in one corner. Bennet recognized the cover of one. That same issue was on top of a pile in his garage destined for the recycling bin. It was eight months old, but the copy on the table looked brand new, even untouched. In fact, all of the magazines appeared unread—

"I'm sorry, there's nothing under Bennet," Dahlia announced, interrupting his train of thought. "Maybe if you remembered the doctor's name."

Bennet smiled. "I wish I could." He pulled the Lumiere Ophthalmology card from a suit pocket, turning it over in his hands. "'See more clearly'."

"Sorry, we have no doctor named Seymour."

"Oh, no. That's just what's written on the back of the card." He held it up for her to see, but Dahlia was already staring at him. Bennet felt the hairs on his neck prickling.

Dahlia sprang up from her chair, aiming a pistol at Bennet's head. He laughed. So his instincts weren't completely rusty. "I knew something seemed off about this place."

"It's okay," a familiar voice said. "He's a friend." Bennet twisted round to find one of his most trusted allies standing in a doorway.

"Rene?"

"There's a bench across the street," Rene replied. "Wait for me there."

Bennet nodded, his mind racing twenty to the dozen. As he left the waiting room, Bennet glimpsed the room from which the Haitian had emerged. Inside were half a dozen people on computers. Lumiere Ophthalmology was no medical center—it was a control room of some kind. So why was Rene there, and who was he working for now?

TOKYO, JAPAN

Miko had done her best to ignore Ren's wild claims, to push them out of her mind, but it was no use. His words had struck a chord in her, chiming again and again until she could ignore it no longer. Now she was standing before the Shoji door in her apartment, the threshold to her father's study, a place she had revered and avoided for so long.

Her eyes slid down to the Evernow manual in her right hand. There was no denying the resemblance she had to Katana Girl—or that Katana Girl had to her. Miko wished her father was there so she could ask him which came first—the daughter, or the character? But she was alone in the apartment. She had to find her own answers, her own truth. She couldn't hide away in the shadows any longer.

Miko slid the paper-panelled door to one side, revealing the room beyond. Aspects of it were a throwback to Japan of the past—ornate artwork decorating the walls, shapes and swirls in the architecture and furniture, her father's origami dragons on the desk, a low table with curved legs. But there were also modern touches, intricate level designs for a video game on one wall, electric lanterns hanging from the ceiling.

Mustering her courage, Miko crossed the threshold. She moved round the study, searching for proof: something that would disprove Ren's words, or validate them. *Her sword is the key.* But Miko could see no sword, nothing that even resembled a... there, on the wall, an empty sword mount. She looked at the Evernow manual again. What had he said? *Hidden under the floor of her father's study.*

Miko studied the floor. Wide panels stretched across it in one direction, east to west, supported by thick wooden beams that ran north to south, cutting between the panels. It all appeared uniform, regular, even ordinary—except for a thin wooden panel in the middle of the room. Moving closer, Miko saw small circular notches cut into the ends of the panel. They were finger holes! She knelt in front of the panel, setting the game manual by her knees. The wood was a tight fit, not wanting to be lifted out, but her deft touch persuaded it. Miko moved the panel aside, gasping when she saw what lay beneath it.

A sword!

Still in its scabbard, the sword was nestled in a hidden compartment under the study floor—just as Ren had said. It had a glyph on the hilt, a narrow S with three horizontal strokes, exactly like the symbol he had shown her in the manual. But there was more: a note lay atop the sword, waiting to be read. Miko unfolded the paper and read the handwritten Japanese kanji: *Save me... The sword is the key.*

She put the note beside the game manual and carefully lifted the sword from its resting place. Miko held it out in front of her, staring at the weapon with reverential awe. Though it was still in its scabbard, holding the sword felt... natural. As if it belonged in her hands. As if it were part of her, an extension of her will. As if this sword was the thing she had been missing all these years, the solution to an absence deep inside her.

As if she was born to wield this weapon.

Miko raised the sword above her head, right hand on the hilt, left hand clasping the scabbard. Holding her breath, she pulled the sword free. As she did, a feeling like an electric shock surged through her. Transfixed, she saw the weapon and her body transforming, changing from flesh and bone and metal into digitized pixels! She opened her mouth to cry out and—

—found herself transported to another world, another reality! No longer in her father's study, she was kneeling atop a rusty train carriage, abandoned and incongruous in a vast, overgrown park. Her body had changed, too. She was taller, stronger—more powerful. Instead of flesh and fears, she was made of pixels, energy, and steely resolve!

Miko rose to her feet, overwhelmed by a thousand different sensations, not even noticing as her left hand slipped the scabbard over her shoulder and clipped it to her back. Her mind was too busy rebelling at this impossibility—what had just happened?

She turned in a slow circle, absorbing her new surroundings. The sky was alive with swirls of orange and red. There were tower blocks in the distance, beyond the boundaries of the vast, neglected park. Closer stood a tall building with the distinctive curved roof of a pagoda, but several stories in height. Blossom-laden cherry trees dotted the edge of the lush green clearing around the neglected carriage. Vines reached up from below, ensnaring it with their tendrils.

Something about this place nagged at Miko. She had seen it before, but where? Of course—the game manual! This place, it was a scene from Evernow. Had she somehow been pulled into the game? That would explain her lithe, elongated body, the new strength in her arms and legs. Even her clothes fit better! Had she become the hero of Evernow? Was she now Katana Girl? No, it was madness, an impossibility.

The sound of a sword sliding from its scabbard and a cry of attack forced Miko to abandon thinking for instinct. Three evil bandits in medieval Japanese armor leapt high into the air, their swords already drawn. Miko ran toward them, her blade pulled back, ready to repel their attack. She locked swords with the lead bandit as he landed on the carriage roof, the other two just behind him. Miko parried the leader's next thrust, then kicked him in the gut, propelling him sideways off the carriage.

No sooner had he fallen than the other two were upon Miko. One strode past her, a slash of his blade forcing her to twist round in defense, while the other moved to attack her back. She raised her sword over her head, blocking the bandit behind from cutting her in two. At the same time she lashed out with one leg, kicking the bandit in front of her backwards. Then she spun round in a circle, her sword bisecting the armor of both bandits, slicing each man apart. Their corpses fell from the carriage, vanquished. But the lead bandit was back, leaping up onto the carriage, sword clasped in both hands.

He ran at Miko, face hidden behind the grinning, skeletal mask strapped to his shaven head. The bandit swung his sword sideways through the air, but Miko bent over backwards to avoid the slashing blade. The bandit continued his attack, swinging the sword up over his head and bringing it straight down where Miko was standing. But she had already danced back out of the way, and the blade buried itself in the carriage roof. Miko ran forwards, stepping on the bandit's sword to hurl herself up into the air! She flew high above his head, somersaulting over the bandit to land behind him.

Miko dropped into a crouch, one knee on the rusted red metalwork as the bandit leader pulled his sword free. He charged at her, eager to finish the duel. Miko lowered her sword behind her back, blocking his clumsy attack. She raised the blade once more and then plunged it straight through the bandit's stomach—a mortal wound!

"You will… never save him," the bandit sneered.

His words stung Miko for a moment, then her face hardened with hatred as she ripped her sword free. Leaping into the air, Miko spun round and sliced the bandit's head clean from his body! He tumbled off the roof, leaving Miko triumphant.

She had been reborn as Katana Girl, warrior princess in the strange world of Evernow. She was strong, confident, even dangerous. She was now… a hero!

DALLAS, TEXAS

Bennet waited on the bench in the shadows beneath an overpass. Getting older had taught him a few things, like the value of patience and how a delay could still be valuable.

It gave you time to think, to reflect. He wasn't sure if any of that qualified as wisdom, but planning ahead had proven useful over the years. He didn't have any special powers, and he certainly wasn't an evolved human. All he had were his wits, his experience, and his instincts. They had gotten him this far in one piece.

Twenty minutes had passed by the time Rene emerged from across the street. He was sharply dressed, as always— light grey suit, pale blue shirt, a Haitian emblem hanging round his neck. As usual, his face betrayed little emotion. Inscrutable, some would call him, even cold. To Bennet, it was just the way his old friend looked. A hard man to read, but somebody you could trust with your life.

Rene was carrying a manila envelope, little bigger than a paperback. The Haitian sat down beside Bennet. They had shared a park bench just minutes before the explosion at Primatech, twelve months ago. Now here they were again, side by side.

"You have been more than a friend over the years, Noah. You've been a mentor."

"Thank you, Rene. But now I'm coming to you for help."

The Haitian nodded, an unusual sadness in his expression as he handed Bennet the manila envelope. "You left these behind the last time I saw you."

Bennet lifted back the unsealed flap, letting the envelope's contents slide into his hand—a pair of horn-rimmed glasses. He stared at them, a little surprised by how one simple object could trigger so many memories. Sitting at the counter in his kitchen with Claire when she was thirteen or fourteen, choosing a pair of glasses with her help. The moment just before a bullet exploded through one lens, such a close brush with death. So many moments, they all came flooding back to him.

He put the glasses on and looked round. Everything was that little bit crisper, clearer. For the first time in a long time, Bennet felt whole again. Complete. He smiled.

"Didn't know what I was missing."

Suddenly a narrow line passed in front of his eyes, moving downwards. No, not a line—a garrotte! It snapped into his neck, wrapping around him, choking him! Bennet grabbed at the garrotte, trying to force his fingers between it and his throat—but without success. His windpipe was being crushed, cutting off his air supply. He could feel blood pounding in both ears, his brain was crying out for oxygen. Unless he did something to change that in the next few moments, he was a dead man.

Bennet reached back, fingers clawing at Rene. He managed to get both hands on the Haitian, gripping the collar of his jacket. Bennet leaned back a moment, then pulled Rene forward with all his strength. The Haitian tumbled over Bennet's shoulders—but Rene still wouldn't let go of the garrotte! The pair of them fell to the ground, locked in a death grip with Rene underneath. Neither one of them was willing to give an inch. In the struggle, Bennet managed to slip three fingers under the garrotte, easing the pressure on his neck the tiniest amount and letting some air back into his lungs.

His other hand reached for the gun hidden behind his suit jacket, but Rene knew him too well, knew just where Bennet kept his pistol. The Haitian grabbed Bennet's wrist as he pulled the gun free. They battled for control of the weapon, rolling across the ground, fingers desperate to close round the trigger—

BLAM!

The noise was shocking, so close and so loud, echoing beneath the overpass.

For a moment, Bennet didn't know who had been shot. Adrenalin was pumping so hard through his body that he couldn't feel a thing. He pushed Rene away and the Haitian rolled to one side, his body limp. A dark crimson stain was blossoming on his chest. Bennet scrambled to his knees, already reaching for his cell phone.

"Oh my God—Dammit, Rene… What the hell were you—? Hold on, I'll call—"

"No." The Haitian grabbed Bennet's arm, stopping him.

Bennet sank back on his haunches, breath still coming in short gasps. He shook his head, unable to understand. "Why were you trying to kill me?"

Rene gritted his teeth, pain stretched across his face. "You told me to."

"What?!"

"You made a perfect plan… You needed to forget."

Bennet frowned. He had no recollection of that conversation, couldn't imagine why he would ever give his friend such an order. That meant there was only one possible explanation. "You wiped my memory."

Rene nodded, wincing as he did.

Bennet looked up at the overpass. Of course, it had to be true. That explained so much. He'd never been a person to trust others easily, always suspicious by nature. Now it seemed he couldn't even trust his own memories. How much of his recollection from June thirteenth was true? Only one man had the answers, and that man was dying on the ground beside him.

"What did I need to forget? What?!"

"Not what. Who." The Haitian's eyelids were fluttering. Blood spilled out beneath him, forming a crimson pool on the cement. "It's coming," Rene whispered. "It's coming."

Bennet leaned closer, putting his ear next to the Haitian's

mouth. All he heard was the last breath leaving his friend. "Rene? Rene? No!" He grabbed the dead man's lapels, shaking him. "Who did I need to forget? Rene!" But it was no use.

He let the body sink back to the ground. His own head fell forward on his chest, numbed by the speed at which everything was unravelling. The day before, he had been certain about so many things. Now one of his few true allies in the world was dead beside him, dead by his hand. Twenty-four hours earlier, he had known beyond any shadow of a doubt what had happened on June thirteenth. Now all he had were doubts and gaps and questions—and precious little hope of finding the truth.

Bennet pulled himself upright, Rene's body sprawled at his feet. Years of training took over, his mind casting aside grief to form a new plan. What did he know for certain? That whatever was coming—and it must be something big for him to have entrusted Rene with such a deadly order—involved Renautas. That he had devised a plan to stop Renautas, and the thing most likely to sabotage that plan was his own intervention.

So what should he do now? Trust his younger self to have put in motion all that was required? Or should he risk undoing that strategy—a strategy that had just cost the life of a close and trusted friend—by investigating further? For Rene's death to mean something, Bennet could not simply return to his life as Ted Barnes, selling cars and singing a happy tune in his head while hoping against hope that everything would be okay.

Nope, that wasn't him at all. What he needed was information, and the most likely source for that was sitting in a police cell back in Austin, cooling his heels after being arrested outside the home of car salesman Ted Barnes.

Bennet took one last look at Rene, burning the memory into his mind before setting off on a quest for the truth. He made a silent promise to his old friend. This was not the end. This was just the beginning.

EPILOGUE

Where does it come from, this fear, this quest? This need to hide in a simpler past when the future cannot be avoided. The planet is changing, no matter how we deny it. An imperative. So the question arises— how do we ensure our survival in the dark days to come? Who will live, who will die? And who among us shall inherit this brave new world?

> —extract from *Escalating Evolution* by
> Mohinder Suresh (unpublished)

THE ARCTIC CIRCLE

The monarch butterfly had no right to be this far north. There was no logic in a creature with such delicate black and orange wings flying through the air above a landscape made of ice and snow. In normal circumstances, the butterfly would have frozen long before reaching this point on the planet—but these were not normal circumstances.

The monarch fluttered across the sky, dropping down to land on the shoulder of a solitary figure facing the distant horizon, clad in a sealskin parka, head and face hidden beneath a fur-lined hood. The lone figure raised its arms, as if preparing to conduct an orchestra. Startled, the butterfly rose back into the incongruously warm air and flew away, borne on a glorious thermal.

Gloved hands gestured at the sky and the sky responded, clouds swirling in vibrant hues, curling and building into an aurora borealis that rose from the horizon. The hands caressed the air again and again, each movement coaxing a corresponding swirl of spectacular color in the sky. The slightest movements by the solitary figure created a powerful response from the clouds, the very air at one with its commands.

Above the horizon, the air became red and pink, swirling the clouds into new shapes. But the center of this incredible light show remained empty, untouched, a void. To the naked eye, it looked like an eclipse, that moment when a heavenly object passes between the earth and the sun, a corona appearing round the central circle of darkness.

The figure turned away from the horizon. It was a teenage girl called Malina, her long blond hair spilling out of her parka's hood. There was beauty in her face, even prettiness, but a haunted look to her eyes. Malina bore a mighty power, but she also had a mighty responsibility to fulfill, a powerful weight on such young shoulders.

She called back to someone in the distance: "It's happening faster than we thought." Malina bit her bottom lip before continuing, the strain of commanding the heavens all too evident. "I don't know if I can control it much longer."

HEROES REBORN

EVENT SERIES

BOOK TWO
A MATTER OF TRUST
TIMOTHY ZAHN

"O Lord, may the glory of your Holy Spirit spread His protection like a cloud throughout the heavens above us," the woman in the cramped back seat of the battered pickup prayed loudly.

Louder than usual for that particular prayer, Mauricio Chavez noted sourly as he wrestled with the steering wheel. More than loud enough for him to hear even over the noise of the pickup's engine and the crunching of the scrub brush they were driving through.

As she no doubt intended. Maria was a good mother, but her strict Catholic upbringing colored everything she ever said or did.

Usually Mauricio was okay with that. But there was a time and place for sentimental words and pious distractions. Driving in the middle of the night across the Mexican wilderness toward the U.S. border wasn't one of them.

Next to Mauricio, hanging on to the passenger armrest for dear life, his younger brother Paco was apparently thinking the same thing. "Hey, *Madre*, give it a rest, okay?" he called toward the back seat.

"Don't talk to your mother that way," their father

admonished from beside her.

"*Look—*"

"It's all right, Paco," Mauricio interrupted the boy. "We're fine."

"She's not distracting you?" Paco asked. "I mean, this road—this *is* a road, *no*?"

Despite the tension, Mauricio had to smile. He'd been Paco's age—seventeen—when he'd first ridden this route with Condor, and at the time he'd said almost the exact same words.

No, it wasn't much of a road. But after five years of smuggling Mexicans and Guatemalans and Hondurans across the border, Mauricio knew the area like the back of his hand.

Or maybe he knew it like the ceiling of the church his parents had been dragging him to every Sunday since he was christened. The ceiling that he'd stared at while trying to ignore what the priest was saying.

Granted, there'd been a few homilies he'd liked. He liked the story of the Transfiguration, and the cloud that came up and covered Jesus and a couple of the Apostles and then talked to them. That had been pretty neat. He always thought about that story when a fog or mist rolled in, wondering if it would talk to him.

But then, he'd always liked clouds. As a boy, he would sometimes lie on the ground for hours, just staring up at them. He'd pretended he was up there, too, cool and aloof and serene, able to ignore the misery that filled the earth below.

But the clouds were up there, and he was down here, and he'd quickly learned that there was only one way out of misery.

Money.

The truck bucked as it hit a particularly deep pothole.

Paco yelped, and Mauricio smiled again. It was a bad pothole, but nothing like the pits on either side of it. As Condor liked to say, sometimes you had to take a slap to the head to avoid a kick to the stomach.

"Be careful, Mauricio," his father warned. "Condor will be furious if you wreck his truck."

"*No hay problema*," Mauricio called back, his smile fading. Condor was going to be furious, all right, no matter what condition Mauricio brought the truck back in.

Because he wasn't supposed to have it in the first place. He certainly wasn't supposed to be giving anyone a free pass out of Mexico. If the boss caught him, Mauricio was going to get that kick in the stomach, and worse.

But he would take it. This was his family, and after five years he finally had the skill and the money to get them out of Mexico and start them on a new life. This was his shot, and he was taking it.

Condor would hurt him when he brought back the truck. But he'd eventually cool down. And even if he made Mauricio work for nothing for the next two years, it'd be worth it. This was his family, and he would do whatever it took to protect them.

Of course, once in the States, his mother would have to find a new church. It was a shame Mauricio would never be inside it long enough to memorize the ceiling pattern.

Because once this was over, he'd be done with religion. Forever.

A familiar stack of rocks flashed past. "We're here," he announced. "We're in the United States."

The words were barely out of his mouth when everything went straight to hell.

The two off-road vehicles that had been lying in wait just out of Mauricio's view exploded into a blaze of headlights, flashing red lights, and ear-splitting sirens. Mauricio's mother gasped something he didn't catch— probably another plea to God—while Paco broke out into a terrified litany of curses.

But it wouldn't be God who got them out of this. Mauricio was already on it, kicking his speed to just below suicidal, daring the border cops to risk their lives matching it. If he could gain enough of a lead—and he knew he could—there was a spot a couple of miles ahead where his family could hide while he drew the pursuit away.

The cops probably thought they knew this area. But Mauricio knew it better.

It cost a few tense minutes, and probably what was left of the pickup's suspension. But in the end the situation played out exactly as Mauricio had planned. "Get ready," he called to the others as they approached the sloping turn he'd been aiming for. "I'm going to stop just past that curve and let you out. There's a saw-tooth rock formation about fifteen meters off the road to the right— you can all hide there until the cops go past. I'll lead them away and come back for you after I lose them. Do you understand?"

"But what if you—?" his mother began.

"I said, *do you understand*?"

"Yes," his father said stiffly. "Be careful."

"I will," Mauricio promised. "Ready?"

He rocked around the curve, his wheels barely holding the road, and slammed on the brakes. "Go!"

They tumbled out. Mauricio didn't wait to see if they made it to the rocks, but took off again as soon as the doors were slammed shut. He had to get moving before the border cops figured out that they'd gained a little on him and wondered why.

Unfortunately for them, it was the last bit of ground they would gain. The road was twisty and rough, and Mauricio was going to hit it as hard as he could.

There was a reason rational people didn't take certain chances. And if it hadn't been his family back there counting on him to lose the cops and come back, instead of some poor peons who had paid in advance for their passage, Mauricio might not have hit the ravine curve quite as fast as he did.

But it *was* his family. And he *did* take the risk.

And he lost.

It seemed to take hours for the truck to bounce and clatter its way down the rocky slope. Mauricio held on to whatever he could—the door handle, the steering wheel, the seatbelt strap—his brain spinning, his body thrown back and forth, his empty stomach heaving with dry retching.

And then, suddenly, it was over. The pickup lay at the bottom of the ravine, inaccessible to the cops on the road above without rappelling lines or a helicopter. Mauricio lay inside the cab, his hips pinned to the seat by the steering wheel, the world outside as inaccessible to him as he was to the cops.

The world he'd known was inaccessible. But the next world was fast approaching. Even as Mauricio tugged uselessly at the steering wheel, he could smell the lethal aroma of gasoline drifting in through the shattered windows. The fuel tank was leaking… and after that mad dash, there would be plenty of engine parts hot enough to ignite the fumes.

Mauricio Chavez was about to die.

He tugged once more at the wheel. Useless. He pushed the door. Useless.

And with nothing else to do, he began to pray.

O God. I haven't been good. I've been evil. But I only wanted to help my family—

He snarled to himself. This was *not* the time to be lying to God.

Time to change tactics. *If you'll get me out of this, I swear to you I'll change my life. I'll go straight. I'll quit Condor and the coyote business. I'll—I'll go to seminary and become a priest.*

The smell of gas was getting stronger. His mother's favorite prayer echoed in his heart and mind—O Lord, may the glory of your Holy Spirit spread His protection like a cloud throughout the heavens above me—

Abruptly, he found himself floating. *Floating.* Inside the truck.

And as far as he could tell, he no longer had a body.

His first horrified thought was that he was already dead. A heart attack, maybe, before the truck could ignite and burn him to death. Was that God's answer to his prayer? To give him a more painless death than Mauricio's recklessness deserved?

But this wasn't heaven. It wasn't purgatory. It certainly and thankfully wasn't hell.

Besides, if he was dead, where was his body? He was still in the truck, and there was no body trapped behind the wheel. Everything he'd heard about out-of-body experiences said that the actual body was still left there. Where had it gone?

For that matter, with no body and no eyes, how was he even seeing any of this?

And then he noticed something he hadn't spotted before. In the faint reflected glow from the still-burning headlights he could see a cloud of white smoke or mist gathered around him.

No. Not *around* him. The cloud of smoke *was* him.

There was a warning crackle from the front of the truck. Shaking away his fear and confusion, Mauricio lunged toward the broken window.

He was outside, floating rapidly up and away, before he belatedly realized that his lunge had actually worked. He continued onward, moving like a wisp of cloud before a summer thunderstorm, trying desperately to get away.

He was above and past the two cop cars, their occupants now lined up along the ravine edge staring down at the wreck, when the pickup burst into flames.

Mauricio didn't wait to see what the cops would do. Especially since they really couldn't do anything. Not now.

He managed to calm down a little as he headed back to where he'd left his family, at least enough to experiment with this new form of existence. He could move at will, he discovered, with no more thought or effort than walking, though the sky was now as open to him as the ground. He could see and hear, though smell and touch seemed to elude him.

He could also talk, just like the cloud in the Bible story. Somehow, that part freaked him out more than any of the rest of it.

His biggest, most terrifying fear was that the change might be permanent, that he would forever be a disembodied cloud of mist. He tried over and over to return to human form, and each time he failed.

But he kept at it. He couldn't let his family see him like this. He certainly couldn't guide them to safety in this form. Not even if he could convince them that it was truly him.

And he probably couldn't do that, for the simple reason that they wouldn't stand still long enough to let him try.

A voice from a cloud? His mother would drop to her

knees and pray. His brother would run like the devil was after him. His father would probably have the heart attack his mother always worried about.

Maybe they would be stronger than that, or smarter, or calmer. Maybe he should just go up to them and tell them what had happened.

But he didn't dare.

And so, as he neared the saw-tooth rock he slowed his pace, still trying to become Mauricio Chavez again. Eventually, he found himself drifting in a wide circle with the saw-tooth rock just visible in the distance, unwilling to abandon his family but equally unwilling to face them.

To face them with no face. Ironic. He would have laughed if he'd had a mouth to laugh with.

It was probably an hour later when he suddenly turned back into human form.

Unfortunately, he was a good three feet off the ground when it happened, and he twisted his ankle badly when he fell out of the sky onto the rocky soil below. For a moment he lay on his side, clutching the injured ankle and swearing softly. Then, he got gingerly to his feet and limped toward the saw-tooth rock.

To find his family gone.

He looked around, his heart thudding painfully in his newly-restored chest. There was no sign of them anywhere. He climbed up the side of the rock, cursing as every step threatened to rip his ankle apart. Still no one.

Had they been caught by the border cops? But he had seen no indication of flashing lights on his long journey back from the wreck. More likely they'd just given up on him and had set off on their own.

Maybe they'd seen the glow in the sky from his fiery wreck and believed he was dead.

There was no way he could find them. Not in the middle of a nighttime wilderness. Not with an injured ankle. Not when they had this much of a head-start.

At least, not as a human being.

He tried praying first. God had given him this thing; surely He would show him how to make it work. But God had gone silent. Mauricio tried to recreate the fear he'd felt in the wrecked truck, and the terror of the knowledge that he was about to die. Nothing. He tried wishing, agonizing, bargaining, and threatening. Still nothing.

Finally, a half-hour eternity later, he found the right combination of thought, emotion, and sheer willpower needed to make the change. He turned into mist and floated up into the sky, moving in a quick spiral path outward from the rock, fervently hoping that his family hadn't gone the wrong direction.

Spiral movement was strangely tricky, and he often found himself wobbling like he had the first few times he'd tried riding a two-wheeler bike. The height could be a little scary, too, especially when he momentarily forgot that he couldn't fall. But at least his wrenched ankle didn't hurt anymore.

Ten minutes later, he found them.

They hadn't gone the wrong way after all, but had set off in the general direction of the town he'd been planning to take them to. Someone—Paco, probably—had clearly been paying attention when Mauricio originally told them they'd be heading northeast after they crossed the border. Someone else—his mother, probably—had then figured out from the stars which direction that was. They had indeed feared he was dead, and their outpouring of relief and love when he suddenly emerged from behind a large rock made him secretly ashamed of the lies he then spun for them about what had happened and how he'd escaped from the cops.

But he had no choice. He didn't dare tell them the truth. Not yet. Not until he could figure out whether this thing was a gift or a curse.

The town was another six miles away, a long trek in the middle of the night. But they made it, and the border cops didn't come back.

Two weeks later, he had his family settled into the place he'd prepared for them, along with some money and a complete set of documents that one of Condor's forgers, Diego, had created for them.

And then, after promising he would visit as often as he could, he set off to find a seminary that would take him.

Condor would be furious. But Mauricio couldn't be distracted by such things.

He'd made a deal with God. God had done His part.

Time for Mauricio to do his.

Seminary was harder than he'd expected. Harder than anything he'd ever done in his entire life. But he was determined, and he kept at it. Eventually, he passed all the tests, and took all the vows, and Mauricio Chavez became Father Mauricio.

For the next two decades he served the people of his various parishes, giving aid and counsel and comfort, striving to be Christ's representative on earth, heeding the words of his bishop and the Vatican, and moving wherever the Church deemed his services were needed the most.

He never told anyone about his power. Not his parents or brother, not his closest friends, or even in confession with his bishop. He only used it in secret, and just when there was a good and useful reason for it.

Not that there weren't plenty of such occasions. Early on, he developed the habit of checking every nook and cranny of each new church and rectory where he'd been assigned, and at least four times found buildups of lint and dust in the heating or laundry units that could easily have started fires. In the more gang-heavy parishes he sometimes used his gift to secretly follow one of his child or teenage parishioners home, staying high enough that he wouldn't be noticed, making sure the young person he was escorting wasn't bothered or molested along the way. A few of those times, when it was clear that trouble was brewing, he was able to slip away, change back into human form, and call the police to the scene.

He tried to keep such rescues anonymous. But at least one cop figured out who was raising the alarms, and "Padre Vigilant" became a private nickname in certain circles.

Some bishops liked that about Father Mauricio. Others disapproved, and got him transferred out of the diocese as quickly as they could.

And as the years passed, he began to realize that he wasn't alone.

At first it was just rumors, stories about other people with strange powers and gifts. But then it was grainy pictures, and jumpy videos, and loud government denials.

And then there was that massive explosion far above Long Island.

Mauricio wasn't sure what to make of that. The rumors and stories intensified afterward, though the government still denied anything was happening. But slowly, over the next few years, the rumors became more believable and the denials grew more hollow.

Until that night in New York City when Claire Bennet dramatically revealed her awesome secret to the world.

Over the next few months, as more people with abilities emerged from the shadows into public awareness, Mauricio toyed with the idea of similarly coming forward. But something always stopped him. Part of it was the Vatican, which was never more than lukewarm to the spiritual implications of such people and powers in the first place, and Mauricio's concern that revealing his power might get him quietly forced from the priesthood.

But most of it was the distressing roller-coaster ride of public opinion. There was an initial surge of interest in the Evolved Humans—or *Evos,* as commentators soon dubbed them—and their powers. Mauricio watched the debate closely, hoping that the Evos would eventually be accepted. But as the months went by, much of the interest darkened into suspicion. In some places—too many places—it darkened further into revulsion, fear, and hatred. It wasn't long before those who'd revealed themselves were trying to regain their anonymity, while those who hadn't left the shadows were making a concerted effort to stay there..

And as the discussions and arguments continued to rage, Mauricio was transferred yet again, this time to All Saints Church in East Los Angeles.

The neighborhood wasn't a good one. Maybe someone was again trying to get Padre Vigilant out of his diocese, or maybe someone had noted the similarity of the area to the one that Mauricio had grown up in back in Mexico and figured he could handle himself there.

It would be rough, Mauricio knew. But at All Saints he would be out of the political and social spotlight, and he would be where a good priest could make a real difference.

All in all, it was a fair trade.

* * *

He was trying not to cry, of course. In Mauricio's experience sixteen-year-old boys always tried not to cry. But even in the muffled acoustics of the confessional Mauricio could hear the sound of stifled tears in his voice. "Forgive me, *Padre*, for I have sinned."

Mauricio studied what he could see of the boy's face through the grille as they went through the ritual exchange. It was Simon Navarro, he decided, one of the members of his parish. He didn't know the boy well, but whenever he turned up at Mass or occasional youth events he always seemed to be hovering between apprehension and despair. Mauricio had tried a couple of times to draw him out on the reasons for his moodiness, but the boy always dodged his questions.

But today might be different. There was a depth of misery in Simon's voice that Mauricio had never heard there before. Maybe he was finally ready to talk.

"I've been thinking, *Padre*, about killing myself."

Mauricio swallowed hard. Ready to talk, all right.

Still, talking about suicide more often represented a cry for help than serious intent. "Tell me why," he said encouragingly.

"I'm hurting people," Simon said, almost too softly to be heard. "You know? I'm—I almost killed someone."

"Was it an accident?"

"*Si pues*," Simon said. "I mean no. I mean—I meant to do it, but I didn't mean for the *vato* to get hurt."

"I'm sure you didn't," Mauricio assured him. "Why don't we start from the beginning? What happened, exactly?"

Simon gave a long sniff, and Mauricio caught a glimpse of white as the boy pulled out a handkerchief and wiped his nose. "It was Angel Martinez," he said. "He pulled—"

"The Angel Martinez who was hit by a car?" Mauricio interrupted. The accident had happened a week ago, and he'd been called in by the teen's mother to give last rites. Angel was out of the woods now, but it had been a close thing.

"Yeah, him," Simon said, sounding more miserable than ever. "He pulled a *filero* on me—you know? He was going to stab me. I couldn't think of anything else to do."

"Yes, I know what he's like," Mauricio said with some frustration of his own. He'd hoped Martinez's brush with death would bring him back to the straight and narrow, but the teen was already talking about rejoining his gang as soon as he was out of the hospital. "I'm sure you didn't mean to push him into the street that way."

"I didn't push him anywhere," Simon insisted. "He ran there by himself. I just… I just made him blind."

Mauricio ran the words over twice in his brain. *I made him blind*. "You mean blind with anger?"

"No, *Padre*. I made him blind. I just… I can make people blind."

And then Mauricio got it. "You're an Evo."

"You won't tell anyone, will you?" Simon asked anxiously. "My uncle says Evos are from the devil."

"I believe all gifts and talents come from God," Mauricio said.

"That's what my *jefa* said once," Simon said. "Before she…"

"I know," Mauricio said quickly. Simon's mother had died in a horrific car accident two years ago, leaving the rest of his upbringing to his well-to-do but rigidly opinionated uncle. "Don't worry—what you did to Angel wasn't permanent. He was seeing fine when he came out of surgery."

"I know that," Simon said. "It only lasts an hour. Either way, it only lasts an hour."

"What do you mean, either way?"

He sensed the boy shrug. "I can make blind people see, too."

Mauricio felt his mouth drop open. "You can make blind people *see*?"

"But only for an hour." Simon sighed. "Sometimes that's worse. *Vatos* like Angel get really scared. But *abuelos* like old Senor Winslow get their hopes up and then get them smashed."

"Maybe they don't have to," Mauricio said, his mind racing. "How much practice have you had bringing back sight? How many times have you done it, I mean?"

"Not a lot," Simon said. "Senor Winslow. A couple of others."

"So maybe that one-hour limit is just because you haven't mastered the skill?" Mauricio suggested.

"It's not a skill, *Padre*. It's a curse. Aren't you *listening*?"

"Anything that reflects back on the miracles of Our Lord can hardly be called a curse," Mauricio countered. "I'm guessing what you need most right now is practice."

"Sure," Simon muttered. "Maybe I'll run an ad on Craigslist."

"I was thinking something a bit more discreet," Mauricio said with a smile. Simon was clearly pessimistic about the whole thing, but at least he wasn't talking about suicide anymore. "Do you know Inez Bustamante?"

"Who?"

"Elena Gutierrez's mother," Mauricio said. "Oscar Gutierrez's mother-in-law. Oscar runs the garage—"

"Oh, yeah—I know him. Lot of bad *vatos* use his shop."

"That's him," Mauricio confirmed, trying to keep any

hint of judgment out of his voice. Oscar was the sort of man who could stand up to the gangs if he wanted to, maybe set an example for the rest of the neighborhood. Instead, he seemed to go out of his way to be cooperative, even friendly, toward them.

But it was a hard life out there. Oscar had a wife and son, and his brother Carlos was way over in Afghanistan. Like everyone else, the man was just trying to survive. "Inez doesn't come to Mass much anymore," he continued. "Lots of medical problems that keep her home. She's also blind."

There was a long silence from the other side of the grille. "What if she tells? That'd be bad, you know?"

"She won't," Mauricio assured him. "Not if we ask her not to."

"You sure?"

"Yes," Mauricio said. "You can trust me. *And* her."

Simon huffed. "Yeah. Trust."

Mauricio kept silent, waiting for the teen to work it through. Considering Simon's troubled past, he wasn't surprised that trust didn't come easy.

"I guess I can try," Simon said at last. "You'll come with me, right?"

"Of course," Mauricio said. "Thank you—I know she'll appreciate it. When do you want to do it?"

"I don't know. You know—whenever."

"Great," Mauricio said. "I'll talk to her this evening."

"Okay," Simon said. "*Padre*... will this absolve me for... you know? Angel?"

"It will indeed," Mauricio promised. "I'll call you tonight."

* * *

"Let me get this straight," Oscar Gutierrez rumbled, standing far too close to Mauricio. "You want to use some kind of new medical *aparato* on my mother-in-law? You won't tell us what it is, and you won't let us watch?"

"You make it sound more mysterious than it really is," Mauricio protested, fighting the urge to take a long step backwards. Oscar was several inches taller than he was, with a sheer presence that could fill a room to overflowing. "As I said, it's experimental and the developer doesn't want news of it getting out."

"So he wants to try it on my *suegra*?" Oscar demanded. "He thinks because we're poor Hispanic folk we won't sue if something goes wrong?"

"Nothing will go wrong," Mauricio said. "If I thought there was even a chance that it would, I wouldn't have asked her to participate."

For about five of Mauricio's rapid heartbeats Oscar just stared at him. "Inez says she wants to try it," he said at last. "So I guess I've got no say. *But.*" He let the word hang in the air like a small black storm cloud. "I *will* check up on her after you're done. *Very* closely."

"That's fine," Mauricio said. "Thank you."

For another two heartbeats Oscar stared at him. Then, spinning on his heel, he strode back to the bed where Inez was talking quietly with her daughter. Oscar spoke briefly to the two of them, and then he and Elena left the room. A moment later, Mauricio heard the apartment door close behind them.

"*Padre*?" Inez called, her voice thin and raspy.

"I'm here, Inez," Mauricio assured her, hurrying to her side. "How are you feeling?"

"Ready," Inez said, a hopeful glint in her unseeing eyes. "Excited. How soon can we start?"

"Right away," Mauricio said, pulling out his cell phone

and punching in the number of the phone he'd given Simon earlier that evening.

Simon didn't answer until the third ring. "*Bueno*?"

"We're ready," Mauricio said, trying to read the boy's tone. Probably still having doubts. "You in the stairwell?"

"Yeah," Simon said. "Fourth floor, *si*?"

"Right—Apartment 403," Mauricio said. "I'll open the door for you."

Two minutes later, everything was ready. "How does it work?" Mauricio asked.

In answer, Simon took a deep breath.

"Oh, my," Inez gasped. She blinked twice, her eyes darting around as if she was seeing the room for the first time. "*Dios mio. Padre*—it worked. It *worked!*" Her newly opened eyes came to rest on Simon's face. "You must be Simon," she said, her voice trembling with emotion. "*Que Dios te bendiga, mijo*."

Mauricio looked sideways at Simon. The teen's face was a turmoil of emotions. Pleasure that he was able to give her such a gift, plus the bitter knowledge that the gift and her joy were only fleeting. "It won't…" He broke off.

"It won't last," she said gently. "Yes, Father Mauricio told me. *Esta bien*. Nothing in this life lasts. You need to learn to take joy wherever you find it, and drink to the fullest." She smiled. "And I know just how to do that."

She turned and reached behind her pillow. To Mauricio's surprise, she pulled out an embroidery hoop with an unfinished pattern in it. "I started this when Jose was born," she said, lowering her voice conspiratorially. "My *nietecito*. It was going to be for his *primera comunion*. But things got busy, and I somehow never got back to it. And then my eyes…" She paused, her thin throat working. "But now I can work on it again," she said in a stronger voice. She looked at Mauricio. "You won't think me rude, will you?"

"Not at all," Mauricio assured her. "It's your night. Do whatever you want."

"*Gracias*." With a final smile at Simon, she settled down to her work.

For a few minutes Mauricio watched, marveling at the skill still present in those old, thin fingers. Simon had already left the bedside and was staring out the narrow window at the blaze of city lights stretching into the darkness. With a final look at Inez, Mauricio walked over and joined him.

Oscar had left the window open a couple of inches, and a cool April breeze was drifting in across the wide windowsill. "You did well, Simon," Mauricio said quietly.

"It's only for an hour," Simon said. Already his face had lost all of its earlier happiness and had settled into a gloom as dark as the night sky.

"What happens if you try it again?"

"You mean right away?" He shook his head. "Another fifteen minutes. Then five more. Then *nada*. You know?"

"The blindness works the same way, I suppose?"

Simon shot him a horrified look. "You think I've ever done that *twice*?"

"No, of course not," Mauricio said quickly. Stupid question. "If you can't give her another hour right away, how soon *can* you do it?"

"I don't know," Simon said. "I know I can do it a week later—I did that once with Senor Winslow. Maybe it would work again sooner. I don't know."

"I'm surprised Mr. Winslow didn't insist you keep coming around."

"Yeah." Simon sighed. "He didn't know it was me. The first time was… accidental. I was outside his house and it just happened. The second time I was trying to see if I could do it again." He closed his eyes. "He cried afterwards. He cried so hard. I was all the way on the sidewalk, and I could still hear him."

Mauricio put his arm around the boy's shoulders. "Looks like our first job is to see how much longer you can stretch out that first hour," he said. "Let's try it again in three days, okay?"

"I don't know," Simon muttered. "You think she'll want to? I mean… it's hard to lose it again."

Mauricio looked over at the woman bent over her embroidery, her face glowing with happiness. "She will," he promised. "Trust me."

An hour and three minutes later—Mauricio timed it—the darkness returned.

If Inez was disheartened by her loss, she didn't show it. She thanked Simon over and over, clutching his hand as if she wanted to kiss it, blessing him and his gift and imploring him to come see her again as soon as he could.

Mauricio took secret amusement in watching how completely Simon was blown away by her gratitude and lack of despair or reproach. The boy assured her she was more than welcome, and promised he would be back as soon as Father Mauricio thought it was worth trying again.

And as he and Mauricio left the apartment and headed toward the elevator there was a new and hopeful spring to his step.

The guilt over what had happened to Angel Martinez would return, Mauricio knew. But at least now it would be tempered by the memory of Inez Bustamante's glowing face and thankful attitude.

He hoped it would be enough.

Four days turned out to be the magic number, and on that schedule Mauricio and Simon quickly became regular fixtures in Inez's apartment. With every session Simon's confidence grew, and as Inez's embroidery progressed so did the boy's power. As April turned to May and then to June the original hour and three minutes became an hour five, then an hour eight, then an hour twelve.

Inez's enthusiasm at her new lease on life began to spill over into other areas of her life as well. At the beginning Mauricio and Simon usually found her waiting for them all alone, but by June they often had to wait while newly made friends said their farewells and headed back to their own apartments.

Gone were Simon's thoughts of suicide, if they'd ever truly existed. He dropped by the church nearly every day on his way home from school to discuss his latest thoughts and ideas about how to increase his power. Even as the outside society continued to debate the whole Evolved Human question, inside All Saints Church the boy found a cocoon of safety and hope.

But the comfortable situation wasn't to last. It was late afternoon on Tuesday, June 10, when Mauricio got the call.

The family was already gathered around Inez's bedside when he arrived, nearly twenty of them, including cousins, nieces, and in-laws. Mauricio remembered her mentioning her extended family once or twice during their visits, but he hadn't realized there were so many of them in the immediate area.

Oscar's brother Carlos was conspicuous by his absence, despite the fact that he was freshly back from Afghanistan. Mauricio had heard rumors of some kind of unspecified trouble with his return, and was sorry that whatever military red tape was involved had kept the young man from his mother-in-law's last moments.

There were also a dozen of Inez's friends present, some of whom Mauricio recognized from his and Simon's secret visits. Behind and among them, the hospice nurse moved as quietly and unobtrusively as possible as she dealt with the final medical details. Inez lay in the middle of the bed, her face calm, her hands clutching those of her daughter and her grandson, speaking quiet words of encouragement and love.

Oscar stood beside his wife, his face stolid, only his dark eyes showing his pain. He looked over as Mauricio came into the room; giving his wife's hand a gentle squeeze, he worked his way through the quiet crowd to him. "*Padre*," he said, holding out his hand. "Thank you for coming."

Mauricio gripped it, feeling the same ironic combination of strength and helplessness that he could see in the man's face. Oscar was phenomenally strong, but his strength was useless here. "I'm glad I could be here," Mauricio said. Letting go of Oscar's hand, he stepped over to the dresser and laid out the oil and the purple stole for Inez's last rites.

He felt a brush of air as Oscar moved closer to him. "Can you call him?" he murmured in Mauricio's ear. "Please? Can you get him here?"

Startled, Mauricio turned around. "What?"

"I know, Father," Oscar murmured. "I know about Simon and his gift. You need to get him here." He swallowed. "Inez should have a chance to look upon her family one last time."

Mauricio's eyes flicked over Oscar's shoulder at the crowd gathered around the bedside. But if they all saw Simon perform his miracle—

His miracle. Perfect. Mauricio could simply call the opening of Inez's eyes a miracle. Which, of course, it genuinely was.

"You're right," he told Oscar. Pulling out his phone, he punched in Simon's number.

The call went straight to voicemail. He keyed off and tried again.

"Trouble?" Oscar asked.

"He must have turned it off," Mauricio said. Voicemail again. "Simon, this is Father Mauricio. Call me as soon as you get this."

He closed the phone and put it away.

"Why would he turn it off?" Oscar asked.

"Because he's not really supposed to have it," Mauricio said, frowning. "I bought it for him so that we could coordinate our meetings with Inez."

Still, it struck him as a little odd that Simon would turn off the phone. A few days ago Mauricio had broached the idea of the two of them driving to Texas to attend the big Odessa Summit between Evos and normal humans at Primatech Paper this coming Friday. Simon had been hesitant, mostly because he would have to come up with some story to tell his uncle, and Mauricio had promised to find a reason that would satisfy him without the boy having to lie to his face. With only three days to go until the summit, Simon should be waiting by the phone for Mauricio's call.

Unless the boy really didn't *want* to go to the summit.

"I'll try his home," Mauricio continued, punching in another number. This one continued to ring with no answer and no voicemail.

"Keep trying," Oscar said. "Please." Turning, he wove his way through the silent crowd and rejoined his wife.

With a sigh, Mauricio put his phone away, picked up the oil and stole, and joined him.

Two hours later, with Simon still nowhere to be found, Inez Bustamante passed from the world.

Oscar never said a word as Inez's friends and then her family said their farewells and gave their final hugs and drifted out of the apartment. But as he and his wife and son left, he gave Mauricio a parting look that cut the priest to the heart. Not a look of anger or blame, but simply one that spoke of an opportunity forever lost.

Mauricio had no answer for him. God, he knew, was well aware of the futures of each of His children. Why hadn't He arranged for Simon to get Mauricio's message in time to offer Inez one final blessing? Or why hadn't He allowed Inez to remain a while longer before taking her into His arms?

Mauricio had no answer for Oscar. Nor did he have one for himself.

The funeral arrangements took most of the next day. Mauricio's tentative hopes that he might still make it to Odessa faded, then vanished completely as Elena and Oscar decided on a Friday morning service. With Mauricio's presence also required for Sunday Mass, and Odessa a good fifteen-hour drive away, holding the funeral on Friday meant there was no way for him to make the trip.

The funeral was well attended, and as pleasant as such an occasion could ever be. Inez had lived a good, long life, so at least the tears of family and friends could be mixed with laughter and fond memories.

Oscar was moving slowly, Mauricio noted, as if he'd hurt himself. Probably another accident at his auto shop—the man was constantly running afoul of some machine or tool. But Oscar didn't talk about it, and Mauricio didn't ask.

Simon arrived late and sat all the way in the back. He left before the final prayer. Whether he shed any tears Mauricio couldn't tell.

It was only after the last of the family had left and Mauricio had retired to his office to finish his homily that he learned the Odessa Summit had been demolished by a series of massive explosions.

Explosions that had obliterated the Primatech building and killed everyone for miles around it.

For the rest of the afternoon and evening Mauricio remained glued to his television, his unpolished homily neglected, watching as details and names of confirmed casualties dribbled in. Claire Bennet was among the dead, as were many others who had become household names in the great Evo debate.

And through it all, Mauricio felt the icy dampness of a California November fog on his skin and in his soul.

He could have been there. *Would* have been there, had the Lord not taken Inez Bustamante when He had.

Three days ago, Mauricio had dared to question God's timing. Now, he was once again reminded that *el Todopoderoso* could be trusted to know what He was doing.

The dust of Odessa had barely settled when the backlash began.

It started in the worst possible way. An Evo named Mohinder Suresh claimed responsibility for the attack in a bitter, rambling diatribe against humans and their prejudice. Politicians and governments the world over countered with condemnations and challenges of their own, a frenzy of anger that grew in pitch and volume as the world's police and intelligence organizations failed to find and capture the self-proclaimed terrorist.

Some nations responded by tacitly declaring open season on Evos, and reports of riots and lynchings began to fill news reports, opinion pieces, and blogs. The U.S. government's response was less violent, but no less chilling: laws were quickly passed that required all Evos to register and submit to restrictions on travel and round-the-clock tracking.

Mauricio watched in dread, all too aware of how closely the world's response to Evos was beginning to mirror Hitler's actions toward European Jews. He'd hoped humanity had matured in the eight decades since then. Apparently, it hadn't.

Worst of all was the fact that the Church itself was apparently less than interested in speaking out in support of the Evos. While any number of individual pastors, priests, and rabbis spoke out against this newest form of bigotry, the official proclamations from the Vatican were far less vigorous. There was no explicit statement that Evo powers were evil, but there was also no denunciation of those who by words and actions *did* make such pronouncements.

For the first few weeks Mauricio held on to the hope that the Church's public statements might be offset by quiet support for people whose only crime was an accident of birth and genetics. The Vatican might even unofficially authorize bishops and priests to offer sanctuary to Evos in danger, a step that would go a long way toward retaking the moral high ground.

But in mid-September that hope was dashed. A set of confidential bulletins from the *Santa Sede* appeared in Mauricio's email, declaring that some powers *were* indeed sinful and instructing priests to counsel any Evos who came to them to submit to the registration required by the new laws.

The Pope himself made no such statements. But neither did he denounce them, either publicly or privately. All his encyclicals would say was that he was still studying the issue.

For Mauricio, that was the final, crushing blow. The Church—*his* Church—seemed to be turning its back on the very outcasts their Lord had come to earth to seek out, nurture, and save. For a while he pondered sending such thoughts to Rome, with a suggestion that the issue required more thought and prayer than had evidently been applied.

But it would be a futile gesture, and he knew it. At best, he would be ignored. At worse, he would be suspended or laicized, perhaps even excommunicated.

Overnight, the world had changed for the worse. And like it or not, there was nothing one man could do to make a difference.

"Father Mauricio?" The deep, resonant voice came from outside Mauricio's office door. "Father?"

"In here," Mauricio called back, his eyes and thoughts on the half-finished homily on his computer screen, trying to finish his current sentence before putting it aside to focus on whatever his unexpected visitor's needs might be. "The door's open."

He blinked as his brain belatedly caught up with him. His office door was unlocked, yes; but the outer church door *was* locked, and as far as he knew he was the only one with a key.

A former priest who'd never returned his key? An exceptionally polite burglar? The door swung open—

And a man wearing a Mexican wrestler's mask and what looked like military body armor walked in.

It took every bit of Mauricio's willpower to stay seated at his desk instead of turning into mist and getting out as fast as he could. The man striding toward him was tall and muscular, his armored suit gleaming in the circle of light from the desk lamp. His gaudy mask covered everything except his eyes and mouth, rendering him completely anonymous. He stepped up to Mauricio's desk and stood there, the dark eyes behind the mask gazing down at the priest.

Mauricio's mind was frozen like an Alaskan glacier… and with his brain temporarily unavailable, he said the first words that came into his head. "You actually walk the streets like that?"

He winced as the sound of the words blasted away the mental frost. He held his breath, wondering if he would even see the blow coming that would flatten him against the wall. Turning into mist was starting to sound better and better.

But the man merely chuckled, a rumbling even deeper than his voice. "I do indeed, Father," he said. "My name is El Vengador. I stand by my people."

"I'm sure they're glad of that," Mauricio said. "Would you care to tell me how you got in?"

"The bell tower," El Vengador said, waving a hand upward. "The bell has been gone for, oh, at least the last two priests. But the outside is open to the air, and the trap door into the church still works."

"Yes," Mauricio murmured. The trap door worked, all right. It was also secured from the inside by a massive padlock. The hasp was loose enough for someone from the outside to lift the door a couple of inches, but a potential intruder would barely be able to get a pair of fingers through the gap. "And my lock?"

In answer, El Vengador reached into the equipment pouch at his waist and pulled out the lock.

Or what was left of it. The U-shaped shackle had been twisted, stretched out like taffy, and finally broken. The body also showed signs of having been squeezed. "The hasp is mostly all right," the big man added as he set the mangled lock on the edge of Mauricio's desk. "I knew you'd want to secure it again."

"Thank you," Mauricio murmured, gazing at his visitor with new understanding. Breaking the lock had taken tremendous strength. So had jumping up to the bell tower. "So when you say *my people*, you mean your fellow Evos?"

"The Evos, yes," El Vengador said. The words were straightforward and polite enough, but there was a hint of darkness beneath them. "But also the regular people—*all* of them—in the *barrio*. I don't believe there should be an *us* and a *them*." He cocked his head slightly. "Tell me, Father: does the Church believe in an *us* and a *them*?"

And right here was where it could get ugly. "I'm sure you've heard many men of the cloth pleading for understanding, acceptance, and brotherly love," Mauricio said, choosing his words carefully. "The voices speaking from the Vatican have so far been... somewhat less supportive. But I have no doubt that the Holy Father will eventually come out with a statement that will confirm the Evos as merely people with God-given talents." He made a face. "The Vatican is not always quick to come to agreement in such matters."

"So I've noticed," El Vengador said. "And you, Father? Where do *you* stand?"

Mauricio took a deep breath. "I know an Evo," he said. "He hasn't registered, and I've not advised him to do so. Nor have I contacted the police or Homeland Security.

Does that answer your question?"

"It's a partial answer," El Vengador said. "You give me a negative. I ask also for a positive."

"I don't understand."

"I want to know what you're willing to do to protect people like Simon Navarro."

Mauricio felt his eyes widen. "You *know* about him?"

"And about his power," El Vengador confirmed. "I was holding on beneath the window, listening, when he first returned Inez Bustamante's sight."

"No," Mauricio said, frowning as he played back the memory of that night. "No, you couldn't have been. I looked out that window. I would have seen your fingers on the sill."

"*If* I'd hung from the top," El Vengador agreed. "I was instead holding on to the sides." He crouched down and set his fingertips against the sides of Mauricio's desk. His arm muscles flexed, just a bit, and the wood gave an ominous creak.

"All right, yes, fine, I believe you," Mauricio said hastily. The desk was an antique, an honored part of All Saints' history, and it would cost a fortune to replace. "You were hanging and—" He broke off as a sudden thought struck him. The night of Inez's death, and Oscar's quiet request that Simon be called… "Oscar Gutierrez sent you, didn't he, to check up on Simon and me? That's how he knew about Simon's power."

El Vengador inclined his head. "I ask again, Father. How far are you willing to go to protect Evos?"

"How far are you *asking* me to go?"

For a moment El Vengador studied his face. Then, the lips below the edge of the mask twitched in an odd smile. "I'll be in touch," he said. "In the meantime, you should consider Canada."

With that, he turned and was gone. Mauricio leaned across his desk toward the door, and thought he heard the sound of someone climbing the steps that led to the bell tower.

For a few minutes afterward he simply sat in front of his computer, his train of thought completely derailed, waiting for his heart to slow down. Then, closing his homily, he logged on to the internet, pulled up a search engine, and typed in *Evos Canada*.

It took a few minutes, but he finally found what he assumed El Vengador had been referring to. In the midst of all the simmering anger and fear around the world, a town in Saskatchewan had quietly announced that it would welcome Evo refugees with open arms. The only conditions were that the refugees' powers would not be used for criminal purposes or to break any Canadian laws. Though it wasn't explicitly stated, it was hinted that the enforcement of these rules would be handled by other Evos.

To Mauricio, it sounded like the ideal solution. But another half-hour's search revealed the carefully unpublicized fact that the U.S. government had already issued a prohibition on registered Evos leaving the country. For unregistered ones who tried to run, there were a half-dozen tests under development designed to catch them at the border and add them to Homeland Security's trophy room. Another hour spent digging into the details left Mauricio with the clear impression that the new laws were as ironclad as anything he'd ever had to deal with.

Which raised the question of why El Vengador had come to him in the first place.

Had the Vatican set up some quiet escape route for priests to use? If so, Mauricio had heard nothing about it. Were clergy exempt from border testing? Again, there was no indication that would be the case. And he'd already seen that Rome wasn't offering Evos any kind of sanctuary.

He puzzled over the question for another week without finding an answer.

At the end of the week, the answer found him.

It was just after lunch, and Mauricio was checking the votive candles at the side altar when the unexpected visitor arrived.

Most people who stopped by All Saints in off-hours made a point of opening the big outer doors carefully and closing them quietly and reverently. Not this one. This one flung the outer door open with a rush of air and then yanked it shut with a resounding boom.

Mauricio's first thought was that the flinger and yanker was El Vengador, making an even more dramatic entrance than last time. But the person hurrying down the center aisle was a young Asian woman barely half El Vengador's size. She spotted Mauricio as he stepped into her line of sight and veered toward him, picking up speed. "Help me," she begged, her voice strained, her face tight. "Please. Help me."

"Of course," Mauricio assured her. "What's the matter?"

"There's a man," she said, breathing heavily as she stumbled to a halt in front of him. Despite the cool autumn weather, her face was gleaming with sweat. She was about twenty-five, he estimated, clean and well fed. Not a street person, then, though her clothing looked overdue for a pass through a washing machine. "A man in a blue Ford Explorer. I think he's following me."

"All right," Mauricio said, gesturing toward his office and pulling out his cell phone. "You can wait in my office while I call the police."

"No—no police," she said quickly.

Mauricio paused with his finger poised. "Why not?"

"The man might be from a... well, there are some people out there who don't exactly like me," she hedged. "Especially one group. I think he might be from them."

"I see," Mauricio said. "Would this be a criminal group, by any chance?"

"No, they're not criminal," she said. "At least, I don't think so. But they have money. Lots of money." She looked at him, her eyes pleading. "And I think they're looking for me."

"Why?"

"I don't know," she said. "Please. Can you help me?"

"Of course," Mauricio said. "A blue Explorer, you said?"

"Yes," she said. "I saw him parking across the street when I was coming in."

"And you're sure he's following you?"

"Well, no, not really," she admitted. "But..."

"It's all right," Mauricio soothed. She was probably imagining things. People with guilty consciences tended to think everyone they met was out to get them. "That door over there is my office. You can wait in there while I take a look."

She nodded and headed toward the office. "Be careful," she warned over her shoulder. "They're—I think they could be dangerous."

"It'll be all right," he called after her.

He waited until she had closed the door behind her. Then, turning into mist, he flowed across the sanctuary and slipped out through the crack beneath the doors.

The girl had been right about the blue Explorer. It was parked across the street, about fifty yards down from the church. A young blond man was seated inside, a light jacket zipped up to his chin, studying what looked like a tablet propped up on the steering wheel. Rising well above the level of traffic where he was less likely to be seen or hit by sudden air currents, Mauricio headed over to investigate.

The man had lowered the driver's side rear window a crack for air. Slipping a tendril of himself through it, Mauricio eased over the man's shoulder for a look at his object of interest.

It was a tablet, all right. Displayed on it were three of the Catholic churches in the area, accompanied by the names of their priests and support staff. At the top of the page was All Saints Church and one Father Mauricio Chavez.

He also noted that there was a small but distinct bulge in the man's right-hand jacket pocket.

The man made a little grunting noise and closed the tablet's case. He tucked it inside the messenger bag on the seat beside him, grabbed the bag's strap, and opened the door.

Mauricio quickly slipped back out of the window and sped across the street, again staying high. He reached the church, slipped under the door, and returned to human form, his newly reformed heart pounding in his chest. For a moment he wondered whether he should call the police, decided that if the man was looking for trouble there was no way the cops could arrive in time anyway, and took up a position a few feet inside the door.

Unlike the Asian girl, the young man *did* open the door carefully and reverently. He was halfway inside when he caught sight of Mauricio standing silently in front of him. "Oh!" he said, twitching in surprise. "Sorry, Father—you startled me. Usually I have to go hunting to find the local priest."

"My job is to make it easy for those who are searching," Mauricio said.

The man frowned. "Was that a joke?"

"Not really," Mauricio said. "Can I help you?"

"Let's find out." The man reached into his bulging jacket pocket. Mauricio braced himself, ready to turn into mist at an moment's notice.

"I'm Father Gunther Lindhurst," he said, pulling out a thick wallet and flipping it open to an intricate ID card. "Special emissary from the Vatican."

"Ah," Mauricio said, feeling some of the tension flow out of him.

But only some of it. This was the same Vatican, after all, that had declared that certain Evo powers were evil.

"I've been sent to investigate the Evo situation in Los Angeles," Gunther continued. "I've been visiting the various churches, introducing myself, and asking for their assistance."

"I see," Mauricio said stiffly. Did they know about Simon? More importantly, did they know about Simon's connection with Mauricio and All Saints? "I'll help in any way I can, of course."

"Thank you," Gunther said, casually looking around. "Nice church. Especially for this area. Some nice woodwork over there."

"Thank you," Mauricio said. An observant man, clearly. Not surprising, considering his job as an investigator.

"Any Evo activity around here that you know of?" Gunther asked, bringing his eyes back to Mauricio. "I understand there's someone who calls himself El Vengador who wanders around trying to discourage gang activity."

"I've heard of him," Mauricio acknowledged carefully. Fortunately, El Vengador's exploits were starting to come to public attention, so there was no need to lie. "From what I've heard, he's good for the neighborhood."

Gunther smiled thinly. "If he's an unregistered Evo, Father, he's by definition *not* good for the neighborhood."

"Perhaps."

"Not just *perhaps*," Gunther said. "At any rate, I'll be in the area for the next few weeks. Please contact me immediately if you witness any Evo powers, or even just hear rumors. At this point, I want to hear everything." He reached into his wallet, pulled out a business card from a thick wad of them, and handed it to Mauricio. "And remember: it's not me who's asking, but the Vatican." He smiled, a thin, humorless thing. "Have a good day, Father."

"And you," Mauricio said. His smile, he guessed, wasn't any warmer or more genuine than Gunther's.

Mauricio had expected the Asian girl to lock the office door behind her. To his surprise, she hadn't.

To his even greater surprise, she was sitting at his desk.

Typing away diligently on his computer.

"I found your car and your man," he told her, frowning as he came around the side of the desk. Was that the California DMV's website on the screen? It was definitely the DMV logo.

Only this didn't look like the public website, the one where people could renew their licenses or get information. It looked like something a lot more private and confidential.

In fact, as he got closer he could see that it was a listing of California license plate numbers and their owners.

She was running Father Gunther's tags.

"He wasn't from any corporation," Mauricio continued mechanically. She wasn't supposed to be able to do this. Was she a cop? "But I think I've figured out why this corporation you're worried about is after you."

"You have?" she asked, looking up over her shoulder at him. "Why?"

"Because corporations frown on people hacking into their computer systems." Mauricio nodded toward the screen. "So does the government."

"What, *this*?" she scoffed. "Don't worry, I'm not changing anything. I just want to find out who that man is. Only according to this, his car doesn't exist."

"His name's Father Gunther Lindhurst, and he's here from the Vatican," Mauricio said. "And you're not finding his plates because you got the number wrong. The last digit's a three, not an eight."

She threw him an odd look, then turned back to the keyboard and made the correction. The DMV computer thought about it for a few seconds, then produced a new page.

"Hertz rental," she muttered. "Let's see if you're right about his name." She worked the computer for another couple of minutes, and a new site came up, this one with the Hertz logo.

"You're very good at this," Mauricio commented as she punched in Gunther's plate number again. "You run Hertz tags a lot?"

"I run everything a lot," she said. "Looks like you're two for two. Car was rented to a Gunther Lindhurst three days ago at LAX."

Mauricio nodded. "So you're a hacker."

She looked up over her shoulder at him. "Boy, that sounded judgmental. Whatever happened to grace and forgiveness?"

"They come packaged with confession and repentance," Mauricio said. "So who exactly is looking for you?"

She made a face. "It could be… oh, a lot of people."

"That's helpful," Mauricio said. "Let's start with whoever you've stolen the most money from lately."

"I don't steal money," she protested. "Not anymore. At least, not right now. Mostly, I just hack into corporate building security systems to get in at night. Just to have someplace to sleep. I don't steal anything."

"Except some food from the break room?" Mauricio suggested, nodding as the odd dichotomy between clean skin and dirty clothes finally made sense. "I suppose you sleep on the couches and shower in the president's private bathroom. But even the fanciest CEO suite doesn't have laundry facilities."

"Sometimes the staff area has one, if they work with messy stuff," she said. "But mostly I have to get my clothes cleaned somewhere else."

"I see," Mauricio said. "Tell me, how did you happen to come in here today?"

"A man pulled me out of trouble a few nights ago," she said. "A *big* man. He said that if I ever needed help I should come here." She gestured toward the office door. "I really did think your Vatican guy was following me. Sorry."

"Not a problem," Mauricio assured her. "I'm Father Mauricio, by the way. What's your name?"

"Kim," she said. "Kim Pyon."

"Nice to meet you," Mauricio said. "Tell me, was this big man wearing body armor and a Mexican wrestler's mask?"

"I don't know what kind of mask it was," Kim said. "But you got the armor right. You know him?"

"He calls himself El Vengador," Mauricio said. "Did he happen to mention Canada?'"

"I don't think so," she said, frowning. "Why? You going there?"

"No," Mauricio said. "But a lot of Evos would like to."

She snorted. "There's the magic word," she said, closing the browser and standing up. "And I'm out of here. Sorry, but Evos are way too hot to touch these days."

"Relax," Mauricio said, holding out a hand, palm outward. "You won't have to deal with them. And you don't have to leave. We have a sort of informal overnight setup down in the basement: a room with a cot, a bathroom and shower, even a small microwave, hotplate, and fridge. You're welcome to stay for a while if you want."

"What about the rest of your staff?"

"There are only two of them, they only come in a couple of days a week, and they don't go down there unless I send them for something," Mauricio said. "As long as you don't feel an urge to start banging pots together, no one else will know."

Her eyes narrowed. "Sounds great. What's the catch?"

"Remember I said a lot of Evos want to go to Canada? Well, they can't. Not from here. Not if they're registered. Even the unregistered ones will only be able to get out until Homeland Security comes up with a fast test to identify them."

"Which they're already working on, I suppose?"

"Like caffeinated beavers." Mauricio lifted a finger. "But they can only act if the person in question is a U.S. citizen. If not, Homeland Security has no legal right to test them or detain them or anything else. I know—I've been reading up on it."

For a long moment Kim frowned at him. Then, abruptly, her face cleared. "I get it. You want me to break into foreign citizen lists and change them."

"More specifically, into foreign passport lists. I assume that once you're in you can insert names and passport numbers into official government databases?"

"Probably," Kim said hesitantly. "You *do* realize the flaw in this whole plan, right? All the computer records in Bulgaria or wherever won't do a bit of good if your Evo hasn't got a real, physical passport to hand the border guard."

"Which is why we'll also need a top-notch forger,"

Mauricio said. "If we can get someone to make the passports, and you can get into the right computer to confirm that the documents match existing profiles in their database, we can do some real good here."

"Like the Underground Railroad back in the Civil War," she murmured.

"Exactly," Mauricio said, nodding. "But as you said, before we can get it up and running, we need a forger."

"Let me guess. You want me to break into police databases and find one?"

Mauricio winced. When she put it like that... "I don't exactly *want* you to," he hedged. "But I don't see any other way." He frowned as a sudden thought struck him. "Wait a minute—maybe there is. Let's start by doing a search for Diego Rebasa."

"Who's he?"

"A forger I knew a couple of decades ago," Mauricio said. "He worked for the man I ran people up here from Mexico for."

Kim's eyes widened. "Whoa. You priests get around way more than I thought."

"It's the repentance and forgiveness package," Mauricio reminded her. "Can you do it?"

"I can try," she said. "You want me to use the computer here? Or would you rather I do it on a different machine?"

"I've got a laptop you can take downstairs," he said. "Though I suppose if it's using the church Wi-Fi it doesn't really matter which computer you use. If they trace it back here, I'm still sunk."

"Don't worry, they won't," she assured him. "None of what I do will show up in your history, either. In case anybody looks."

Mauricio thought about Gunther. "Someone probably

will," he warned. "Would have been nice if El Vengador had laid all this out for us, instead of hoping you just happened to drop in someday. And *then* hoping we could figure it out before you took off again."

"I get the feeling he's the kind of guy who plays his hand half under the table," Kim said. "Only deals out the cards when he needs to, and then only to the people he wants to have them."

"Probably," Mauricio said. "Though that kind of compartmentalization can lead to trouble down the road." He took a deep breath. "Okay. Let me get the laptop and show you downstairs. There should be a robe down there, too."

"A robe?" she asked, suddenly wary again. "What for?"

"For you," he said. "Because the washer and dryer are at the rectory next door. I want to run your clothes through them."

"Ah. Right." She looked down at her shirt. "Maybe even run them through twice."

It sounded straightforward. Unfortunately, it wasn't.

Kim had no trouble getting into the LAPD's criminal database. Or the FBI's, the Treasury Department's, or Homeland Security's.

But in the end, she found nothing. As far as official records were concerned, Diego Rebasa didn't exist. Or more likely, he'd died sometime in the past twenty years.

Still, even though Kim hadn't found Diego, she'd turned up a lot of other possibilities. A sort-and-download of people with the word *forger* in their rap sheets netted a truly impressive list of names.

The problem was that the police hadn't been obliging enough to rank their criminals by competence level. That left no way to distinguish the true experts from those whose technique consisted of scrawling "20 Dollars" on pieces of green paper and hoping for the best.

Worse, as Kim pointed out on the third day of their efforts, the absolute best forgers wouldn't even show up in the database, because those would be the ones who'd never been caught.

It was frustrating. Every day, it seemed, there were new stories about Evos: running for the border, running amok, or just running. Most of the top politicians, on both sides of the aisle, were united in their firm support of Evo registration. Across the world, official and unofficial action against Evos was increasing, and while social and religious leaders warned against the dangers of mob violence, there was little anyone could do to stop it. In some places, a single, unsupported accusation that someone was an Evo could get that person killed.

Particularly worrisome to Mauricio were rumors of a vigilante couple—a Caucasian man and an African-American woman—who were actively hunting down Evos and murdering them. That kind of publicity inevitably led to copycat killings, and that was something the world absolutely didn't need right now.

It also didn't help that there were a handful of Evos who *did* use their powers to rob, terrorize, or murder. Highly-publicized crimes like those just fanned the flames higher.

Canada, and that one enlightened part of Saskatchewan, seemed to be the Evos' only hope. The problem was, Mauricio couldn't seem to gather all the pieces he needed to get them there.

* * *

"Maybe we should try something different," Kim said when Mauricio came down to her basement apartment at noon to bring her a sandwich and check on her progress. "Instead of a regular forger, maybe we should try looking for an *Evo* forger."

"Why would that be better?" Mauricio asked. "And what makes you think there is such an animal?"

"Nothing, really," Kim said. "But I've been thinking. The Renautas Corporation has been making lists of Evos for a while. All I need to do—"

"Wait a minute," Mauricio interjected. "Are you talking about *the* Renautas Corporation? The behemoth that gobbles up other companies like potato chips?"

"You know any other companies by that name?" Kim asked dryly. "Anyway, like I said, they've got lists of Evos. Maybe I can pull those lists and cross-reference with the police and FBI files and look for a match."

"Let me guess," Mauricio said. A few more pieces of the Kim Pyon puzzle were falling into place. "You know about the Renautas lists because you've already been inside their computers. *They're* the people with lots of money you mentioned the first time you came in here, aren't they?"

"Well… yes," she conceded. "But they didn't spot me."

"Are you sure?" Mauricio countered. "What if they've got some kind of Evo computer expert on their payroll?"

Kim's eyes went a little flat. "Ouch," she said in a suddenly subdued voice. "I never thought of… Wait— wouldn't they have to register someone like that?"

"Who says they haven't?" Mauricio pointed out. "The only way to know for sure would be to get into the government's own Evo registration files. And don't try *that*, at least not from here. If anyone would have Evos guarding their computers, it would be the government."

"Yeah, they would," she said sourly. "Hypocrites." She pursed her lips. "I still think Renautas is worth trying. But you're right, we can't do it from here. An internet café, maybe?"

"A bit obvious," Mauricio pointed out. "Not to mention right out in the open."

"Open's not too bad if—no, wait." A small smile twitched suddenly at the corners of her lips. "Never mind—I've got it." She closed the laptop. "You've got a car, right?"

"Yes," Mauricio said. There was something about that smile that sent an unpleasant tingle up the back of his neck. "Where are we going?"

"A little Thai place on Pennsylvania," she said, stuffing the laptop into a messenger bag Mauricio had given her.

"Let me guess," Mauricio said, a hollow feeling forming in the pit of his stomach. "The part of Pennsylvania right down the street from the Hollenbeck Community Police Station?"

"Bingo." She cocked her head at the look on his face. "Oh, come on. It'll be fun."

"Right," Mauricio said with a sigh. "I can hardly wait."

The Thai place was bigger than Mauricio had expected: long and relatively narrow, with large windows on the street side, and filled to the brim with lunchtime diners. Mauricio had hoped to get a table by an inside wall, where they'd at least be somewhat hidden from the view of passing vehicles and pedestrians.

Kim, naturally, had other ideas. Tipping the receptionist twenty dollars of Mauricio's money, she got them a two-person table right by a window.

"Because if someone comes for me, I want to see him

before he gets inside," she said when Mauricio asked her about it. "They won't know who the hacker is until they can take a look at everyone. If I see them first, we'll have time to slip out the back before they make us."

Unless they already know who to look for. With an effort, Mauricio held his tongue. It sounded crazy to him, but Kim was the expert in these things.

A harried-looking waiter hurried up. They gave him their order, Kim choosing something for Mauricio that she promised would be easy on his stomach.

The minute the waiter's back was turned, she opened the laptop and got to work.

Mauricio sat across from her, dividing his attention between her furrowed forehead and the traffic passing by outside, wondering how he'd let her talk him into this. Yes, they needed the information, and so far they'd been spinning their wheels. But hacking a major corporation like Renautas via a police system was just begging for trouble. He could see the station just down the street, and all the cops wandering in and out the front door. Police cars pulled briskly out of the station parking lot, merging into the flow of traffic—

Mauricio froze. Coming toward them, moving slowly as though the driver was looking for an empty parking space, was a blue Ford Explorer.

It was Father Gunther Lindhurst.

"We have to go," Mauricio murmured, reaching across the table and taking Kim's arm.

To his consternation, she shrugged off his hand. "Not yet," she muttered. "I'm in. I just need to find the right files."

"It's Father Gunther," Mauricio bit out, trying in vain to get another grip on her arm. "If he sees us—"

"If he sees *you*, you mean," Kim cut him off, pausing

in her work for a quick look out the window. "He wasn't chasing *me*, remember?"

Mauricio clenched his teeth. No, Gunther hadn't been following her. But he *had* presumably seen her go into All Saints. If he spotted her here, he might find her presence in this neighborhood odd enough to investigate further.

"That door back there should be the kitchen or a storage area," she said, flicking a finger at the wall behind Mauricio's chair. "Go on—make yourself scarce."

Mauricio glared at Gunther's car as it eased its way into a space right across the street from the restaurant. Now what?

Mauricio was bigger than Kim. He could certainly haul her bodily out of her chair and out of the restaurant, whether she wanted to go or not. But that kind of scene would draw attention, which was exactly what they were trying to avoid.

Should he leave? Kim had a point—his face was probably more recognizable than hers, especially after that brief chat back at the church. Mauricio could use the back door, turn into mist, and get out through a vent or something. It would be risky to travel along a crowded street in broad daylight, but there was a fair chance he could make it to Gunther without anyone spotting him.

Then what? Turn back to human, strike up a conversation, and hope he could steer Gunther away from the restaurant? But if Gunther spotted Kim and started wondering about her and Mauricio being in the same place at the same time…

He paused as a sudden thought occurred to him. He was visible in daylight because sunlight reflected off the particles that made up his mist form. That was just basic physics.

And if he reflected sunlight…

It was crazy. But it might work.

"Hurry it up," he murmured to Kim as he stood and backed toward the service door. Gunther had nearly finished shoehorning his car into the space. Mauricio pushed open the door and let it swing closed behind him, turning into mist and slipping through the gap just before it closed. He headed straight up to the ceiling and, staying out of the light as much as he could, returned to Kim's table.

Lowering himself from the ceiling as inconspicuously as he could, he spread himself evenly across the window, filling the entire pane of glass that separated Kim from the world outside.

The Explorer's door opened and Gunther stepped out. For a moment he stood beside the vehicle, giving the area the same kind of quick but careful look that he'd given All Saints on his first visit. His eyes swept across Kim's window...

And kept moving.

Mauricio watched the other priest closely, almost afraid to believe the trick had worked. But it had. Whether Gunther thought the haziness of the view through that particular window was due to an extra layer of dust or just some trick of the light and angle, he apparently attached no significance to it. A moment later, his informal surveillance completed, he made his way to the sidewalk and headed in the direction of the police station.

Kim, her full attention on her work, never saw a thing.

Mauricio waited until Gunther was a good half block away. Then, returning to the service door, he slipped through the crack beneath it, turned back into his human form, and rejoined Kim.

She looked up as he loomed suddenly over her. "Back already?" she asked. She glanced out the window again. "Is he gone?"

"For now," Mauricio said, reaching out to take hold of the laptop screen. "And we're not giving him any more chances. Close down and let's get out of here."

"I'm not finished," Kim protested, prying at his fingers.

"Yes, you are," Mauricio said firmly. "Close down, or I'll do it."

Kim glared at him. But she obediently lowered her eyes to the computer and tapped out a final sequence. "Okay."

Mauricio closed the laptop and tucked it under his arm. "Come on," he said, pulling out his wallet and dropping some money on the table.

"What about lunch?" Kim asked as he led her past the crowded tables to the main door. "We never got our food."

"Don't worry," he assured her. "There's a sandwich with your name on it back at the church."

Three hours of sifting and cross-referencing later, Kim admitted defeat.

"Sorry," she said, scowling at the screen. "If Renautas has any sublisting of Evo criminals, I couldn't find it."

"So we have nothing?" Mauricio asked.

Kim lifted a finger. "Maybe not. Renautas has a handle on a few places they think Evos might hang out. Very preliminary stuff—mostly just rumors—and they're just starting to look into it. I could go to one of them, see if I can find an Evo or two, and ask if any of them knows a forger."

"Sounds like an invitation to get grabbed," Mauricio said. "A whole nest of Evos would be awfully tempting for the authorities."

"Oh, these aren't Evo clubs," she assured him. "Most of the people who go there are normal humans. Makes it easier for Evos to blend in. And like I said, it doesn't look like Renautas has really started any serious surveillance yet. You want me to go check it out?"

Mauricio chewed at his lip. He'd had enough experience with the Church's bureaucracy and reports to know that just because the records weren't showing any significant attention didn't mean the people who filed stuff in those records weren't already on the case.

But they still needed a forger. This might at least give them a lead. "Fine," he said. "But we both go."

"Seriously?" Kim ran a critical eye over him. "Don't take this wrong, Father, but the club that's our best shot is mostly for teens and twenty-somethings. You don't exactly look like a hipster."

"You'd be surprised how good I look when I take this off," Mauricio said, tapping his clerical collar. "Either way, you're not going alone."

"Okay," Kim said with a sigh. "I guess I can always pretend I don't know you."

Mauricio had never heard of *La Basa*. But the rest of L.A. apparently had. He had to park four blocks away, and even at the relatively early hour of eight o'clock the street outside the black-draped entrance was crowded enough to be Times Square on New Year's Eve. "So this is it?" he murmured to Kim.

"This is it." She shot him a sideways glance. "It's not too late to back out. I can do this by myself."

For a minute Mauricio was sorely tempted. Even out here the salsa music and over-amplified bass spilling out the door were verging on the uncomfortable. God alone knew what it would be like inside. As Kim had predicted, the crowd leaned heavily to the youthful side, which would make a forty-nine-year-old man all the more noticeable in contrast. Not exactly the ideal way to keep a low profile on what was supposed to be a secret mission.

And while most of the crowd seemed fun-loving and harmless, he could see a few knots of darker types scattered around. Maybe Evos; maybe punk rockers; maybe gang-bangers.

Mauricio knew the feel of bad neighborhoods and bad situations. This place was rapidly taking on that vibe.

Kim was still waiting for an answer. Squaring his shoulders, Mauricio gave her a quick smile. "I'm okay," he said. "Let's do this."

There were two lines of people waiting along the sides of the building: those with tickets, he assumed, and those without. Both groups seemed irritated at the slow progress of the lines, and a good half of them were smoking or drinking. Most of the rest were on their phones, chatting with friends or possibly trying to find a less crowded club. The rest of the people filling the street like a sort of block party were apparently a third group: those who'd given up on getting in—or had never planned on it in the first place—and were simply taking advantage of the free music to hold their own open-air get-togethers. The door itself was guarded by a half-dozen bouncer types, all of them massive, all of them dressed in black, all of them with professionally blank expressions. Gazing uneasily at the lines, Mauricio wondered how long this was going to take.

Not long at all, as it turned out. Kim didn't head for either of the lines, but simply walked up to the biggest of the bouncers. "Kim Pyon and escort," she called loudly enough to be heard over the music as she held up her phone. "We're on the VIP list."

The bouncer looked at her, looked at Mauricio a couple

of seconds longer, than pulled a scanner from his jacket pocket and held it up to Kim's phone. A small light flashed and he peered at it a moment. Then, with another long look at Mauricio, he nodded toward the doorway behind him. Kim gave him a smile, took Mauricio's arm, and slipped carefully around the man's massive shoulders and through the doorway.

Inside, it was every bit as loud as Mauricio had feared. And then some. "Don't tell me," he called to Kim over the racket.

"Well, I sure as hell wasn't going to wait in line." She looked at him, her lip twitching as she seemed to suddenly remember who she was with. "Sorry."

"I've heard worse," Mauricio assured her, looking around. The room they'd entered was bigger than he'd expected from what he'd seen outside—clearly, the club extended sideways into what he'd assumed were separate buildings. The center space was dominated by a dance floor, which was flanked on its four sides by two long bars, an area for the DJ and his sound equipment, and a large stage currently featuring six barely-clad girls gyrating to the beat in front of a screen with an eye-prickling light show. In sharp contrast with the light show, the rest of the room was fairly dim, lit mostly by strobing flashes of different colors from lights in the atrium-style ceiling two stories above the dance floor.

In the room's four corners were archways that led back into smaller, more private areas with even murkier lighting. Mauricio was pretty sure he didn't want to know what was going on back there. A balcony wrapped around the entire center room, midway between the dance floor and the ceiling, with tables and chairs for patrons who wanted to take a breather or an alcohol break or just watch the activity below. From Mauricio's current vantage point, he could see hints of more archways and more private rooms up there.

And there were *people*. Lots of people. Everywhere.

"So," Kim called. "How do you want to play this?"

"It was *your* idea," Mauricio reminded her.

"Right." She did a slow circle, taking everything in. "Well, I suppose we could start by looking for people in groups who don't seem to fit in."

Mauricio eyed the kids gyrating on the dance floor. All of them seemed to be dressed pretty much the same: bizarrely. "Good luck with that."

"Well, that's what *I'm* going to do," she said. Even over the noise he could hear the scorn in her voice. "Maybe you should look for someone built like that El Vengador character. Anyone like that's bound to be an Evo."

A couple of heads turned in their direction. Wincing, Mauricio took Kim's arm and pulled her deeper into the milling crowd. "Let's try not to use the *E*-word in public, shall we?"

"Right," Kim said. "Sorry."

"And I'm thinking we should stick together," Mauricio continued, looking around. *Like a needle in a haystack*, the old cliché whispered through his mind. A needle, moreover, that was trying very hard *not* to be found.

He frowned. Had someone just called his name? He looked around, started to turn—

And started as a hand snaked out of the crowd and grabbed his arm. "*Padre!*" a voice shouted. "*Padre Mauricio!*"

Mauricio exhaled a relieved puff of air. It was only Simon Navarro. "What are you doing here?" the teen called out.

"A friend invited me," Mauricio called back.

"One of *your* friends?"

"It's not exactly my usual music," Mauricio conceded. "But I thought about all the people here who need to be saved." He gestured. "What about you? I would think your uncle would frown on places like this."

Simon's throat worked. "Not any more. God, *Padre*— you don't *know*?"

"Know what?"

"My *tio*—" Simon broke off. "Come on—we can talk better outside. You know?"

"Just a second." Mauricio looked around. But his brief pause and moment of inattention had allowed Kim to disappear into the crowd.

Still, she was used to taking care of herself. She should be all right alone for a few minutes. "Never mind," he said to Simon. "Lead the way."

Earlier, before they'd entered the club, Mauricio had found the noise spilling into the street painfully loud. Now, as he left the even louder environment inside, the decibel level outside seemed almost calm by comparison. Simon worked his way deftly through the knots of people chatting or smoking as they waited their turn to get in. Mauricio, for his part, struggled to keep up, trying not to bowl anyone over.

They'd made it to the outer edge of the crowd before Simon finally stopped and spun back to face Mauricio. "You didn't know?" he demanded. "My *tio* died in a car crash, and you didn't *know*?"

Mauricio felt his eyes widen. He'd been so focused on Kim and their underground railroad project for the past few days that he'd totally neglected both his phone messages and his emails. "Simon, I'm so sorry," he said. "When did this happen?"

"Last night." Simon sniffed loudly and swiped his

sleeve across his eyes. "I thought you'd call." He dug the phone Mauricio had given him out of his pocket and waved it accusingly in Mauricio's face. "You should have *called*!"

"I know," Mauricio said. Behind Simon, one of the small clusters of people was starting to notice their conversation. It wasn't one of the harmless-looking groups, either. Gang-bangers for sure. "Look, let's head back to the—"

"Why didn't you *call*?" Simon cut him off. He took a step backward toward the gang-bangers. "They threw me out. You know? My own *primos*. They threw me *out*. I had no place to go."

"You could have come back to the church," Mauricio said, taking a step toward him. The boy was gesturing wildly, his swinging arms coming dangerously close to the people behind him. "Come back—we'll talk."

"What could I do but come here?" Simon raged on. "I thought there might be a *vato* here who could help me. You know? Only there's no one. No one *anywhere*." He waved his arm over his shoulder in emphasis.

And as he did so, the back of his hand slapped against the cheek of the man directly behind him.

It wasn't a hard blow. But it was hard enough. Even as Simon spun around to see what he'd hit he was thrown off balance as the man spat a curse and slammed the heel of his hand against the teen's chest.

Simon gasped something and tried to scramble away. But his feet were tangled up with each other, and the man was coming toward him. The man's hand dipped into his side pocket—

And suddenly he was holding a knife.

"No!" Mauricio barked, hurrying forward and trying to put himself between them. "Please don't—he didn't mean it. Come on, I'll make it up to you."

The gang-banger didn't even slow down. "Out of the way, *ruco*," he snarled, not taking his eyes off Simon as he shoved Mauricio aside. Mauricio took a couple of quick steps sideways and again tried to get between Simon and the knife. This time the gang-banger backhanded him across his cheek, sending a dazzling haze of pain across his face and nearly knocking him off his feet. "*Por favor!*" Mauricio pleaded, fighting for balance as he fought against the pain. "It was an accident."

The gang-banger spared him a single, burning glare, then started to turn his eyes back to Simon.

And without warning he jerked to a halt, his mouth dropping open, his arms and torso twitching violently, his eyes going wide.

Wide… but unseeing.

Simon had blinded him.

Not just him, either. A quick look at the man's companions showed that Simon had used his power against all of them.

Mauricio mouthed a word he hadn't used since his days running the border. The gang-banger's knife was slashing back and forth now as his bewilderment and growing panic began to degenerate into fear and paranoia. His flailing attack caught one of his buddies across the upper left arm.

The other man jerked back with some vicious curses of his own. He grabbed for his pocket, pulled out a knife and snapped it open, and suddenly there were *two* blades sweeping randomly through the night air. "It's all right," Mauricio called, trying to get between the knives and a nearby group of young people who hadn't yet noticed the threat behind them. "You—all of you—go," he snapped, shoving the two nearest girls out of reach of the knives. "*Por favor*—put the knives down—"

He barely managed to get out of the way as both men jabbed their weapons in the direction of his voice. "You'll be all right in an hour," Mauricio finished, getting the words out as fast as he could. Simon was standing a couple of feet out of stabbing range, his face wooden as he surveyed his handiwork. Mauricio circled warily around the flailing knives and pulled the boy back into the throng of people.

"*Lo siento*," Simon said when they were once again in the relative anonymity of the milling crowd. "Sorry. I just—"

"It's all right," Mauricio said, keeping a tight hold on his temper.

But it wasn't all right. Not by a long shot. The gang-bangers had gotten a solid look at Simon before he'd blinded them, and once their vision cleared Mauricio had no doubt they'd come looking for the kid who'd done that to them. Worse, with Simon's home situation suddenly up in the air, the boy had nowhere to go except the streets.

Even at the best of times, life on the streets was dangerous. Right now, sleeping out in the open—especially in this neighborhood—would be a death sentence.

Which left Mauricio only one option. "You have anywhere you can go tonight?" he asked, just to be sure.

"No." Simon pointed toward the club door. "That's why I came to the club. I hoped I could find an Ev—could find someone like me who would let me crash with them for a few days."

Mauricio sighed. "Fine," he said. "Once we're finished here, you can come back with us. There's a guest bedroom in the rectory—you can sleep there for now."

"Really?" Simon breathed. "*Gracias, Padre.* I really appreciate it." He pointed at the club again. "You say you're doing something here? What is it? Can I help?"

"I don't know," Mauricio said hesitantly. The more

people he pulled into this underground railroad thing, the greater the chance that someone would talk.

Still, he and Kim had been prepared to talk to total strangers about their situation. At least Simon was a known quantity. "I'm looking for a forger," he said, lowering his voice. "Someone who can make falsified documents. You know any Evos who can do that?"

"I don't know any Evos," Simon said, scratching thoughtfully at his cheek. "But there's a *moyo* named Jackson Tarbell who I heard works for a guy who does documents."

"Really?" Mauricio asked, a hint of cautious excitement tingling down his spine. "Is Jackson in there?"

"I think so," Simon said. "He was at the bar a couple of hours ago. Come on, we'll go see."

"Assuming we can get back in," Mauricio cautioned, eyeing the group of bouncers dubiously. "Let's hope they remember me."

"Hey!" a voice called from beside him. Mauricio turned, tensing—

"What happened?" Kim asked as she walked up to them. "Music get to you?"

"I needed to talk to Simon," Mauricio said. "Simon, this is Kim. Kim; Simon."

"Yeah, it's a little loud for conversation in there," Kim agreed. "But don't do that again, okay? I was afraid you'd been grabbed by the cops."

"There are *placas*?" Simon asked anxiously. "Where?"

"There, for starters," Kim said nodding toward the edge of the crowd Mauricio and Simon had just left. "That gray sedan, parked third back on the left side of the street? Those two guys sitting in it are cops."

Mauricio's mouth had gone suddenly dry. "You sure?"

he asked carefully, peering through the crowd at the car Kim had identified.

"Positive," she said. "I've seen that car and those two guys before. Don't worry—they're just there to watch for trouble."

Mauricio took a deep breath, the muscle tension that had been fading away suddenly reversing direction.

Because Kim was wrong. The gang-banger who'd pulled the knife on Simon had been in full view of that car. Cops who'd been tasked with keeping order should have been charging toward the scene well before Simon was forced to use his power.

But they hadn't even opened their doors. Which meant they were there for some purpose other than keeping order.

Looking for Evos?

Possibly. Kim had warned him that Renautas suspected *La Basa* was frequented by Evos. If Renautas knew about the place, then the government probably did, too. Maybe the cops were trying to spot evidence of powers.

In which case, depending on how observant they were, Simon's picture might already be wending its way through a facial-recognition computer somewhere. Mauricio's might be, too.

Or else the cops were setting up for a raid.

"Jackson's going to have to wait," he said, digging out his car keys. "You two need to get back to the church—right now. Kim, you know how to drive?"

"Sure," Kim said, her eyes narrowing. "What's going on?"

"I think we're about to get raided," he said, handing her the keys. "Go on, get out of here."

"What about you?" Kim asked, fingering the keys.

"I'll get a cab or something." More likely, he would just turn into mist and float home. But of course he couldn't tell her that. "Don't worry, I'll be all right."

"Come *on*, *chica*," Simon urged, tugging at Kim's sleeve. "You heard him—it's not safe. Let's go."

Kim gave Mauricio one final, lingering look. Then, spinning around, she headed away through the crowd, Simon close behind her.

Mauricio waited until they were out of sight. Then, again trying not to knock anyone over, he headed toward a cross street angling away from the club.

The street was lined with cars, but none of them seemed to have cops sitting in them. The far end of the block wasn't cordoned off, either. Apparently, whoever was setting up the barricade was doing it slowly and casually, with small steps designed not to give the show away. Mauricio still had time.

Though time to do *what*, he still hadn't figured out.

Looking around carefully to make sure he wasn't being observed, he turned into mist and headed back toward the club.

In broad daylight, he could be seen in his mist form. At night, though, as long as he stayed out of the full glare of streetlights or headlights, he was as good as invisible. Staying well above the crowd, he circled the building, looking for a way in.

An opportunity presented itself almost at once: a side window on the third floor with the upper part open a few inches. The room behind the window was dark, but given the murkiness of the club's back rooms, that didn't necessarily mean anything.

For that matter, he didn't even know if this floor was part of the club. It could just as easily be apartments or something else that just happened to share the same building. Either way, he needed to be careful. Alert for signs of life, he slipped through the cracked window.

Straight into an X-rated movie.

Or possibly several of them. There were at least five couples grunting and gyrating on the giant mattress that covered half the floor.

Mauricio flowed across the room, wishing he could at least look away from the display. But he couldn't. Like a hologram, where each piece somehow held the entire picture, each bit of his cloud form seemed to be all of him: eyes, ears, heart, and mind. As long as any part of the cloud was in the room, there was no way for him to turn a blind eye. All he could do was get out as quickly as possible.

The hallway outside was better lit than the orgy room had been, but it was still darker than the dance floor in the club below. He moved through the gloom, searching for a way down into the main part of the building. Along the way he passed an open door leading into another room, this one featuring an even more horrific orgy of drug use. Again wishing he could close his eyes, he hurried past.

Finally, following the sound of the music, he reached a thick door with just enough room beneath it for him to get through. As he moved out of the private area the heavy beat of the music once again slammed into him with full force, fully as uncomfortable as it had been when he had physical ears.

At least the raid hadn't started yet. The dancers, drinkers, and music were just the way Mauricio had left them, with no hint of trouble.

But that was an illusion. By the time the trap was sprung, it would be so airtight that not a single Evo would escape the net.

Assuming that the Evos were indeed the target.

Mauricio paused, hovering against the ceiling beside one

of the pulsing strobe lights as that thought suddenly struck him. Given what he'd seen on the third floor, was it possible that the drug dealers up there were the actual targets?

In which case, the raid would have his complete blessing. He'd seen what those drugs did to the kids and adults in his parish. Anything that would get even a small percentage of that poison off the streets would be a good thing.

But it was a false hope, and deep down he knew it. Drugs and drug use were low on every official priority list these days. No, the raid was for Evos, all right. And he had to stop it.

But how? El Vengador could probably neutralize every police car in the gathering cordon, tossing the cops into the next block or just flipping each vehicle up on its side. But Mauricio couldn't do anything like that.

Should he call in a bomb threat at the other end of the city and hope that the cops assigned to the raid would be diverted to the more immediate threat?

Again, not an option. A bomb threat might draw away some of the cops outside *La Basa*, but a lot of the response would probably be requisitioned from elsewhere in the city, leaving other neighborhoods unprotected. Besides, with modern electronic equipment, no matter how he called in the warning they would likely be able to trace it back to him.

No, his best move—his only move, really—was to get the Evos out of here before the cordon could be completed.

He looked down at the DJ's area. It would be simple enough for him to float down there, turn back into human form, and use the sound system to call out a warning to the Evos to get out.

But they might not believe him. And even if they did, if the Evos were the only ones who left, the police spotters would have their job done for them.

No, if Mauricio got anyone out, he had to get *everyone* out.

And then, as the strobe beside him began lighting up the dance floor again, he spotted something he hadn't noticed before.

A ceiling-mounted smoke detector.

He spent the next couple of minutes flying around the club, locating all the detectors. A single alarm going off might be seen as a glitch and ignored. *All* of them going off in rapid succession would hopefully do the trick.

Finally, he was ready. Steeling himself, he gathered himself into a tight, dense mass.

And like an insubstantial skier running a bizarre slalom course, he was off.

He'd thought the music was loud. It was nothing compared to the smoke alarms. Especially since he was right there, flowing through the detector, when each of them went off.

He was halfway through his planned course when the music was suddenly cut off. He'd nearly finished when the mass exodus began.

Or rather, the mad scramble.

Mauricio had hoped the kids would leave in some kind of nervous but relatively calm order. Not even close. The screams and shouts were audible even over the blaring alarms as the patrons shoved and clawed their way through the exits.

Mauricio gazed down at the chaos, once again unable to look away, aching with the cold knowledge that he was responsible. He'd done it for good reasons, but it was still all on him.

And having engineered a potentially lethal situation, there was no earthly way for him to stop it.

Slowly, the shouts and screams faded as more and more people made it out through the doors. Every time he caught a glimpse of the floor by the exits he felt himself tensing with new apprehension, wondering if he would see the bodies of those who'd been trampled in the frenzy. But he could see no mangled figures, at least not from his position by the ceiling.

Moving down to the balcony level would probably give him a better view. But he was too afraid of what he might see to go any closer.

Finally, they were all out... and with an overwhelming sense of relief he saw that, by incredible luck and the pure grace of God, there were no dead or dying bodies stretched out across the floor.

And with that settled, it was time to see if he'd accomplished what he'd set out to do. Retracing his path through the upper floors—the occupants in the private rooms, he noted, had also made their escape—he slipped through the open window and out into the Los Angeles night.

It was everything he could have hoped for. Maybe a third of the people who'd been inside and outside the club were still hanging around, watching from a safe distance. The rest were streaming down the streets and alleyways, heading for cars or buses or apartments.

Hopefully, all the Evos were among them.

Rising a little higher, Mauricio oriented himself above the city streets and headed for home. He had saved them.

This time.

Kim was cooking her morning egg on the hotplate when Mauricio and Simon arrived from the rectory. "Good morning," Mauricio greeted her. "I hope you slept well."

"Mostly," Kim said. "Some weird dreams. I see you got home safely. Keys are by the laptop."

"Thanks," Mauricio said, stepping over to the desk and picking them up. On the laptop's screen, he saw, was a picture of a sullen-looking man, his dark eyes staring accusingly. "Jackson Tarbell?"

"One of them," Kim said. "I put together a slideshow of every Jackson Tarbell in the L.A. area, or at least the ones in the DMV database."

"Thanks." Mauricio caught Simon's eye and gestured to the desk chair. "Simon? You're up."

"Just a second," Simon said, peering at the neat row of bacon slices Kim had set to drain on a folded paper towel. He chose one and stuffed it into his mouth, snagging another paper towel and wiping his fingers as he headed for the desk.

Kim watched in silence, her eyes following him until he sat down and started scrolling through her slide show. Then she shifted her attention to Mauricio. "I presume you heard the news this morning?"

"You mean the border-tightening announcement?" Mauricio asked. "All the more reason we need to get our railroad up and running."

"No, I mean someone setting off the smoke alarms at the club last night," Kim said.

"Oh. Yes. Yes, I did."

"Crazy, huh?" she persisted. "And weird timing. You know—right after Simon and I left?"

"God works in mysterious ways," Mauricio said, forcing himself to meet her gaze. His initial relief at not seeing any bodies on the floor last night had been tempered somewhat by the morning's reports of bruises, lacerations, and a few broken bones.

Still, no one had died, and the injuries were for the most part minor. And there was nothing on the news about any Evos being nabbed.

Though of course there wouldn't be any such reports, whether it had happened or not.

"It's not God's timing I'm worried about," she said. "Let me put it another way: are they going to find your fingerprints on the fire alarm?"

"No, of course not," Mauricio said, putting some offended dignity into his voice, relieved that she'd phrased the question in a way that didn't require him to lie.

"I hope you're right," Kim said, clearly not convinced. "I've got enough people sniffing at my rear without adding the city's arson squad to the list."

"We'll try to keep it that way," Mauricio assured her. "Simon? Anything?"

"Only Jackson Tarbell," Simon said, gesturing to the screen. "*Orale!*"

"That's him?" Mauricio asked as he and Kim walked over.

"That's him," Simon confirmed. "Corona, huh? How far away is that?"

Mauricio leaned over Simon's shoulder for a closer look at the screen. "About forty-five minutes in good traffic," he said, making a quick mental calculation. "Maybe two hours in bad."

"*If* that's really his address," Kim warned, peering over Simon's other shoulder.

"Why not?" Simon countered. "This *vato*'s clean—trust me. *Placas* won't be looking for him. Just maybe his partner."

Behind his back, Mauricio caught Kim's eye and raised his eyebrows questioningly. The cops might not be interested in Jackson, but Renautas very well could be.

But she shook her head. *Not on any of their lists*, she mouthed silently.

At least, not on the lists she'd been able to look at. But there was no point in complicating things any more than they already were. As Mauricio had learned in his coyote days, a certain level of paranoia was useful in helping a person dodge potential trouble. Too much paranoia, and a person would spend his life hiding under his bed. "Let's find out," he said. "You up for a drive, Simon?"

The boy shrugged. "*Vamos pues.*"

"Good," Mauricio said. "Let me go upstairs and take care of a few things—" *like checking my messages and emails*, he thought with a twinge of guilt "—and then we'll go. And don't eat any more of Kim's bacon. You had plenty of breakfast already."

After missing out on the news of Simon's uncle's death, he found himself approaching his phone and computer with a certain dread. Fortunately, there were no urgent or traumatic emails or voice messages waiting for him. There was a follow-up note from Simon's uncle's brother, informing him that the funeral would be held at the church the brother attended instead of All Saints and hoping Mauricio wouldn't feel slighted or offended. Mauricio sent a return message assuring him that he was fine with the decision, offering his condolences, and urging them to contact him again if there was any way he could help. After that he cleared out a few more emails, did a quick proofreading of the Sunday Mass bulletin, and closed down the computer.

And with that, he was ready. For a moment he considered changing clothes, wondering whether clerical garb would help or hinder this first contact with Jackson and his forger friend. But this was who he was, and the forger should probably know the truth right from the start.

He had just checked his cell phone to make sure it was charged when he heard the sound of someone pounding on the church door.

The police! was his first, guilty thought. But surely there wasn't any way for anyone to connect him with last night's nightclub incident.

Unless the cops who'd witnessed the assault on him and Simon had seen his face, tracked him down, and were here to ask a few pointed questions.

Even worse, one of them might have seen him turn into mist.

The pounding came again, louder this time.

There was nothing to do but let them in. Mauricio left his office, walked across the church, and unlocked the door. Steeling himself, he swung it open.

And felt a flash of relief. It wasn't the police after all.

"Father Mauricio," Father Gunther greeted him. He was smiling genially, but there was a hardness around his eyes. "I was afraid you were sleeping in. May I?"

"Certainly," Mauricio said, stepping aside. "Is there a problem?"

"Possibly," Gunther said, reaching back to pull the door closed behind him. "Did you hear about that nightclub panic last night?"

"That—? Oh. Right," Mauricio said. "*La Basa*. Someone pulled a fire alarm?"

"That's the place," Gunther said, looking casually around the sanctuary. "And a whole bunch of people scrambled out the exits. Including, apparently, some dangerous Evos."

Mauricio felt his skin prickling. "Did the police catch them?"

"No idea," Gunther said. "But I did hear some disturbing

news this morning from one of the other priests in the area. Apparently, he got to his church this morning to discover someone had broken in and spent the night there."

"You're kidding," Mauricio said, for once not having to pretend he was startled. "Where was it? Was the priest hurt?"

"Fortunately, no," Gunther said. "The fugitive—or whoever it was—apparently just wanted a place to crash for the night. But it seemed prudent to check the rest of the churches in the East L.A. area. That's why I'm here."

"Yes, of course," Mauricio said, feeling his chest tightening. And Kim and Simon were right below them in the basement. He had to find a way to get them out of there before Gunther found them. "How can I help?"

"Let's start with a grand tour," Gunther said, turning and again looking around the church.

With his visitor's back turned, Mauricio slipped a hand into his pocket and activated his cell phone. He didn't know if Simon had his own phone with him, and even if he did Mauricio could hardly give him a warning with Gunther standing five feet away.

But there might be another way.

"Let's start with the bell tower," he suggested. "I've heard stories about kids climbing up the outside of the church. Before my time, but I'm told it can be done."

"Hard to get to, and not at all obvious," Gunther said, nodding. "A perfect route for a clever person. Is there a way into the church proper from there?"

"There's a trap door," Mauricio said. "Let's see if the lock's been tampered with."

"All right," Gunther said, nodding. "Which way?"

"There," Mauricio said, pointing toward the door that led to the library and classrooms. "We can look in on the classrooms along the way."

And with Gunther's back again turned, he surreptitiously punched the church's phone number into his cell.

They'd gotten three steps when his office phone began to ring. "Sorry—I need to take that," Mauricio said, shifting direction toward the office. "One of my parishioners died the day before yesterday—this might be about that. The stairs to the bell tower are at the end of that hallway if you want to head on up."

"No, that's all right," Gunther said, falling into step beside him. "I'll wait for you."

Mauricio clenched his teeth. He should have guessed that Gunther wouldn't let him out of his sight.

And now, there was only one way left to pull this off.

They reached the office, and Mauricio stepped inside. "I'll just be a minute," he promised, starting to close the door behind him.

Gunther caught the door before it could close. "Take your time."

"Conversations in this church are private," Mauricio said firmly. "If I may…?"

Gunther pursed his lips, but obediently took a step backwards. Mauricio closed the door and crossed to the ringing phone. He picked up the handset, simultaneously shutting off his cell. "Father Mauricio," he said, loudly enough for someone pressing his ear against the door to hear.

He waited long enough for his imaginary caller to utter a few sentences. "Yes, I understand," he said, setting the handset quietly down on the desk. "Let me grab a pencil… okay. Can you repeat that?"

And with a final look at the closed door, he turned into mist.

He'd studied the church's ventilation system when he was first assigned to the parish, and had traveled the ducts several times since then. It took him less than ten seconds to make his way from the office to the vent just outside the basement room door. He slipped through, reformed into human shape—

"Get out of here," he whispered loudly to Kim and Simon. "The back stairs—that door over there."

"*Que paso*?" Simon asked as they both turned to look at him. "The *placas*?"

"Just go," Mauricio said. "There's a hedge behind the church—"

"Yeah, I saw it," Kim cut him off. "I'll get us clear."

"Make it fast." Stepping away from the doorway and out of their sight, Mauricio turned back into mist and made his way back through the vents to the office.

The door was still closed. Taking human form again, he picked up the phone. "Yes, I've got it," he said. "Thank you for letting me know. I'll call you later."

He hung up the phone, tore a piece of paper from his notepad, and folded it in half as he walked over to the door.

Gunther was waiting just outside, looking nothing like a man who might have been eavesdropping. "Everything all right?"

"As well as can be expected," Mauricio said, slipping the folded paper into his jacket pocket. "Thank you for your patience. Let me show you to the bell tower."

"On second thought, let's do this from the other direction," Gunther said, putting out an arm to block Mauricio's path. "I assume All Saints has a basement. We'll start there."

Mauricio took a careful breath. "Certainly. This way."

The whole way down the stairs to the basement room door he desperately hoped that he'd given Kim and Simon enough time to get out. To his surprise, not only had the two of them vanished, but so had the laptop, Kim's breakfast, the robe he'd given her, the frying pan, and even the hotplate.

"Nice little hideaway you've got here," Gunther commented, glancing at the cot as he walked over to the bathroom. "Shower and everything. All the comforts of home."

"Sometimes one of our members needs a temporary place to stay," Mauricio explained. Kim's breakfast might be gone, but the scent of bacon lingered on. "The previous priest had this room set up for such occasions."

"You use it often?" Gunther frowned, sniffing at the air. "What's that smell?"

"Some kind of mold in the vents, the heating people think," Mauricio said. "They've tried three times to get rid of it, but it's still there."

"Smells familiar," Gunther said, sniffing a little harder.

"I've heard it called everything from a wood fire to maple syrup," Mauricio said. "Of course, most of the people who stay here don't complain about the lack of five-star ambiance."

"Do they give out no-star ratings?" Gunther said dryly. "Still beats sleeping on the streets. Anything else down here?"

"The furnace and AC units are behind us on the left, and there's a big storage room on the right," Mauricio said, gesturing back toward the door. "They're on the other side of the stairs."

"Okay," Gunther said. "We'll take a look, then head back upstairs."

Gunther's inspection was quick but thorough. Mauricio watched him as closely as he could, but saw no indications of suspicion. The most precarious moment was in the bell tower, where the trap-door hasp was still slightly bent from

El Vengador's nighttime visit a couple of weeks earlier. But Gunther merely glanced at the hasp and the new lock Mauricio had installed and asked no questions.

Half an hour after his arrival, with the tour finally over, Gunther thanked Mauricio for his time and left.

Mauricio sat in his office for ten minutes after that, his hands shaking with reaction. If Gunther had found Simon and started questioning him... but there was nothing to be gained by dwelling on that.

His cell phone vibrated suddenly in his pocket, sparking a reflexive jerk. He pulled it out, muscles tensing.

But it was only Simon. Shaking his head with annoyance at his own reaction, Mauricio tapped the button and held the phone to his ear. "You two all right?"

"So far," Simon said. "What's going on? Can we come back in yet?"

"I don't know," Mauricio said. "Let me check, and I'll call you back."

He closed the phone, put it back in his pocket, and again turned into mist.

Five minutes later, after a quick but careful survey of the neighborhood confirmed that Gunther had truly left, he called Kim and Simon back inside.

"You think he was looking for us?" Kim asked as she set the laptop back on the desk.

"Probably not specifically," Mauricio said, taking the hotplate and frying pan from the collection of items Simon had staggered in with. "But he was definitely looking for someone or something."

"*Que onda* with our road trip, then?" Simon asked, dumping the rest of his stuff onto Kim's cot.

"On hold, I'm afraid," Mauricio said. "Until Father Gunther turns his attention elsewhere, there's no telling where or when he might pop up. I don't want him to see us together right now."

"That won't be a problem," Kim said, a studiously casual expression on her face. "In fact, I'll bet you ten dollars he'll be spending his afternoon and evening in a holding cell somewhere."

Mauricio felt his eyes narrow. "Kim, what did you do?"

"Nothing serious," she said. "I just put out a BOLO for his car in connection with a B and E in Chinatown last night."

"A *what* and a *what*?" Simon asked, frowning. "If you can't talk Spanish, *chica*, at least talk English."

"A BOLO is a be-on-lookout alert," Mauricio said, frowning hard at Kim. "B and E is breaking and entering. Kim—"

"I know, I know," she said. "Dangerous and I shouldn't have used the church's Wi-Fi to do it. But you have to admit it was clever."

"Only if he doesn't figure out who fingered him."

"He won't," she assured him. "Besides, I thought you priests all had this turn-the-other-cheek thing."

"Most of us do," Mauricio agreed, frowning to himself. He'd known a lot of priests, both in seminary and during his years in the ministry. And while they'd come in all sizes, shapes, and personalities, they'd all had that underlying sense of nurturing or compassion that he'd always considered a vital part of their holy calling.

All of them except Gunther.

It was more than just a lack of empathy. There was an active hardness about Gunther's face and eyes, a hint of darkness that never quite disappeared. Even when he was smiling the darkness was still there, just beneath the surface.

But of course Gunther wasn't a normal priest. His skills

and aptitudes would naturally be different from those of the other priests Mauricio had known.

"I don't suppose there's any way to tell if and when he gets picked up?" he asked Kim.

She shrugged. "I'd just need to hack the police system again. One more thing. I checked Jackson's address, and it turns out he lives in a four-story apartment building above a copy shop."

"Clever *vato*, eh?" Simon put in. "Any paper or ink he needs gets delivered to the shop. Perfect cover."

"Of course, that means security cams," Kim warned. "And they don't close until seven, so you'll probably want to wait until then to make your move."

Mauricio sighed. Why, he wondered bleakly, did each step of this process seem more complicated than the last one? "Okay," he said. "We'll hang out here for a while, and head out later this afternoon."

"Just about in time for rush hour?" Kim suggested.

"Just about," Mauricio agreed. "Let's just hope he's home."

The drive to Corona took about an hour and a half, nicely midway between Mauricio's two original time estimates. He and Simon were still fifteen minutes out when Kim called with the news that Gunther had just been picked up via the BOLO she'd inserted into the LAPD computer system.

Kim was maliciously pleased that her trick had worked. Simon openly crowed at the result. Mauricio was merely relieved that he had one less thing to worry about for the evening. Certainly he had plenty of others.

The copy shop closed at seven. Five minutes after

that, Mauricio and Simon were standing at the apartment building's back door.

The good news was that there were no cameras watching the rear of the building. The bad news was that the door was protected by a heavy wrought-iron gate that was securely locked.

"I don't suppose you know Jackson well enough for him to let you in," Mauricio suggested, eyeing the line of intercom buttons set into the wall outside the gate.

"Don't be *loco*," Simon said with a snort. "But I guess we have to try."

"Let's try one other thing first," Mauricio said. "Go around to the front and see if that door's locked. It might not be."

"It's got cameras on it," Simon pointed out.

"Just keep your head bowed low," Mauricio said. "Chin to your chest. You'll be all right."

"*Si*, that should work," Simon said sarcastically.

"Just try," Mauricio said.

Simon gave a theatrical sigh. "If I'm not back in five minutes it means I got in."

Mauricio waited until the teen had disappeared around the corner of the building. Then, turning into mist, he slipped through the bars of the gate, under the heavy wooden door, and into the small foyer.

He was standing outside again, the gate and door both unlocked and open, when Simon returned. "Hey, *machin*," the teen said incredulously. "What, he *opened* for you?"

"Someone else did," Mauricio said. It wasn't *exactly* a lie. "Come on."

Jackson's apartment was on the third floor. "Someone else going to open this one, too?" Simon asked as they reached the door.

"We'll just try knocking," Mauricio said.

He did. After a short pause, he knocked again. This time there was the soft double-click of a pair of locks. The door opened wide—

"*Que onda*, Jackson," Simon greeted the big African-American man who all but filled the doorway. "I'm Simon Navarro—we met at *La Basa* awhile back. I'm the *vato* who—"

"How'd you get in here?" Jackson demanded, looking back and forth between them.

"We need to talk to your *guey*," Simon said. "You know? The forger who lives—"

The sentence ended in a gasp as Jackson reached out, grabbed Simon's shirt, and pulled him bodily into the apartment. He shoved the door closed; moving fast, Mauricio managed to slip inside before the door thundered shut behind him.

They were, he discovered as he regained his balance, in a large living room. From one side, an archway led to a small kitchen; from the other side, a hallway headed toward the rear of the apartment. The living room was only sparsely furnished, with a couch, a couple of leather club chairs, a coffee table in the middle of the room, and a professional drafting table in the back corner.

Plus lights. *Lots* of lights. A pair of balanced-arm lamps were clamped to the drafting table, there were floor lamps at each corner of every piece of furniture, the ceiling sported three overhead lamps, and there were four rows of track lighting along the upper walls. All were equipped with high-wattage incandescent bulbs, and all of them were blazing at full power. Briefly, Mauricio wondered what kind of eye trouble the forger had that required this much light for him to work.

"It's cool—it's cool," Simon said hastily, his voice coming out in a frightened squeak as Jackson dragged him across the room and tossed him into one of the club chairs. "It's business. You know? We're just here to do business."

"The boss does business *his* way, not yours," Jackson growled. "Who sent you?"

"No one sent us," Mauricio said. "Like Simon said, we're just here on business."

"And he *sure* as hell doesn't do business with priests," Jackson snapped. He stretched out his hand toward Mauricio—

And Mauricio's chest suddenly blazed with heat.

Reflexively, he dropped into a crouch and half-dived, half-rolled to the side. "That was your warning," Jackson said, throwing a look over his shoulder to make sure Simon was staying put. "One last chance. Who sent—?"

Suddenly he stiffened, his voice cracking in mid-threat, his eyes widening.

"That was *your* warning, *puto*," Simon spat out. "Now, knock it off and let us—"

He barely made it out of the chair in time as Jackson sent another bolt of heat arrowing toward him, blasting the cushions into a smoldering blaze of smoke and flame. "Jackson…" Mauricio began, taking a step across the room toward the fire extinguisher fastened to the wall by the kitchen door—

And also just managed to get out of the way as Jackson sent another blast in his direction. There was a loud crackle, and Mauricio looked back to see a circle of blackened and smoldering drywall behind the spot where he'd been standing. "Please—"

"Enough," a clipped voice came from the hallway.

Mauricio turned to look. An elderly man was standing

there, wrapped in a black-and-burgundy smoking jacket and silk pajama pants, one hand resting casually in the jacket's side pocket. He gestured to Jackson, his eyes on Mauricio. "You made a mess, Jackson. Fix it."

"I can't," the big man said, his voice trembling. "I can't see."

"Really?" The old man looked at Mauricio and raised his eyebrows. "You?"

Mauricio shook his head. "May I?" he asked, gesturing toward the fire extinguisher.

The old man seemed to think about it, then nodded. Mauricio crossed the room, pulled the canister from the wall, and took it over to the chair. A handful of cold blasts later, the fire was out. He directed a couple of blasts at the damaged wall, then gave the chair two more shots, just to be sure. "You have very forgiving smoke detectors," he commented as he set the canister down on the floor beside the chair.

"We don't have *any* smoke detectors," the old man corrected him. "Exhaust fans do a better job and don't disturb the neighbors. You don't remember me, do you?"

Mauricio frowned. Now that he mentioned it, his voice—

His *voice*? "*Diego*?" he breathed. "Diego *Rebasa*?"

"Very good," the old man—Diego—said. "I certainly remember *you*, Mauricio. I don't suppose you have any idea what Condor did to all of us when you took his truck and ran off."

Mauricio winced. For twenty years he'd been trying to put Condor and his insane temper out of his mind. Now, it all came flooding back. "None of you were responsible," he said. "It was all me."

"You think that made any difference?" Diego retorted. "You think *that*—" he waved at Mauricio's clerical collar "—makes any difference now?"

Mauricio sighed. No, nothing would have made a difference. Not to Condor. "For whatever it's worth, Diego, I'm sorry."

"It's worth nothing," Diego said flatly. "So, fine; you're here. State your business, then get out."

Mauricio glanced at Simon. The teen was still crouched on the floor where he'd landed after dodging Jackson's heat blast, clearly afraid to risk drawing any more attention to himself. "I'm trying to set up an escape route for Evos who want to leave the U.S. and go to Canada," Mauricio said, looking back at Diego. "We need someone to forge foreign passports and documents so they can cross the border without being—"

"No," Diego said.

Mauricio stared at him. "Don't you at least want to hear the details?"

"Twenty years ago, you ran out on us," Diego said. "That's the only detail I care about. Now fix Jackson's eyes and get out."

"Diego—"

"Or just keep talking," Diego offered. "There's more than enough light in here for Jackson to burn you to a cinder right where you stand."

Mauricio swallowed. Anger, a lingering bitterness… and a dead end.

And ultimately, it was Mauricio's fault. "All right," he said quietly. "I'm sorry, Diego, for everything. Don't worry, Jackson's sight will come back by itself in about an hour."

"It had better," Diego warned. "Otherwise, I'm hunting you down."

"No need," Mauricio said. "I'm at All Saints Church. If you change your mind—"

"Good-bye, Mauricio. Don't come back."

Five minutes later, Mauricio and Simon were back in the car. "Now what?" Simon asked.

"I don't know," Mauricio admitted, resting his hands on the steering wheel and staring out the windshield at the apartment building half a block away. "I really just don't know."

"Yeah." Simon was silent a moment. "You know, *Padre*, they say the best thing you can do when you've had a big disappointment is eat."

Mauricio snorted. "Actually, that's the *worst* thing you can do."

"Not if you're hungry," Simon said. "I don't know about you, but I haven't eaten since that slice of bacon I got from Kim this morning."

"The slice of bacon you *stole* from Kim."

"I just don't want her getting fat. Forget her, huh? I'm hungry."

"I know," Mauricio said apologetically. With the day's focus first on Kim's hacking, then Gunther's unexpected visit, then their drive to Jackson's apartment, they'd somehow missed lunch. "Fine. Let me call Kim and bring her up to speed, and then we'll find a place to eat."

Mauricio had noticed a café tucked away just off the street half a block from Diego's building. Over Simon's objections—the teen wanted a burger joint—they went there.

The café was crowded, and the service was slow. But once the food finally arrived, it proved decent enough.

"So why here?" Simon asked as he finished off his second slice of pie. "You thinking Diego might change his mind?"

Mauricio pursed his lips. "Is it that obvious?"

"We can see their apartment from here," Simon pointed

out. "They said twenty minutes for a table, and you didn't leave and go somewhere else. No, *Padre*, you wanted here. *And*—" he checked his watch "—Jackson's eyes came back fifteen minutes ago. You're going to go talk to them again, aren't you?"

"I have to try," Mauricio said, feeling a tiredness that went straight to the bone. Diego would never agree, he knew. In fact, there was every chance he'd turn Jackson loose on him.

But he couldn't just give up. This underground railroad was too important for too many people. "He probably won't listen. But I have to try."

"There *are* other forgers out there, you know."

"But probably not many with as much incentive as Diego," Mauricio pointed out. "He's got an Evo friend—he knows what's at stake. More than that, we know he won't betray us, because if he did Jackson would be scooped up with everyone else. If he won't help us…" He shook his head.

"Maybe it's not *us* he won't help," Simon said. "Maybe it's just *you*."

"That thought has not escaped me," Mauricio admitted. "The problem is that if I back out, who'll run things? Kim?"

"Or me," Simon suggested, turning his head to peer out the window beside them. "'Course, we'll need a bigger *canton* to make it work. A real house, maybe. And lots of *lana*—" He broke off, his eyes narrowing. "That's funny."

"What is?" Mauricio asked, trying to follow his gaze. The sky had darkened and the streetlights had come on while they'd been eating, and the car and pedestrian traffic had thinned down to the city's normal mid-evening levels.

"Diego's building," Simon said. "It's gone dark."

Mauricio focused on the apartment building. Sure

enough, there were no lights showing in any of the windows. At the same time, the buildings on either side seemed to have normal power and lighting.

And of all the apartments in the neighborhood, Jackson Tarbell's would be the *least* likely to have all its lights turned off. Not with his power apparently dependent on having them blazing away.

Which could only mean one thing.

"Go to the car," he muttered to Simon, digging out his keys and sliding them across the table. He glanced at the bill, took out enough cash to cover their meals and a decent tip, and laid it on the table.

"You think it's the *placas*?" Simon asked as they headed for the door.

"Only one way to find out," Mauricio said. "Get in the car and lock the doors. And *don't* leave until I'm back."

Their car was parked down the street to the right of the café's entrance. Once outside, Simon turned right and Mauricio turned left

And the moment Mauricio was around the corner, he turned into mist and headed for Diego's building.

The cordon around *La Basa* the previous night had consisted mostly of unmarked cars. But as Mauricio was heading for home after chasing everyone out, he'd also noted a dozen or more black-and-whites forming a backup barricade a couple of blocks further out. That alone had made it clear that the raid was an official government action.

Not so here. There was no double ring, no marked cars; in fact, no obvious indication that a raid was even underway. More significantly, none of the vehicles on either side of the street or in the small adjacent parking lots carried government tags.

This wasn't a police operation. This was someone else.

Renautas?

For the moment, though, the *who* of it didn't matter. All Mauricio cared about was getting Diego and Jackson out before it was too late. Floating up along the side of the building, he headed toward what should be the apartment's rear windows—

And dodged reflexively back as a six-inch-diameter black tube dropped straight out of the sky past him.

It took him a confused second to realize that the tube wasn't just falling past him, but was somehow also still sitting there in front of him. It took another, longer second to realize that what he was seeing was a telescoping fire-escape pole, installed under the building's eaves and just now triggered.

A moment later he was once again forced to dodge sideways as Jackson slid past him down the pole, with Diego five seconds behind him.

Only it was too late, Mauricio realized with a sinking feeling as the two men reached the pavement and took off at a fast walk down the street. The raiders in the building wouldn't be caught off-guard by such a simple escape ploy. They would have left plenty of backup waiting on the streets below.

And they had. Jackson and Diego had gone barely ten yards when a pair of cars driving at opposite ends of the block suddenly made sharp ninety-degree turns, screeching to a simultaneous halt perpendicular to the street, sealing off traffic along the entire block. Even as the handful of cars caught in the trap squealed to panic-stops, a half-dozen of the vehicles parked along the curbs hit their lights and pulled out into the street, all of them swiveling toward the two fugitives. Jackson and Diego came to a sudden, jerky halt, and the cars began disgorging men waving handguns and big flashlights.

It was a tactic Mauricio had seen many times before, usually sprung on some coyote whose luck had run dry. The attacker surrounded the target with people and guns, then threw as much light in their eyes as possible to dazzle them and keep them from getting a good view of the situation. It was a classic and time-worn technique, and if executed properly it nearly always worked.

Only in this case…

In the center of the blaze of light, Jackson made a horizontal sweeping gesture with his arms. The flashlights within that arc jerked abruptly, wavering off their targets as a smattering of shouts of surprise and pain drifted up to Mauricio. Jackson didn't wait for the freshly burned assailants to recover; spinning on his heel, he repeated the gesture at the semicircle behind him, generating a second wave of jerking lights and outraged snarls.

Someone in the group barked an order. In the reflected glare from the still-twitching lights, Mauricio saw the entire group raise their guns from standby to fully aimed.

Fully aimed. All of them.

Around the entire circle.

Mauricio had to stop it. Somehow, whether by shouted warning or physical action, he had to stop it. Men were about to be hurt, maybe even killed, and he couldn't just stand by and do nothing.

But hard on the heels of that thought was the realization that it was already too late. He was up here, the drama was down there, and there was nothing he could do in time.

And so he floated above the ground, watching helplessly as the neatly orchestrated raid went straight to hell.

Again, Jackson waved a hand toward the men still converging on them. But this time, instead of simply spinning around to target the rear half of the group, he executed a corkscrew-like maneuver that sent him dropping into a crouch as he spun. Diego was right with him, dropping flat on his stomach on the ground as Jackson waved at the men behind them.

And in a rapid-fire staccato of ear-shattering blasts, the heat-triggered rounds chambered in each of the guns went off.

Causing each man to unintentionally shoot the man directly across the circle from him.

Once again screams and shouts rose into the night air, though after the stuttering thunderclap of the massive volley the cries of the wounded seemed almost subdued by comparison. The flashlight beams swung crazily as the men holding them dropped to the ground, their lights and guns lying where they fell or skittering for a few feet across the pavement. In the still-steady glow of the car headlights Mauricio could see the injured clutching at arms or legs or torsos, some of them writhing in pain, others perhaps already slipping toward death. A couple of the men clutched bloody hands where bullets from their guns' magazines had also ignited, blasting through the weapons' grips to shatter hands and fingers.

And as for Jackson and Diego...

Mauricio tensed. The two fugitives should have been back up and running by now. But they weren't. Instead, Diego was crouching over Jackson, who was lying in a curled pretzel-shape on his side, both hands gripping his torso just above his left hip.

Hands that were bright red with blood.

Somewhere, in all the chaos of the melee, one of the guns had ended up pointed at the fugitives when Jackson ignited the bullets.

Diego looked up as Mauricio strode through the

broken circle, doing a double-take as he saw who it was. "*Mauricio*? What the hell—?"

"How bad is it?" Mauricio asked, dropping to one knee beside Jackson.

"Not too bad," Jackson panted. His eyes, too, were narrowed as he looked at Mauricio. "Our car's… in the garage…"

"Back there," Diego finished for him.

Mauricio nodded. Unfortunately, the garage was within the barrier created by the two sideways cars at the ends of the block. No escape that way.

And speaking of the barrier cars, after what had just happened their occupants were almost certainly heading their way. "Come on," he said, getting a grip on Jackson's left arm and levering him to his feet.

For a second Diego just stared. Then he scrambled to his feet and got under the big man's other arm. "My car's half a block away on the other side of the building," Mauricio continued. "If we can get to it before they block that street, too, there's a chance we can get out of here."

"We'll get to it," Diego promised darkly.

From the direction of one of the blocking cars came a shouted order to stop. Mauricio looked over Jackson's shoulder and saw a pair of shadowy figures charging toward them, flashlights bobbing in time with their pace. He tensed, his own pace wavering as he automatically started to comply with the order—

He had almost lurched to a halt when Jackson lifted his arm from Diego's shoulder long enough to make a gesture. The distant shouts became bellows of pain as the newcomers' lights and guns went flying. "Like I said, we'll get to it," Diego repeated. "Or we'll light up the night trying. Come on, Jackson—move it."

* * *

Earlier that day, Mauricio had estimated that Jackson's apartment would be a forty-five-minute drive in good traffic.

With an injured man bleeding in the back seat, he made the return trip in thirty minutes flat.

Mauricio had had Simon call ahead, and Kim had the church basement ready.

"There's all the first-aid stuff," she said, pointing to the desk that she'd moved across the room to the head of the cot. The cot itself had been covered with a couple of cheap plastic tablecloths, Mauricio noted as he and Diego eased Jackson down onto it, with the tablecloths further covered by blankets to absorb any additional blood.

Blood which Jackson really didn't have to spare. Diego had managed to stop the worst of the bleeding during the wild drive back, but along the way the big man had slowly stopped cursing, then talking, then even groaning. The walk in from the car had been a nightmare all its own, with Jackson barely able to help with the move, and Mauricio and Diego nearly dropping him twice as they maneuvered him down the back stairs into the basement.

Now, with the injured man's eyes closed to slits and the makeshift bandages from the car wet with seeping blood, Mauricio wondered if it was already too late to save him.

But they had to try. "First thing is to clean the wound," he said, surveying the array of medical gear Kim had laid out on the desk. Along with everything from the church's first-aid kit, she'd made a quick run to the drugstore down the street and picked up more bandages, antiseptic spray, and a couple of rolls of gauze. "Diego?"

"Don't look at me," Diego said, his voice strained. "My

medical training stops at treating paper cuts."

"Right," Mauricio said, clenching his teeth as he picked up the antiseptic and one of the rolls of gauze. His own medical training consisted of a three-hour first-aid course the church had made him take fifteen years ago.

But he was all they had. Sending up a quick, silent prayer, he turned back to the cot. "Simon, grab that floor lamp and bring it over here. Kim, angle the desk lamp in this direction. Let's see exactly what we've got."

The wound wasn't as bad as he'd feared. But it was bad enough. The bullet had been a through-and-through, leaving entry and exit wounds through Jackson's lateral muscles. An inch further left and it would have been barely a graze; two inches further left and it would have missed him completely.

Two inches further right, and it probably would have taken out his kidney. Mauricio sent up another prayer, this one a prayer of thanks.

As he'd already noted, the two wounds were still seeping blood through their coverings. Removing those coverings increased the flow from seepage to a trickle. Mauricio cleaned the entry and exit holes as best he could, which briefly brought Jackson out of his stupor long enough to groan. He gave each wound a hefty dose of antiseptic spray and sealed them with bandages, which he then strapped into place with strips of gauze.

And with that, he'd done all he could.

"Is he going to make it?" Diego asked quietly from the bathroom doorway as Mauricio washed his hands in the sink.

"I don't know," Mauricio said. "He's lost a lot of blood. On the plus side, there's no bullet lodged in there and nothing but muscle got damaged. If he makes it through the night, I'd say he's got a good chance."

"Yeah."

Mauricio went back to his washing. Blood, he'd long ago learned, was hard to get off. This much blood was *very* hard to get off.

But with persistence and a lot of soap, he managed it. "Why did you come back?" Diego asked as Mauricio toweled his hands dry. "I'd already told you I wasn't going to help."

"I know," Mauricio said. "But I've always believed that people deserve a second chance."

Diego snorted. "You talking about me? Or about you?"

"A little of both," Mauricio admitted. "Look. When I decided to leave Condor's organization, it was for what I considered to be good reasons. I thought about what the consequences might be for me, but I never thought about what they might be for you and the others. For that I'm both embarrassed and deeply sorry."

"Yeah," Diego said. "Well, it looks like we're going to have some time together. I want to hear about this grand epiphany, or whatever it was."

"Of course," Mauricio said. "You've earned it."

"Father Mauricio?" Kim called from the other room, her voice strained. "You need to come out here. Right now."

Diego was already out the door and heading across the room toward the cot. Mauricio dropped the towel in the sink and followed.

His first thought was that Jackson must have taken a turn for the worse. But the big man was still just lying there, his eyes fluttering as he drifted in and out of consciousness, his chest moving slowly up and down with steady breaths. Kim and Simon were standing a little way past the bathroom door by the makeshift kitchen, their backs stiff, their eyes on the door that led out of the room toward the stairs up to the main part of the church. Frowning, Mauricio followed their gaze.

Father Gunther was standing just inside the open door. Motionless and silent.

A gun held casually in his hand.

Mauricio stumbled to a confused halt. "Gunther," he breathed. "What are you…?"

"Hello, Mauricio," Gunther said coolly. His eyes darted to his right, to Kim and Simon, then to his left, to Jackson, and then back to Mauricio. "I see you've collected a few friends for me. Excellent."

"He's hurt," Diego said, nodding toward Jackson. Like Mauricio, he'd stopped midway across the room when he spotted Gunther and the gun. Now, cautiously, he started walking again, heading toward the cot.

Mauricio tensed, wondering if Gunther would shoot him. But the other priest merely watched Diego without comment. "What do you want?" Mauricio asked as Diego reached the cot and dropped to one knee beside it.

"You want money?" Diego put in before Gunther could answer. "I have money."

"I'm sure you do," Gunther said. Reaching behind him with his free hand, he pulled the door closed. "But I doubt you can match my current employer's bankroll." He gestured to Kim and Simon. "You two. Go over by the good Father."

Silently, they obeyed, Kim coming to a halt close beside Mauricio, Simon stopping a couple of feet away from her. "Let me guess," Mauricio said. "You're angry about the BOLO and getting hauled in."

"Oh, no, not at all," Gunther assured him. "As a matter of fact, as far as the police are concerned, I'm still in custody." He smiled at Kim. "You're not the only one who can manipulate databases, Ms. Pyon. No, actually, being on their blotter gives me a perfect alibi if anyone should start to wonder afterward."

"Wonder about what?" Mauricio said. "If it's me you're looking for, I'm right here. You can let the others go."

"Don't make me laugh," Gunther said contemptuously. "You're just the conduit. *These*—" he gestured at the others "—are the prizes." He cocked his head. "Or so I assume."

Mauricio frowned at Kim. "So you *were* following her?"

"Of course," Gunther said, smiling again. "And I will say, you've led me a merry chase. First that thing in Hollywood a couple of weeks ago, then sneaking into the church here, then the hack into the police station database—they're still trying to figure out how you pulled that one off—and finally *La Basa* last night. I was always close, but never quite in position to grab you. This time, I am. So. Let's find out what your power is."

"I don't know what you're talking about," Kim said, her voice starting to shake. "I'm just a hacker. I don't have any power."

"I hope that's not true," Gunther said. "I'd hate to have gone to all this trouble for nothing." Keeping his gun leveled, he lifted his other hand and held it out toward her.

Kim stepped closer to Mauricio and gripped his arm. "Father?" she whispered.

"Gunther, please," Mauricio said. "Whatever you're planning—"

"You especially should appreciate this, Mauricio," Gunther said. "One of your old Catholic requiem melodies, of all things, seems to work best for me." He took a deep breath.

And to Mauricio's astonishment, he began to sing.

Quietly at first, but gradually increasing in volume. And as he'd already indicated, the words and tune were very familiar:

"*Dies irae, dies illa, solvet saeclum in favilla, teste David cum Sibylla...*"

Mauricio caught his breath. It was the ancient "Day of Wrath": *Day of wrath and doom impending. David's word with Sibyl's blending, Heaven and earth in ashes ending...*

And then, without warning, the pressure of Kim's grip on Mauricio's arm shifted. He turned his head—

To find her floating six inches off the floor.

Gunther stopped singing. Kim hovered a moment longer, then settled back onto the floor. "Excellent," Gunther said, smiling. "A flyer. They do so like fliers."

"I don't understand," Mauricio said, looking from Kim to Gunther and then back to Kim. "Kim?"

"I'm sorry, Father," she murmured, a pained expression on her face. "I couldn't—I didn't want to tell you." She looked at Gunther. "How did you *do* that?"

"Quite easily," Gunther said. "My power happens to be forcing *other* powers to manifest. It's why I'm so good at my job."

"You're an *Evo*?" Mauricio asked, thoroughly confused now. "And the Vatican *knows* about this?"

"The *Vatican*?" Gunther snorted. "Don't be ridiculous. The Vatican doesn't pay nearly well enough for me to hunt Evos for them. No, I work for someone with considerably deeper pockets."

"Renautas?" Kim asked.

"Hardly," Gunther said, his lip twisting. "Actually, they're the competition. Let's see; who's next? Don't worry, it won't be him," he assured Diego, nodding toward Jackson. "We wouldn't want to strain him, now, would we?

Anyway, from the frantic reports still clogging the police and FBI systems, I'm pretty sure I know what his power is. And yes: once he's healed my employers will definitely want to meet with him."

His eyes turned back to Simon. "You, I think." He leveled a finger at the teen and began singing. "*Dies irae, dies illa, solvet saeclum in favilla—*"

And without warning, the world went black.

Gunther broke off his song with a startled curse. "What the *hell—*"

And broke off with another curse. "*God—*"

"Shut your mouth, *guero*," Simon's voice came blackly from somewhere across the room to Mauricio's left. "There's a *padre* here." There was a sudden scuffling of feet. "Don't be stupid," he added. "You're blind, you know? I can see, and I've got this little gun of yours… So just stand there and shut your mouth while I figure this out."

"It's all right, Simon," Mauricio said, feeling a stirring of hope. "I can help you. Get your phone—"

"You shut your mouth, too, *Padre*," Simon cut him off. "Let me think. Let me think… Okay. Okay. Diego, Gunther—you're the ones I need to talk to."

"What about?" Diego asked.

"I'm looking to trade up," Simon said. "Find a new *casa*—a new place to live. And someone with money."

"What in God's name are you talking about?" Diego demanded.

"What do you think?" Simon's voice had changed to something dark and bitter. "Okay, so I got the *padre* to let me stay here. But he's a priest—he's got nothing."

"You had your uncle," Mauricio said, frowning. "He had money."

"And he hated me," Simon retorted. "Or he would have.

He'd just about figured it out, too."

"Figured what out?"

"What do you think? What I am. You know? What I am."

"Ah," Mauricio said. "And your mother? Did she figure it out, too?"

Simon snorted loudly. "You think she ever figured out anything in her life? She was stupid. And she had nothing. My *tio* had money. I knew he'd take me in if I didn't have anywhere else. Just like you did, *Padre*."

"It's called compassion," Mauricio said mechanically, the world suddenly tilting around him as everything Simon had ever said or done ran at dizzying speed through his mind. The poor, lost, helpless boy, transformed in an instant into something cold and manipulating. "You killed them, didn't you? Both of them."

Beside Mauricio, Kim inhaled sharply. "You killed your own *mother*?"

"Who asked you, *chica*?" Simon demanded scornfully. "You want to make it in East Los, you do what you have to. So I go *madre* to *tio* to *padre*—*madre* to *padre*; funny. And now I go up again. Someday, I reach the top."

"How did you do it?" Mauricio asked, driven by some obscure need to make absolutely sure the boy wasn't lying just to puff himself up. "Did you blind your uncle while he was driving?"

"No, *that's* how I did my *madre*," Simon corrected him calmly. "My *tio* was too slow and careful for that. If he'd suddenly gone blind, he'd have hit the brakes and stopped."

"So what *did* you do?"

"I blinded a driver coming toward him," Simon said. "A quick little T-bone—you know? And that was it."

Mauricio swallowed. "And Angel?"

"Who?"

"Angel Martinez. The boy who ran into traffic after you blinded him."

"Oh. Him. No, you were right. Everyone was right. He was messing with me, so I blinded him and shoved him into the street."

"Only he didn't die like you'd expected."

"He was tougher than I thought," Simon admitted. "I knew if he remembered afterward I'd need someplace to run. Hey, but the big stupid trusting *padre* would hide me, *no*? That's why I came to you first."

Mauricio felt his stomach tighten. "Maybe."

"But now you don't have to anymore," Simon said. "Now I've got two other people who want me. You *do* want me, right?"

"I'm sure we do," Gunther said calmly. "Tell us about your power."

"Okay, it's like this," Simon said. "I can blind people for an hour at a time. I can also make blind people see, but you probably don't care about that. So what will you give me to work for you? Diego? You start."

Kim's fingers tightened a little harder around Mauricio's arm. He reached over with his free hand and wrapped it reassuringly around hers.

"All right," Diego said warily. "I'm a forger. I make a good living and can offer you a very comfortable life. The only real danger is from the authorities. Sometimes there's a pushy rival, but Jackson can usually chase those away before they make any real trouble. Having you on my team would eliminate both those problems."

"Okay," Simon agreed. "Gunther?"

"Comfort is all fine and good," Gunther said, his voice smooth and persuasive. "But a man like you shouldn't settle for just comfort."

"So what you got that's better than comfort and money?"

"Power," Gunther said flatly. "When my people take over—and they will—you'll have everything you've ever dreamed of. Power, wealth, respect—everything."

"Sounds good," Simon said. "But you know, there's a problem. The way you talked before it was like you were collecting Evos for these *gringos*, whether we wanted to go or not. Like we were going to be slaves."

"Not at all," Gunther said. "As I said, my organization needs you to help take over. They'd be fools to then turn against the very people who got them there."

"So you're saying I'd have power?"

"Absolutely," Gunther said. His voice was still dripping with assurance.

But to Mauricio's ear his tone was starting to crack a little around the edges. Perhaps he was beginning to suspect that Simon was playing him. "All the power you want," Gunther continued. "I guarantee it."

Simon laughed. It was the coldest sound Mauricio had ever heard. "You *guarantee* it?" he echoed. "*You*, who told us you were a *padre*, and then told us you were picking us up off the streets like stray dogs? I'm supposed to believe you'll just give all this power to some poor street Chicano?"

"Fine, don't believe it," Gunther said. "Actually, I like a man who doesn't simply swallow what he's being fed. Let me prove it."

"How?"

"Let me take you to my people. You can talk to them and see first-hand what they're offering. If you don't like it, you can walk away."

"Hey, I can walk right now," Simon said. "I walk, and you get *nada*. How does that sound?"

"It sounds stupid," Gunther growled. "Because they'll

find you. They'll find you, and they'll make you work for them."

"No, they won't," Simon said. "Because they don't know about me. You know *why* they don't know about me?"

Suddenly, the room exploded with a violent crack. Mauricio jerked, trying to figure out what the sound could have been—

And then, even through the ringing in his ears, came the thud of something heavy hitting the floor.

"Because you're not going to tell them," Simon said, his voice faintly audible throughover the ringing. "Hey, that was a lot quieter than I thought. This is one fancy gun."

"My God," Kim said, her voice shaking, her fingernails biting into Mauricio's arm. "You *shot* him?"

"Hey, chill, *chica*," Simon said scornfully. "He was going to make you a slave, too."

"But you can't—" She broke off as Mauricio squeezed her hand warningly.

"So, Diego—you got a deal," Simon continued. "You got me."

"I'm so pleased," Diego said, his voice under tight control. "What about Mauricio and the girl?"

"What do you care?"

"I thought we could take them with us," Diego said. "A girl who can fly could be very useful to have around."

"And the *padre*?"

"He could be our spiritual advisor," Diego said, his voice tinged with dark sarcasm. "At the very least, I want to hear why he ran out on us."

"Oh, hey, that's right," Simon said. "How about it, *Padre*? You want to do it again?"

"What do you mean?" Mauricio asked.

From across the room came the sound of the door

opening. "I mean the door's open," the teen said. "You can go—just you—right now. You want to? Go ahead."

Mauricio smiled, tasting the irony of the whole thing. He didn't need an open door to escape. All he needed to do was turn into mist, slip into the vent above the door, and he would be free. And there was nothing Simon could do to stop him.

But it would mean leaving Kim and the others behind. And that was something he would never do again.

"I appreciate the offer," he said. "But I'm a priest. My job is to care for God's people."

Simon snorted. "You think Evos are God's people? Even the Vatican doesn't—"

Without warning, Kim suddenly pulled her hand away from Mauricio's arm and out of his grip. There was a sudden movement of air beside him.

"*Mierda!*" Simon snapped. There was the sound of quick footsteps, a dull thud, a stifled gasp of pain.

And then silence. "Kim?" Mauricio called into the darkness, his heart thudding painfully. He groped to the side, but Kim was no longer there. "*Kim!*"

"I'm okay," her dull voice came from somewhere near the door. "He—I'm sorry, Father."

"Simon?" Mauricio asked carefully.

"Oh, relax," Simon growled. More footsteps, followed by the sound of the door closing again. "I just slapped the *puta* with the side of the gun. You really think you could get past me?"

"If we'd been upstairs you'd never have had a chance," she shot back.

"Because of the high ceiling?" Simon asked. "Yeah—up there I would have had to shoot you. You know she could fly, *Padre*?"

"No," Mauricio said. "It wouldn't have made any difference if I had."

"No, all you wanted was for her to hack computers for you."

"Which is a skill you still need," Mauricio pointed out. "Diego was right—you need her."

"She's a hacker, too?" Diego asked, picking up on Mauricio's cue. "Even better. Come on, Simon—let's bring her along, okay?"

"And the *padre*?"

"Just leave him here," Diego said. "He can figure out how to sell this—this other thing—to the cops."

Mauricio held his breath. If Simon bought it—if he let Diego and Jackson take Kim out of here—

"Yeah, not gonna work," Simon said regretfully. "He won't just let me walk away. And the *chica* will be gone as soon as we hit open air. No, it's just going to be you and me and Jackson."

Turn into mist, a small voice at the back of Mauricio's mind urged. *He doesn't know you can do that. Turn into mist, get out of here, and call the police.*

Only he couldn't. The moment he escaped Simon would kill everyone in the room and run. And whether he got caught later or not, Kim and the others would still be dead. There had to be another way.

And then, the flicker of an idea drifted across his mind. *Turn into mist...*

It was a desperate idea. A desperate, dangerous idea.

But it was all he had.

"It won't work, Simon," he said. "You kill Kim and me and the police *will* hunt you down."

"Hey, this is East Los," Simon growled. "People get shot all the time."

"Priests don't," Mauricio pointed out. "Not in their own church basements. It's not like a murder-sui—" He broke off abruptly, wincing.

"What you say? A murder-suicide?" Simon finished his sentence for him. "Let me guess. You want me to put the gun in your hand so the stuff they talk about on TV will be on your sleeve?"

"You're wasting time," Mauricio said between stiff lips. "If you're going to be stupid enough to shoot us, get it over with."

"Sure, okay." There was the sound of quiet footsteps coming toward Mauricio, then circling around to his right—

And suddenly a foot slammed down on the back of Mauricio's right knee, sending a jolt of pain through the leg as he went sprawling to the floor. He clenched his teeth against the agony.

"See, now we skip the part where you try to jump me," Simon said. Mauricio winced again as a knee pressed down on his back with Simon's full weight behind it. "Give me your hand," the teen ordered. "Come on. Give it, or I'll wreck your other leg. Makes no difference to me what they think Gunther did to you before you shot him."

Mauricio lifted his arm. A hand closed tightly around his wrist, locking it in place, while another hand pressed the hard metal of a gun grip into his hand. Mauricio closed his fingers around the weapon—

And turned into mist.

And suddenly, he could see again.

The scene laid out in front of him was exactly how he'd envisioned it. Jackson was still on the cot to his right, propped up on one elbow, pain in his open but unseeing eyes. Diego was crouched beside him, his hand gripping the edge of the cot, his head turning back and forth as he tried to sort out what was happening. Kim was sitting on the floor halfway to the closed door, her hand pressed against the side of her head. Simon was staring up at him, eyes wide with disbelief, his hand rubbing his knee where it had slammed into the floor when Mauricio vanished from beneath him.

And to Mauricio's left, midway between the cot and the bathroom, was Gunther, his shirt soaked with blood.

Dead.

"*Maldito*," Simon breathed, still staring at him. "What the—?"

"Diego, Kim, I've got the gun," Mauricio called. "Kim, I need you—"

"And it talks, too," Simon said. "Hey, you're just full of surprises, *Padre*."

"Kim, I need you to get to Gunther's body and see if he's got any restraints," Mauricio continued, ignoring Simon. "Handcuffs, cable ties—"

"Hold it, Dusty," Simon cut him off. "You think you won? Because unless you can shoot like that, I'm still in charge."

"How do you figure that?" Mauricio asked.

"Like this." Keeping a wary eye on Mauricio, Simon backed over to Kim. He stepped behind her and caught hold of her arm. "On your feet, *chica*," he ordered. His other hand slipped around behind her.

Mauricio tensed. Simon's other hand was no longer empty, but was gripping a switchblade.

A switchblade that was now pressing against the side of Kim's neck. "So don't try anything stupid," Simon added quietly.

Kim's hands had been starting to curl into claws, ready to gouge at her unseen captor. Now, with the blade against her neck, her hands reluctantly went limp again. Slowly, she got to her feet and stood motionless. "So now you see—*do* you see like that?" Simon interrupted himself.

"We can still make a deal," Mauricio told him. "Let the rest of them go. I'll come back, and you can do whatever you want to me."

"You don't listen so good, do you?" Simon growled. "I don't do this because I *like* it. I do this to make my future."

"Kim has a future, too."

"Not if I say she doesn't."

Mauricio focused on the air vent behind Simon and Kim, trying desperately to think. If he left the room just long enough to turn back into human form and drop the gun somewhere out of Simon's reach...

No. It was way too bright down here for him to sneak past Simon without being seen. The minute it looked like he was trying to get out, Kim would be dead.

Could he turn back and threaten Simon with the gun? But as soon as he changed he would be blind again. Not to mention half crippled from Simon's kick.

Another thought struck him: the church's breaker box was also in here. If he could cut off power to the room and douse the lights, at least he and Simon would both be blind. And he would still have the gun.

But no. The minute Mauricio headed toward the box Simon would figure out what he was doing. He'd be standing ready with his knife for the moment Mauricio became human again.

"Could you ease up a little with that thing?" Kim asked, her voice shaking. "It's not like I'm going anywhere."

"Relax, *chica*," Simon soothed. "As long as the *padre* behaves you'll be fine." But he nevertheless wrapped his left arm securely around her chest and lifted the knife a couple of inches away from her neck. "Okay?"

Kim took a deep breath. "Yes. Thank you."

And without warning, she shot straight up from the floor, flying toward the low ceiling, carrying a startled Simon up with her. Mauricio tensed.

At the last second Simon let go, dropping back to the floor. Kim slammed into the ceiling with an agonizing *thud*, her head twisting sharply sideways with the impact. She dropped back to the floor—not flew, but dropped— and lay still.

For a couple of seconds Simon stared at her, his breath coming in short gasps. Then his eyes snapped back to the cloud floating above him. "Don't," he warned.

"I wasn't going to do anything," Mauricio assured him, silently cursing himself. Kim's failed effort had nevertheless bought him a few crucial seconds of confusion in which he could have made a move. Instead, he'd been so startled that he'd wasted her gift. "Simon—"

"Shut it." Simon huffed out a breath, dropping his gaze again to the unconscious woman. "You know, if she'd tried flying me into the wall it would have worked." He shrugged. "I'd have killed her on the way, but she might have knocked me out." He looked back at Mauricio. "So now it's just you and me."

Mauricio focused on Jackson and Diego. Neither had moved, but both were listening intently to what was happening.

And in their faces, he could tell they'd figured out what Mauricio already knew.

They might survive the night. But sooner or later Simon would see a chance to move up again on the perceived ladder of his future.

And when that happened, both of them would be in the

boy's way. Just as surely as Mauricio and Kim were in his way now.

The question was whether they were ready to do what had to be done. If they were, Mauricio still had one chance left.

"There must be another way," he said, floating down from the ceiling to Simon's eye level. "Some way we can all walk out of here and you can still get what you want."

"Sure," Simon said, frowning at him. "Don't come too close, hey?"

"I'm not," Mauricio assured him. Slowly, he began drifting to the side, toward where Gunther's body lay halfway across the room. "Let's talk, shall we? What you want—"

"I said *not too close*," Simon snapped, straddling Kim's unconscious form and pointing his knife warningly down toward her.

"Easy," Mauricio said hastily. He moved further back from the two of them, continuing to drift to the side and closer to Gunther. Another couple of feet, and he would be in position. "I'm not going to hurt you."

"Yeah, sure," Simon said. "If you're trying to stall, forget it. No one's coming about that shot. Not in this *barrio*."

"I know," Mauricio said. He was nearly above Gunther's body now. "Tell me, Simon: did you ever pay attention in church? Or were you always just sitting there figuring out your next move?"

"Get away from him," Simon ordered.

"What?"

"I said get away from him," Simon repeated. "I heard what you said before. You think he's got something you can use on me. Try it, and the *chica* dies."

"I'm not trying anything," Mauricio promised.

"Then back off. Now."

"Whatever you say," Mauricio said. He floated away from Gunther's body and eased a little more to the side. "You haven't answered my question."

"What, church?" Simon snorted. "Yeah, I listened sometimes. You going to tell me the part that talks about murder?"

"I was thinking more of the verses about sheep," Mauricio said. "Especially the ones about the sheep hearing their Master's voice and obeying Him."

"Yeah, like you're the Master," Simon scoffed. "And I'm not a sheep."

"No, of course not," Mauricio said. Nearly there… "I was also thinking about idols and false gods. Wealth and power can be idols, you know. A lot of people in our world struggle with that. So did the kings of Israel. Do you remember the story of Elijah and King Ahab?"

"Never heard it."

"Too bad," Mauricio said, moving the last remaining few inches. "It's a good story. It was up on Mount Carmel. Elijah assembled the prophets of Baal and built an altar to God."

And finally he was ready. Gunther's body was two feet to his right. Simon was in front of him, still standing over Kim. Directly behind Simon were Diego and Jackson.

"And when all was ready," Mauricio called as loudly as he could, "Elijah stood behind the altar—*directly* behind it—and stretched out his hand, and called down fire from the Lord."

Perhaps in that final second Simon realized what was about to happen. But it was too late. Half propped up on the cot, directed by the sound of Mauricio's voice, Jackson stretched out his hand—

A strangled scream filled the room as Simon's back burst into flame.

And once again, Mauricio wished that he could close his eyes.

Simon had been wrong about no one caring enough to investigate a gunshot in the vicinity of All Saints Church. There was, in fact, someone who did.

"Sorry I couldn't get here sooner," El Vengador apologized as he carefully wrapped a bandage around Mauricio's throbbing leg.

"I'm sorry, too," Mauricio said, clenching his teeth against the pain. But at least he could see again. "We could have used you."

"So I hear," El Vengador said. "Kim and Diego told me about it."

"Are they all right?"

"Define *all right*," the big man said, the lips below his mask twitching in a wry smile.

"Sorry," Mauricio said. "Poor choice of words."

"But I think they'll *be* all right," El Vengador continued. "Jackson's lost a lot of blood, but he seems to be stable. I have a doctor who'll take a look, no questions asked. Diego will call him after he has them settled somewhere safe. The doctor will look at Kim, too. She might have a slight concussion, but I think she'll be okay." He cocked his head thoughtfully. "They're all very confused about what happened there at the end. Jackson was sure he was going to fry you along with Simon. But you're not even singed."

"I was on Simon's far side."

"That's what he figured you were trying to tell him," El Vengador said. "Still a little confusing."

Mauricio shrugged. "What are we going to do with the bodies?"

"You're not going to tell me, are you?"

"Not now. Maybe later."

"Fine." El Vengador finished tying off the bandage. "Well, Gunther's the easy one. We'll drop the body and his gun near the morgue. They can try to figure out how he got himself shot when the computer says he's still in police custody."

Mauricio winced. "That's going to be a little hard on the police, isn't it? This one's hardly their fault."

"Maybe," El Vengador said, his voice darkening. "The way I see it, anything that gets Gunther's people and the cops chasing each other is a good thing for us." He looked over at Gunther's body, now covered with one of Jackson's bloody blankets. "Any idea who he was working for?"

"He said it wasn't Renautas," Mauricio said. "That's all I know."

"The Renautas Corporation?"

Mauricio nodded. "Kim told me they were making lists of Evos. I don't know anything more."

"Hmm," El Vengador murmured. "Okay. We might want to look into that."

Mauricio braced himself. "And Simon?"

El Vengador was silent a moment. "Seems to me that as far as the world is concerned, he's a runaway."

"Not exactly," Mauricio said. "He was thrown out by his cousins."

"*After* he murdered their father."

Mauricio grimaced. "True."

"So I'm thinking we bury him out in the hills," El Vengador said. "Just you and me."

Mauricio sighed. It wasn't right. But all things

considered, it was probably the best they could do. "Would it be okay if I said a service?"

"Of course," El Vengador said. "We can go tonight, if you're up to it."

Mauricio got carefully to his feet. His leg ached horribly, but he was able to limp a couple of steps on it. "I may need a cane," he warned. "And you'll have to do all the heavy lifting."

"No problem," El Vengador said, taking his arm and helping him hobble toward the back stairs. "I'll get you to your car, then come back for the others. After we're done, we'll take the car to Oscar Gutierrez's shop. He'll know how to clean out the blood."

"You think we can trust him?"

"He knew about Simon and didn't turn him in," El Vengador pointed out. "I think we can trust him on this, too."

"Yes," Mauricio murmured. *Trust...*

"I know you're doubting yourself right now, *Padre*," El Vengador said as they reached the stairs. "But don't."

"Why not?" Mauricio said, hearing the bitterness in his voice. "Two people are dead because of me. Three, if you count Simon's uncle. I need to be less trusting."

"You don't need to trust *less*." Adjusting his grip on Mauricio's arm, El Vengador started the two of them up the stairs. "You just need to trust *fewer*."

Mauricio snorted. "If this is a grammar lesson, your timing stinks."

"It's not about grammar," El Vengador said. "You may need to trust fewer people. But once you find the ones worth trusting, you can give them as much as you've got."

"People like you?"

"People like me," El Vengador confirmed.

"Uh-huh," Mauricio said. "You know, trust needs to

work both ways. I've confessed my involvement in two killings, and you won't even show me your face."

El Vengador flashed him a smile. "Let's just say you're still on probation," he said. "We'll get around to that."

"I look forward to it."

"I'm sure you do," El Vengador said. "In the meantime, there's an underground railroad to get running. With Kim and Diego handling the documents—did Diego tell you he's decided to help?"

"No," Mauricio said, blinking in surprise. "Last I heard he was a solid no."

"Because he didn't trust you," El Vengador said. "After tonight, he does. Like you said, trust runs in both directions. Watch this last step."

They negotiated the final step, and with his free hand El Vengador pushed open the door. A wave of cold air flowed over Mauricio, sending a shiver down his back. "It's still an uncertain world," he pointed out.

"It'll always be an uncertain world," El Vengador said. "But that's all right. Because we'll always have people like you."

Mauricio smiled. "Priests?"

The big man put his free hand on Mauricio's shoulder. "Heroes."

EVENT SERIES

BOOK THREE
DIRTY DEEDS
STEPHEN BLACKMOORE

James Dearing pulls his black, unmarked Crown Vic that couldn't scream cop any louder if it had sirens going up to the garage door and lets it idle. He wants Hugo Gallegos to know he's there. He wants him to know who's in charge.

Because he's been getting the distinct feeling that Hugo is forgetting that very important point.

Gallegos is standing at the back of the chop shop behind a torn-apart Mustang, ignoring him. Dearing gives it a few more moments, then kills the engine and steps out of the car, his holstered gun obvious on his belt.

"Lieutenant," Gallegos says, looking all surprised, like he's just noticed Dearing for the first time. He wipes engine grease off his hands with a shop rag. "I didn't see you there."

In a lot of ways they're opposites. Gallegos is a big guy, bigger than Dearing by a couple sizes. Dearing is all hard angles—lean muscle, flinty eyes, sandy brown hair. Gallegos is made of waves and curves. Rolls of muscle and sinew, long black hair pulled back in a ponytail, a swollen, bulbous nose from too many punches. Dearing can't tell if the guy should be a luchador or playing guitar for a mariachi band.

"We need to talk, Hugo." Dearing heads into the chop shop, eyes wary for any of Gallegos' crew, but the two men are alone in the garage.

"Detective Murphy tattled, didn't he?" Hugo smiles with too many teeth. Makes him look like a monkey. It's all a goddamn game to him. He doesn't get that if the wrong word ends up in the wrong ear, it all comes crashing down.

"You want to tell me the hell your problem is?" Dearing says, getting in Hugo's face. "We have an arrangement."

It's an arrangement that's worked out well so far. Dearing and his men give Gallegos information, Gallegos gives them money. It's that goddamn simple. Dearing does not, and will not, kill his own people.

Gallegos' smile somehow gets even bigger. "Big, scary policeman's grown a conscience. Fine. Don't do it."

For the better part of a year, Dearing and two of his men, Murphy and Evans, have had an arrangement with Hugo that's put a lot of money in all their pockets. Gallegos is one of Sinaloa's L.A. shot callers, a man who works the drug trade the way a sales exec copes with a flagging market. With marijuana next to legal and nobody doing cocaine anymore, the cartels have moved into cheap heroin, sending it up from Tijuana through San Diego to points north.

That's all fine and good. Dearing doesn't much care if a bunch of junkies who can't get their oxy move on to something uglier, as long as he gets his cut. But Hugo is proving to be an ambitious little prick. His request that Dearing, Murphy and Evans kill a Narcotics detective for him makes it apparent that their control is slipping. And they can't have that.

"It's not about conscience, you jackass. It's about exposure. Your money's good, Hugo. But it's not that good."

Hugo steps back, puts his hands up. "I get it, man. Too

risky. Wish you'd reconsider. Be a shame if the press were to hear about our little arrangement."

Dearing stares hard at him. He knew this was coming. He has been talking about it for the last couple of weeks with Murphy and Evans. Taking bets on when Gallegos was going to snap and do something stupid. Dearing figured it would be today. Guys like Gallegos always pull this crap sooner or later.

"You're gonna wish you hadn't said that," Dearing says, stepping back and drawing his pistol.

Gallegos picks up a rag from the workbench, wipes grease and oil from his hands. "Oh, what, you gonna arrest me?"

"No," Dearing says and pulls the trigger.

Or at least he tries to. Searing pain engulfs his hand as dark blue crystals appear around the pistol and grow across his fingers like in a time-lapse film, encasing his hand in stone. The stone is cold, so cold it burns. He can feel his skin blistering. He cries out from the pain and tries to drop the gun, but it's stuck fast to his hand in a prison of dark blue stone.

Shock. Then anger. "You're an Evo," Dearing says through gritted teeth.

"Damn right, *puta*. Whatcha have to say to that?"

"It's going to make this next part a lot easier." Dearing flexes his fingers with unnatural strength and the stone cracks, splinters. It shatters into a hundred razor-edged shards. The gun is still frozen, but at least his hand is free. Gallegos' jaw goes slack and his eyes bug out like a fish. The look of surprise is almost worth the pain. "What, you think you're the only one around who's got powers?"

"But you're a cop."

"Yeah. Means I'll get away with it." He throws the stone-locked gun at Gallegos, missing him. The gun embeds itself three inches into the brick wall, sticking hard, its stone shell cracking. Dearing jumps at Gallegos, his strength shooting him across the room at inhuman speed.

Dearing takes a swing, but the air in front of him turns into a solid sheet of blue rock, deflecting his fist and shattering when he hits it. Cobalt blue shards scatter across the room, peppering Gallegos' face. His surprise gives way to pain as the shards draw blood.

Gallegos rolls behind the gutted Mustang he had been working on, but Dearing doesn't let him stay under cover for long. He grabs the front end of the car with one hand and yanks, casually throwing the car out of the way and onto its side with a tremendous crash of metal and glass.

Which turns out to not be the best idea. A dozen needle-sharp stone projectiles the size of tree branches shoot toward Dearing's face, and he's not fast enough to duck them all. One skims along the side of his skull just above the ear, digging a long furrow across his scalp. The rest embed themselves into the wall behind him like javelins.

Dearing recovers quickly, steps in, feints with his left, and when Gallegos ducks, he catches him in the chest with an uppercut that shatters ribs, pops a lung and sends Gallegos flying across the garage. His body slams into a workbench, scattering tools. He starts to wheeze, hands clutching ineffectually at his chest. He tries to stand but only manages to fall onto the floor, cracking his knees on the hard concrete.

Any second now he'll turn purple and start suffocating to death. He looks up at Dearing with bugged-out eyes. He's mouthing something, 'Please' or 'Help me', maybe. Dearing isn't sure.

Dearing considers just letting him die that way but

decides against it. He's a bastard, but he's not that big a bastard. Besides, he doesn't want to watch it. A bullet in the head is one thing. A slow death by asphyxiation is just torture.

He picks Gallegos up by his neck, drags him over to the back wall of the chop shop and slams his head deep into the wall. Once, twice, three times. The back of Gallegos' skull shatters, craters into the brick, blood and brain oozing out like a burst ketchup packet.

Gallegos' body spasms, eyes rolling back into his head, legs and arms jerking as the nerves misfire. He goes still, his body hanging limply from the broken skull lodged in the wall.

Dammit, Gallegos. Stupid bastard. Why couldn't he have made this simple? One bullet is all it would have taken. Dearing had it all planned out. Shoot Gallegos, drive out to a spot in the desert he's already got picked out where he can dump the body. But now he's got a slice in his head he'll have to explain and all this mess. The first person who comes in here is going to know an Evo destroyed the place.

He needs to clean this crap up fast. Some of the blood on the floor is his. His fingerprints are going to be on the Mustang. There's only so much he can do to hide his presence here, and it won't be enough. SID, the Scientific Investigation Division of the LAPD, is going to be crawling all over the scene. Even if he gets Gallegos' body out of the garage, provided he can find all of the pieces, there's no way he can clean up the scene enough to hide what's happened. They're going to know an Evo was here. And there's plenty of forensic evidence to show he was here, too. It's a lost cause, but he has to try anyway.

He reaches for his gun to pull it out of the wall and has a thought. Gallegos has been slowly attracting more interest from Narcotics. They've been poking around him for a while now. Waiting for him to screw up. They've suspected he's a shot caller for some time, but they haven't been able to pin anything substantial on him. That's less down to Gallegos' skill or good fortune and more to Dearing and his men's ability to bury evidence.

If they'd thought Gallegos was an Evo, they'd have jumped on him a long time ago. He'd be sitting inside a concrete bunker somewhere, or under a surgeon's knife as they pried all the secrets from his genes. It's an ugly world for his kind. Dearing thinks it isn't entirely undeserved.

Ever since the June 13th attack in Odessa that killed so many people, Evos have been seen as monsters, enemies, mankind's greatest threat. They're synonymous with terrorists.

Evos lose their rights, have to be registered, are constantly tracked. Finding work is difficult. Finding a place to live is even harder. They can't have government jobs, can't join the military, can't run for office.

Can't be cops.

Which is why Dearing has stayed hidden for so long. He likes being a cop. It's not about justice or righting wrongs. It's about power. The power of authority, to come and go as he pleases, to get away with damn near anything. Even murder.

He's not about to give that up. Whether it's for being a crooked cop or for having super-strength, he's not going to let anyone find him out and take his life away from him.

If Dearing scoops up and buries Gallegos, or even if he leaves him stuck in the wall like that and bails, there will be questions. Questions that will lead back to him.

But what if he doesn't do either?

What if he were to call it in? Show that Gallegos is

an Evo. Point to the damage and say, "Isn't it a miracle I survived?"

Gallegos is an Evo shot caller working for a Mexican cartel. Alive or dead but better dead, that'd be a hell of a feather in Dearing's cap. Take some of the scrutiny off of him. So many people view Evos as a group, never seeing the actual individuals. Like they're a club or a softball team or something.

For some reason, a stupid number of people don't think Evos are going to kill other Evos. They imagine that the mutants are all on the same side. One big, happy band of terrorists and thugs. He doesn't understand why. They're just people. And people kill, lie, cheat, murder. Doesn't matter if someone can fly, turn the air to stone or water into wine. They're still just people.

People are monsters, and Dearing's no different.

Gallegos might just be his ticket to the fast track from Lieutenant to Captain. He, Murphy and Evans have been hiding evidence showing what Gallegos did for a living. But they weren't stupid enough to destroy it.

Now that Gallegos is dead, all that evidence can suddenly appear. After all, things get misfiled all the time.

Captain. That would be useful. More power. It's always about more power. Being a cop, climbing the ranks. He can think of a few things he could do with that much power.

Mrs. Dearing didn't raise any fools, and he knows an opportunity when he sees one. If he's going to do this, he has to be very careful. He prowls around the shop, wiping prints off of anything he might have touched that won't support his story.

He grabs a crowbar and pries the stone-encrusted gun from the wall. He could just yank it out with his hands, but he wants to make it look like he had to work for it. Chips of rock flake from the metal, scattering blue dust on the floor.

Dearing hopes he can keep this quiet, out of the news for a little while, but he doubts that will happen. Evos don't get taken down by cops that often. And once word gets out who Gallegos worked for, the media will eat it up.

He opens the door on the Crown Vic and winces. His right hand is blistering and red from where Gallegos' stone enveloped it. It was more than just a rock. His skin burns and itches. Cold and hot at the same time.

He gets into the car, turns his key in the ignition and activates the radio. "This is 1-Henry-12," he yells into the handset. "Officer needs help. 4th and Dacotah, Boyle Heights."

"Roger, 1-Henry-12, dispatching cars to your location."

Dearing sets the radio back in its cradle and takes a deep breath. He thinks about buckling his seatbelt, but he knows what that will look like, the bruising it will leave. That'd just complicate things.

He puts the car in gear, guns the engine and lets it go.

This probably won't kill him, but it's still going to suck.

The car slams into Gallegos and the wall at forty miles an hour. The airbag goes off in Dearing's face as the windshield explodes, the front end crumples like it's made out of cardboard, driving Gallegos' body further into the wall. His corpse pops, a blood-filled piñata, viscera spraying across the crushed hood.

Dearing's head whips forward. The car fills with the acrid stench of gunpowder and the plume of talcum powder and cornstarch that gets released as the airbag inflates, catching his head just in time. He feels it punch into his face, stars blooming in his eyes. He's going to look like hell when he gets out of this. Black eyes, probably cuts on his face. Good. The worse he looks, the better.

He pushes the car door open. It groans with a squeal of twisted metal. He pulls himself out of the car, staggers outside. He leans against the building and slides to the ground. In the distance he can hear sirens.

Now all he has to do is sit back, wait and hope he's as good a liar as he thinks he is.

Agent Tracy Weller leafs through a dossier on her team's latest acquisition in her office at the Pelican Bay state prison. She's young, younger than most in her position. Short, blonde hair cut close to her head, sensible flats, a navy pants suit. She's not dressed for show.

When she was first starting at the FBI, she thought she needed to stand out. That turned out to be a mistake. Women at the Agency who stand out too much get stomped on. She changed tactics. Played the game. Learned who to throw under the bus. Pretty soon she was the one doing the stomping. Surprised more than a few people who'd given her shit about her age.

It's been two years since she was brought in as part of the Federal Evo Taskforce, and a year since her team moved into the Security Housing Unit, an X-shaped set of buildings at the north end of the prison that had been converted to hold powered individuals. And as her team ran into stranger, more powerful Evos, the facility had to be constantly upgraded to secure them. She was glad all she had to do was catch them. Dealing with that level of budgetary politics and bureaucracy gave her a headache.

The file Agent Carson has handed her is for an Evo named Pat Barton. They picked him up in Des Moines during a bank robbery. From the report, it looks like they had a hell of a time bringing him in. Put up a fight. Three agents in the hospital, five police officers dead.

"He turns into a toxic gas?" she says.

"Yeah," Carson says, drumming his pen against the table, a habit Weller has grown accustomed to. Carson is almost a stereotype of an FBI agent. A lean African-American with a boyish face. Black hair cut military short, a holdover from his tour of duty in Iraq with the Marines. "Near as we can tell it's a combination of different agents, though we haven't isolated them all yet. It's got properties of sarin, hydrogen cyanide, phosgene and chlorine. It's a trip to watch. Just don't be anywhere near it."

Weller scans down the page, raises her eyebrows in surprise. "But that's not how he killed them," she says.

"Seems our boy's impatient. Didn't want to wait the ten or fifteen minutes it would take to kill them, so he got into their lungs and turned solid. It's as messy as it sounds. Fortunately, he holed up in the bank vault. We were able to pipe a hundred thousand volts through the wiring for the security system and create enough of an electric field to suppress him."

"Shock batons didn't work?" Her team has protocols. Their charter prioritizes capture and detainment. They want to get dangerous Evos off the streets, not to mention study them.

Shock batons, Tasers. If those don't work, aerosolized fentanyl, an anesthetic gas that leaves people dead or in a coma almost as often as it simply knocks them out. Dosages are almost impossible to control. The Russians tried using it in a hostage situation in a theater in Moscow back in 2002, and it was a disaster. A hundred and seventy people died, most of them from the gas.

After that, the subdual protocols get a little more... direct. They've had to put down more than a few Evos in the field with a bullet to the head.

Once they're subdued, the nasal shunt goes in, a bulky piece of equipment strapped to the Evo's chest with a cannula stuck deep into the maxillary sinus. It pumps out a constant dose of a gas that blocks the use of powers. Unwieldy, messy. Fails often.

"The batons slowed him down," Carson says. "When we connected. He was gas most of the time. Even with masks, folks got some nasty burns. And even when he looked solid, he wasn't always. I'm not sure we actually hit him with the batons, just got close enough for the electricity to arc. When we did tag him, it made him go solid, but it didn't last. We'd cut the voltage, and he'd gas out again. We couldn't keep him down long enough to get him locked up."

"The fentanyl?"

Carson shakes his head. "We think he's got a natural barrier between him and any surrounding gasses. We're not even sure he breathes when he's in that form. Or how he moves. Since the shock batons worked, we figured we'd try electrifying the bank vault through the security system wiring. We got lucky and it worked. Knocked him out enough for us to sedate him and get the shunt in."

"The shunt worked but the fentanyl didn't?"

"As long as he's solid, sure. Once it's in, it stays in."

"Well, that's something, at least," she says. Barton is going to be a fascinating one to study. A person who can turn into toxic gas? Imagine the things they'll learn. She wonders if there would be a way to bleed off some of that gas. Would he replenish it? Would it be like healing a wound? People died to bring him in. She's not going to let that go to waste.

"How are we containing him?" she says.

"Nasal shunt, shock manacles, sealed cell, negative room pressure. Even if he can turn to gas—doubtful with the shunt and the manacles—he shouldn't be able to flow out of the room. And if he does, we've installed an incinerator outside his door. We've been keeping him in an isolation ward in the infirmary while we get his cell prepped."

Weller winces. It feels a little like overkill, but with a power like this, they can't afford to mess around. The nasal shunt should handle things just fine, but the gas has to be replenished, and so the manacles provide supplemental control for more dangerous Evos.

The manacles operate like the shock batons. Hardware embedded in the cuffs detects minute changes in galvanic skin response that might indicate a power about to be used. When the circuit trips, it sends fifty thousand volts through the wearer for a minute and a half, like a Taser on steroids. They're notoriously unreliable.

The nasal shunts are better, but even they sometimes fail. Weller hopes to change that today.

"I hope the manacles work," Weller says. "Let's go talk to him."

Carson hesitates. "What? You sure you want to do that? See him in Room One?"

Weller understands his concern. Most of the interview rooms, a euphemism if Weller has ever heard one, are split in two by a thick Plexiglas partition. Protocol requires that dangerous Evos be interviewed in one of these rooms in case they get out of hand, and Barton might be one of the most dangerous ones they've ever had in this facility. Room One is only used when there needs to be some sort of hands-on work. Like enhanced interrogation.

In her jacket pocket, Weller feels the weight of the package she received from Quantico earlier that morning.

She's eager to try it out. Barton will be the perfect Evo to use it on.

"I'm sure."

"You didn't hire me to cave easily, so I'm going to ask you again. We've got him in the room. We have the shunt out, like you asked us. It's just the manacles keeping him in place. But if he turns into gas and the manacles don't catch it—"

Weller places her hand on his shoulder. Carson's a good man. Good soldier. "Thank you for the concern, but for this we need the shunt out. And no, I'm not wearing a gas mask. I want him to see I'm not afraid of him."

"All right. Don't die," Carson says. "I so don't want your job."

Weller and Carson walk down the utilitarian gray corridor, following the orange line painted on the floor that leads to Room One. Like the rest of the facility, the room is an oppressive shade of gray, the only furnishings a couple of light plastic chairs and a flimsy plastic table. They'd learned the hard way that anything heavy was a bad idea when a woman with super-strength ripped out a bolted-down metal table and beat three guards to death. Instead, there are U-bolts sunk deep into the floor with a thick chain to attach to the prisoner's manacles.

Pat Barton sits in a chair, his hands in front of him, the heavy chains of the manacles tight against his wrists. His head is shaved nearly bald, and he sports a red goatee that could use a trim. His face is set in a scowl, eyes burning and full of hatred. His left nostril is swollen and red from the shunt being pulled out.

Weller returns his look with one of disinterest. He has only himself to blame for his predicament. He could have registered. He could have not knocked over banks. He could have not been a murderer. He could have not been born a monstrosity.

Evos have been getting more common, and it pisses Weller off. She's not scared of Evos—she hates them. Abominations that need to be watched, controlled. Left unchecked, they'll take over the world. And where will regular people, real people, be then? Barton is an example of the worst of his kind. It's bad enough that Evos are protesting for rights as if they were true humans. But then Evos like Barton decide to use their powers to steal, to hurt, to kill.

He should be grateful they didn't put him down in the field.

Guards stand at each of the four corners of the room, shock batons at the ready. They wear gas masks, which isn't standard procedure, but then Barton isn't your run-of-the-mill Evo. Carson holds a mask of his own, but he doesn't put it on.

Weller sits across from the prisoner, not saying anything. Just looking. Studying. To his credit, he keeps his scowl going longer than most. But eventually it starts to crack. Anger turns to fear.

"The hell are you looking at?" he says.

"An experiment gone wrong," she says. "That's what you are, you know. That's what all evolution is. Experiments. Sometimes they work. Sometimes they don't. You're one of the ones that failed." She doesn't think it will take much to rile him up, and he doesn't disappoint.

"Yeah? I'll show you something that works." Wisps of green gas lift gently off his skin. He begins to appear hazy, indistinct. The guards start forward, but the manacles kick in before they get more than a step, sending electricity coursing through the Evo's body. He convulses, the gas disappearing.

The manacles keep kicking out voltage for a good long while. Sometimes they'll trigger seizures. But Weller gets the impression that Barton can take the punishment.

She takes a breath. The moment he started going gaseous, her lungs seized up, some primal fear deep in her brain kicking in. She masters it, breathes normally. She won't let him see her afraid.

Barton slumps against the table when the manacles finally shut off, his body shaking, breath coming in a ragged wheeze. He's trying to say something, but Weller can't tell what. Some form of 'Screw you', no doubt.

"Hurts, doesn't it?" she says. "The manacles are messy. Expensive to run, too. Cruel, honestly." She pulls a small box from her jacket pocket, flips it open and retrieves a small white device with silicone nasal cannulas on the back, minute gas cartridges protruding from the sides. She shows it to him, putting it on the table next to his head so he can see it. She isn't sure he's tracking quite yet, but she keeps going anyway.

"This is a new type of nasal shunt," she says. "Renautas tech. Brand new stuff. It keeps a steady flow of gas going into the subject's sinuses. Shuts down powers just like that." She snaps her fingers under Barton's eyes, and he jerks away from her.

"It's more reliable, more secure. Lasts longer, too. Doesn't have the problems of the current tech. It'll make Evos no more powerful than the rest of us. Imagine. No more bulky equipment. No more manacles. Quick, simple. You won't have to get shocked anymore. Doesn't that sound great?"

Barton whimpers, tries to lift his head. Doesn't get very far.

"I know," she says, as if he's answered her. She stands,

stepping around the table and kneeling down next to him. "Now, this is largely untested tech. We've tried it on a lot of Evos, but we know what to make of most of them. We haven't run into one with your powers before. You're a trailblazer, Mister Barton." She pulls his head back and shoves the device against his nose. A probe from the cannulas extends into his sinuses, lodging there. She slams the palm of her hand up against it to really shove it in there.

Barton starts whimpering, a sound just on the edge of a scream. His body thrashes, but there's no strength in it. The manacles might not be reliable, but when they work, they do a pretty good job. Blood oozes from around the shunt. Weller lets his head fall back onto the table.

"You killed five people," she says. "You hurt three of my agents. I'd just as soon kill you as look at you. But you've got some use left in you, and by god, I will use up everything you have if it means carving you into little slices to look at under a microscope. Goodbye, Mister Barton. Enjoy your new life."

Dearing's phone rings while he's sitting in traffic on the 101 freeway near downtown. He thumbs the answer button. "Dearing," he says.

"I come bearing good tidings," Murphy says. "You're cleared from administrative leave."

Dearing hasn't seen Murphy or Evans in a couple of weeks. They met after everything went to shit in order to strategize, get stories straight. After that, they decided Dearing should lay low until things died down. Too many eyes on him.

Mostly, Dearing's been bored. He doesn't have a lot going on outside of his work for the LAPD and his more lucrative extracurricular activities. He lives alone, doesn't date. Hard to have a relationship when you're constantly hiding the fact that you can bend steel with your bare hands. Keeping secrets is what he does, but that level of secrecy is just exhausting. He's tried it a few times. It's always ended in disaster.

So he's been down at a casino in Gardena playing Hold 'Em and Pai Gow poker. Normally he goes once a month, but with so much free time and not really wanting to do anything that might attract attention, he's been going a lot more.

Murphy and Evans have been splitting his job between them, mainly just collecting payments from the gangs they have deals with.

They need to show their clients, mostly gangsters and thugs with the odd higher-end businessman, that nothing has changed. That they're still watching out for them. And that if anybody steps out of line, they'll be dealt with just like before.

"That was faster than I expected." Use of Force investigations usually take a while, and the high-profile ones even longer. It didn't get much higher profile than taking down a suspected cartel shot caller who was an Evo. The department had put Dearing on administrative leave as they tried to sort through what the hell had happened.

He'd kept his story simple. Anonymous tip. Sounded like a string of GTA cases he'd been working on. So he went down to see what was up. Things went south from there. Gallegos pegged him as a cop and showed his powers. Dearing hadn't even been able to get a shot off. If he hadn't gotten to his car and rammed it into the gangbanger, he'd be dead.

The garage was trashed enough to support the story, though he got an ass-chewing for stepping on an active

Narcotics case. He feigned ignorance. How was he to know Narcotics was on this guy? Acted surprised that Gallegos had been anybody important. He's not sure they bought it.

To make matters worse, the media was all over the story. The department had kept his name under wraps for now, but that wasn't going to last. It was weird to be in the spotlight without actually being in the spotlight. Some were calling him a hero, others a monster.

"They rammed it through," Murphy says. "Autopsy was cut and dried. DNA came back showing he was an Evo. SID supports your story. You're free and clear, man."

"It's never that simple."

Murphy laughs. "Yeah, there's a wrinkle. But it's a good one. The way they're talking, they want to fast-track you for Captain. Put your name out in the news and everything."

"Shit."

"What? I thought you'd be happy about that."

"You remember what we do, right?" The added scrutiny was going to make things difficult. Not just for their little side jobs, but also for Dearing's attempts to keep his powers under wraps.

"Dammit."

"We'll deal with it. So are you the official welcome wagon, or do I have to act surprised when I get a phone call from the Captain?"

"I'm it. Narcotics still thinks you're an asshole for jacking up their case, but everybody else loves you."

Murphy might buy that, but Dearing doesn't. "So nothing else? Nobody from the *Times* poking around? Narcotics isn't asking questions?"

There's a pause. "Well, yeah, but it's nothing. Some federal agent's in a pissing match to get the body. They want to study it or something."

Dearing's hands are suddenly slick with sweat. His heart pounds in his chest. Everything feels tight and close as his paranoia spikes to eleven. "Are they asking about me?" he says.

"No idea. Why would they?"

Why indeed? "Because if they want Gallegos' body, they're going to want to talk to the guy who killed him."

Best case, they take everything he says at face value, nod their heads and go home. Worst case, they dig. Even if all they do is find out about the side jobs, he's screwed. There's no way he'll be able to hide what he is in prison.

"So? They've got an Evo corpse and a good crime scene. Everything you've said checks out. You worry too much."

But that's just it. Dearing doesn't think he's nearly worried enough.

"They're still stalling," Carson says, coming into the LAPD interrogation room with two coffees. He hands one to Weller, who's going through a file, and sits down across from her.

"That's fine," she says. She expected the LAPD wouldn't want to give up the body. Jurisdiction is murky, and this is the sort of case that can make or break a career. Soon enough, the news will cycle around to the next celebrity meltdown, and nobody will care anymore. When that happens, she'll push for a court order and take the corpse back to Pelican Bay, where they'll cut it up and yank out its secrets. Two, maybe three days, tops.

"Oh?"

She slides the file across to him. "I want to talk to this Lieutenant Dearing. He's the one who killed the Evo. I want to know what he knows. What he saw. The only thing

I have is his report, and it's crap. They're not releasing any of the other information yet."

"I can get Judge Horner on the phone," Carson says. Horner's a FISA judge who's good at cutting through interagency bullshit, but Weller shakes her head.

"Not yet. The last thing we need is the press to turn their eyes on us. We'll give the police their time in the spotlight. It won't be that long."

"I can't say I don't appreciate the change of scenery," Carson says.

The door opens, and a young officer sticks his head in. Earnest, puppy-dog eyes, hair high and tight. "Excuse me, Agent Weller? Lieutenant Dearing is here."

"Well, show him in, then."

The officer pauses. "Uh. I'm supposed to take you to him. To his office."

"You can bring him here," Weller says. She smiles at him, as if this was perfectly normal. "We've got the paperwork here. It'll be easier for all of us."

"I—Okay."

"Appreciate it," Weller says, still smiling. He nods, the nervousness never leaving his face, and disappears, closing the door behind him.

"You know that smile doesn't actually look friendly, right?" Carson says. "Way too many teeth."

"Who says I want to look friendly?"

"That's not gonna win you any points with this Lieutenant," Carson tells her.

"I'm okay with that," Weller says. "Look at his file. Everything about that record screams ambition."

Carson skims through the file. "No wonder you don't like the guy. This file looks just like yours."

Is that why her gut is telling her to look into this guy?

She just doesn't like him? Sure, the report's incomplete, but that doesn't mean anything. Does it?

The door to the interrogation room opens. Not too hard to be threatening, but not so delicately that it doesn't get the point across. A square-jawed man with short brown hair stands in the doorway, scowling.

"Lieutenant Dearing?" Weller says, all smiles. "I'm Special Agent Weller, and this is Special Agent Carson. Pleased to meet you."

Dearing isn't buying it. "I don't have time for this," he says. "You've got my report. Everything's in there."

"Have you ever dealt with an Evo before, Lieutenant?" Weller says.

A pause, a little too long. Then, "In the station. A few get brought in from time to time."

Something about that pause bothers Weller. Is he lying? Why? Possibly because he knows one and isn't reporting it? Interesting.

"You do get a few of them out here, don't you? I was reading some of the station reports. People who fly, phase through walls. Those must be a pain in the ass. I saw a report about one who can turn into smoke. They haven't killed anyone, have they? I've got one in custody like that. Only he does poison gas. He's a real monster."

"Not that I've heard," Dearing says.

"Well, if they had, I'm sure you'd know. One of the things we've found is that when someone encounters a person with powers, they tend to be shaken up. Initial reports aren't always, well, reliable. They're often... incomplete."

He says nothing for a moment, and Weller swears she can hear gears turning in his head. He's taking too long to decide between sitting down and telling her to kiss off.

"My report's complete," he finally says. "And like I said, I have work to do. I've been away for a few days, and cases are piled up on my desk."

"I understand," Weller says. "But we won't take up much of your time. Just a couple of questions. Promise." She smiles, this time not showing as many teeth, trying to be as disarming as possible. Part of her wants him to balk again. Because if he's going to resist that much, well, that would mean something, wouldn't it?

"Fine," he says and sits down at the interrogation table. "What do you want to know?"

"It says that—What was his name?"

"Gallegos," Carson says. "Hugo Gallegos."

"Gallegos, right, was exhibiting super-strength and some kind of crystal powers? Can you elaborate on that at all? I mean, I understand the strength, but what do you mean by crystal powers?"

"He made rocks form out of thin air, over objects." Dearing says. He shows her his hand. Where there isn't gauze, the skin is pink, bordering on red. "Like my hand. Covered the whole thing in this blue rock. I don't know what kind. Docs say I'm suffering from mild frostbite. They think when the rock crystals formed, it sucked all the heat out of my hand."

"That looks nasty," Carson says. "Healing okay?"

"They tell me it will."

"The Evo had multiple powers?" Weller says. "That's rare. Almost unheard of, actually."

"I thought all Evos were rare."

"Well, yes, but two distinct powers? That doesn't happen often."

"It's usually just one and done," Carson says.

"Even when we see multiple powers, it's a lot more than

that. I don't think we've run into anyone with just two."

Weller watches Dearing. That was one thing about the story that bothered her. With Evos, there were commonalities. A ridiculous number of them could fly, for example. So if he'd had super-strength *or* this crystal power, she wouldn't have thought much about it. But both? Possible, yes. Likely? No.

"Huh. Good to know," Dearing says. "Anything else?"

"You drove your car into him?"

"Well, my gun was covered in stone and stuck in the wall, and I wasn't about to try punching the guy. He'd just tossed a Mustang onto its side."

"Really made a mess of his body, didn't you?" Carson says.

"Cars do that when you ram them into people. I wasn't exactly thinking about how tough it was going to make the coroner's job. Sorry."

"Pretty resourceful of you," Weller says. "Thinking of the car. Why'd he let you get all the way over to it, do you think?"

"I didn't ask," Dearing says. "I was busy running."

"Your report says you received an anonymous tip about a chop shop. Any idea who called it in?"

"You do know what anonymous means, right?" Dearing says.

"Fair enough. How come you didn't take anyone with you? Is that protocol?"

"Didn't think it would lead to much. We're stretched thin. The LAPD doesn't have the resources to throw a bunch of people at a rumor."

"But they have the resources to throw a Lieutenant at it? That seems like something a patrol officer should be doing."

"Agent Weller, what is it you're looking for? I know a grilling when I see one."

"I'm just trying to get to the meat of what happened," Weller says, her tone hardening. "We're talking about someone suspected of being highly placed in a Mexican cartel who turns out to have powers. I don't know about you, Lieutenant, but that scares the hell out of me. So if I sound like I'm looking for something, I am."

And it does scare the hell out of her. When things changed, she was already a veteran at the Agency. She'd handled drug cases, murders, money laundering, terrorism. She cut her teeth on the Fort Dix attack in 2007, broke a Russian human-trafficking ring in 2009. Young women brought over in cargo containers, sold into slavery—when they survived the journey, that is. She'd seen the worst that humanity had to offer.

When the Evos showed up, everything changed. Whole new ballgame. Whole new terrors. She understood the fear, or thought she did, but she clung to the idea that they were still American citizens.

And then Odessa happened. She was on the ground in the first days after the attack. She saw the dead. Saw the destruction. So many bodies that they had to stack them up outside of town.

It was worse than anything she'd ever seen before. Something inside her snapped. Human beings hadn't done this. Monsters had.

"Gallegos was under surveillance by your Narcotics division," Carson says. "How did this guy manage to keep his powers under wraps? Did he never use them around people? Or did he just happen to kill everyone he ran into? I'm not sure which one worries me more."

"Maybe he just didn't want to get locked up," Dearing says. "How hard could it be for an Evo to hide their powers? People lie all the time."

"They're not people, Lieutenant," Weller says. "They're abominations. And all liars slip up now and again."

"Everything you need to know is right there in my report," Dearing declares, his voice flat. "Nothing more, nothing less. Now, if you'll excuse me, I have work to catch up on."

"Of course, Lieutenant," Weller says. "Thank you for your time. It's been illuminating."

Dearing gets up, his scowl somehow deeper than before. "Yeah. Whatever." He leaves the interrogation room, slamming the door behind him.

"That went well," Carson says.

"Better than I expected, actually. Interesting guy."

"He was pushing back a little too much there," Carson says. "What do you think he's hiding?"

"I don't know," Weller says. "But I'm going to find out."

Dearing leaves the interrogation room, his palms sweating. He's screwed himself. He should have been more cooperative, more conciliatory. But goddamn if he's going to give these people the satisfaction.

He should have played it straight. Cooperate. Tell the same story he's been telling. So what if there are inconsistencies? He should have played up the unreliable witness angle. Said he was still shaken after his run-in with the Evo. Anything.

There are half a dozen things he did wrong in there that he would have exploited if he was in their shoes. But then, if he was in their shoes, he'd have kept pushing until something cracked.

So why didn't they?

Because they know there's more going on, but they

don't know what it is. That means they're falling back to dig some more. Dammit. He's acting like an amateur. His unanticipated battle with Gallegos must have thrown him more than he's been willing to admit to himself.

A commotion at the front of the squad room pulls him out of his thoughts. Five uniforms are hauling in a guy who looks like he's been living on Skid Row. He's screaming an incoherent rant about black helicopters and shadowy agents.

Closer to the truth than you know, buddy.

And then he bursts into flame.

Three of the officers holding him go up like Roman candles. Rolling around on the floor, screaming as the flames consume them. Somebody pulls the fire alarm, kicking off the sprinklers. Dearing bolts for the fire extinguisher on the wall, pulls the pin—and stops.

The blazing homeless man doesn't seem to mind that he's on fire. He's standing in the middle of the room, everything catching fire around him despite the downpour of water; papers, desks, the floor. A black, smoldering stain is spreading across the ceiling.

And he's laughing.

"Evo!" Dearing yells. He runs over to the two officers and lets loose with the fire extinguisher, covering them in a cloud of white powder. They're badly burned, but at least they're not on fire anymore. Dearing turns to see the burning Evo lock eyes with him. The man puts his arms out and starts walking toward him.

"Free hugs!" the Evo yells, cackling. "Love for everybody!" Inside his shroud of flames, Dearing can see that the man is untouched by the fire. It dances off his skin like he's wearing it as a suit, his hair unsinged, his skin unblistered. Even his clothes are fine.

With each footstep, the linoleum on the floor ignites.

Desks are catching fire, phones are melting. Papers curl brown and black in the heat before going up like so much flash paper.

Officers with stun batons come running at the burning man, but they can't get anywhere near him. The flames are too hot. He turns toward one of them and a jet of flame arcs from his fingers to the officer's baton. It explodes in the officer's face in a shower of molten slag. The man falls to the floor, screaming.

Dearing drops the fire extinguisher while the man's attention is elsewhere, draws his sidearm and puts two bullets into the Evo's back. The flames disappear as suddenly as they had appeared. The man's knees give way and he falls onto his back in a flooded patch on the floor, steam rising as the sprinklers rain down on his face. He peers up at Dearing with a look like he's just stepped in something foul. Not pained, not confused. Pissed off.

Then his eyes roll back into his head and he dies.

Dearing stares at his body, gun still in his hand. The man's ranting echoes through his mind. Love for everybody. Sure, pal. Kumbaya and all that crap. We're just one big bunch of understanding motherfuckers in this world.

Out of the corner of his eye, he catches Weller watching him from the doorway of the interrogation room. He turns to her, face flat, holsters his gun. Yeah, he just killed another Evo.

Let her chew on that.

The mess takes hours to sort out. The whole station is a crime scene now. Ambulances come to cart away the wounded and the dead. Weller's probably going to want this Evo's body, too. There are statements to take, reports to file.

Dearing is looking at another Use of Force investigation. Just what he goddamn needs.

To make things worse, most of the computers are fried from the sprinklers, and the ones that aren't can't connect to the network. They boot up, the screens go weird and then they die. By the time everything's cleared out and the computers come back up, it's almost midnight.

Dearing has Evans and Murphy meet him in the parking lot outside the station. All three are exhausted and still wet from the sprinklers in the squad room, but they have things to talk about.

"Agent Weller is going to be a problem," Dearing says. He needs to tread carefully here. He knows he can only trust these two so far. Something about thieves and an overwhelming lack of honor.

"What does she know?" Evans says.

"Nothing yet. But she's digging." He gives them a rundown of his talk with Weller.

Murphy scowls. "She doesn't know shit."

"She's going to want to talk to Gallegos' crew," Dearing says.

"They've scattered," Murphy says. "She won't find anything there."

"Still, we need to watch her and see what happens."

"I really don't want to do surveillance on a Fed," Evans says.

"And I don't want to have to dismantle everything we've built," Murphy says. "I got too much money riding on this."

Dearing gets it. They've put a lot of time and effort into contacts, side deals, protection rackets. It's not a big network, but it's theirs. He's damn well not going to watch it all go to shit.

"We won't have to do either. Pay attention to her. She'll

be making noise. We'll hear about it around the station. As for everything else, we take it down a notch until things calm down. Patience and calm."

He's telling himself this as much as he's telling them. He has more to lose than they do. They get caught, they'll do ten years, tops. Dearing gets caught, he'll disappear into a hole and never come out again.

They nod in agreement. He's hoping that's at least one thing he can trust them on, but he wonders when, not if, they're going to screw him. "All right. Watch yourselves."

"Yeah, you too," Evans says.

They break up, each going to their separate cars. Dearing's is parked on the other side of the lot. He stops when he gets to his car. The cab light is on. He knows he didn't leave it on. Most of the time he forgets it's even there.

Did Weller bug his car? No. He doesn't see her as the sloppy sort. She's too organized, too by-the-book. If she'd put a bug in there, he'd never know it.

He unlocks the car and pulls the door open. A thick manila envelope is sitting on the driver's seat. He opens it warily, like he's expecting a snake to jump out of it. He's made use of enough blackmail material in his time to know that the right photo can be just as dangerous as a bomb.

He pulls out an unlabeled DVD and files from his investigation stamped with LAPD evidence numbers. Tire prints, crime-scene photos, coroner files, DNA reports.

And a cell phone that starts to ring.

Dearing stares at it. Whoever's calling is doing it from a blocked number. He picks it up and answers.

"Good evening, Lieutenant Dearing," says a man's voice.

"Who the hell is this?"

"Someone with a vested interest in your welfare," the

voice says. "The envelope contains the paper copies of your Use of Force investigation. The DVD is the only remaining copy of the computer records. Do with them what you will."

Dearing thinks back to the problem with the computers after the fire. Even the ones that hadn't been affected by the sprinklers were malfunctioning.

"Why?" he says. He looks over the resolution report from the police commission and the medical examiner. "Says here I was in the right. As far as everybody's concerned, I'm free and clear. Even the M.E. said it was a good kill."

"Look at Gallegos' cause of death," the man says.

Dearing looks. Massive blunt force trauma to the parietal and occipital bones. The rest of Gallegos' injuries are listed as post-mortem.

"The back of his skull was crushed and then he was rammed into the wall by your car after he was dead," the man says. "Now, how do you suppose that happened?"

Shit. The only reason he isn't locked up right now is sheer luck. If Weller catches a glimpse of this, she'll see the problem. And then he's screwed.

"And these are the only copies?"

"They are. I suggest you destroy them." The man hangs up.

Dearing knows he's lying. Anyone who would, or even could, go to this much trouble to get the evidence in the case wouldn't just hand it all over to him. They'd hold onto it for leverage. This guy wants something.

But what? And why?

He checks the phone's history. Nothing. He's not surprised. Of course he's covering his tracks. Even tracing the call through the cell tower probably won't get Dearing anything. He gets out of the car and looks around. Whoever's watching him could be in a hundred different places. He checks under the dashboard for a camera, peers into the vents. He doesn't find one, but that doesn't mean there isn't one.

He's just spinning his wheels. When the mystery man wants to get hold of him, he will. There are more important things to think about. Like what to do with these files.

By the time he gets home, he's decided to shred and burn them. He checks the DVD to see whether the man was at least telling the truth about it. Sure enough. Everything nicely scanned and filed away. He nukes the DVD in his microwave until it's nothing but a sparking, smoking mess.

He goes through all the papers, looking for any holes that might screw him over and can only think of two: the pathologist who conducted the autopsy, and the body itself. The records might be missing, but if anyone were to talk to the M.E. or do another autopsy, he's screwed.

He knows the pathologist, Katherine Reese. She's not the type to turn down a little extra cash. She could conveniently forget the details and get Gallegos' body carted off to a mortuary for a nice, quick cremation. It'll cost, but it beats getting locked up, or worse.

After a fitful night of his stomach twisting into knots at all the things that could go wrong, Dearing calls the Coroner's Office from the burner phone. If his new benefactor wants to listen in as he digs himself deeper into trouble, that's fine. The important thing is that the call doesn't get traced back to his apartment.

"Hi, this is Detective Horton," he says, "Hollenbeck Division. Is Doctor Reese in today? I can't get hold of her."

Silence. Then, "I'm sorry, sir, but she was in a car accident yesterday."

"Oh," Dearing says, suspicion growing in his gut. "I hope she's all right."

The receptionist's voice starts to crack. "She was killed," she says.

This cannot be a coincidence. He takes the burner phone away from his ear and looks at it for a moment. Did they kill her? What about the body? Did they take care of that, too?

"I'm very sorry to hear that," he finally says. "Is there another pathologist I could talk to?"

"I'll redirect you to Doctor Martinez."

"That would be great, thanks."

He's heard of Martinez. A stick up his ass so far it's a wonder the guy can bend over. Reese, he could work with. If the rumors about Martinez are true, the doctor would just turn him in. He doesn't want to talk to the guy, but he needs to know about Gallegos' body.

A new voice, gravelly with age, comes on the line. "Martinez," the man says.

"Hi, Doctor Martinez, Detective Horton, LAPD. Working on an Evo case that Doctor Reese did the autopsy for. I understand she had an accident."

"Yep," the doctor says. "Got her in a drawer right here. Don't know what I can do for you, though. All our computers went to shit yesterday."

At least that part's true. "Sorry for your loss," Dearing says.

"Eh, shit happens," Martinez says. "Said you're calling about the Evo?"

"This one landed on my desk this morning, and I had a couple questions. Is the body still there?"

"Oh, yeah. Looked at him this morning. He's a mess. Car accident or something. Almost cut the poor bastard in half."

"Oh, good. I'll see if I can find the info she sent over.

There's something here. Really sorry to hear about her."

"Yeah, it's a drag. But hey, all our luck runs out eventually, right?"

"Right," Dearing says. He hangs up, wondering if his luck has run out, too.

Weller's morning has been one frustration after another. The squad room is still flooded enough that she's working from her hotel room. She's been on the phone with the LAPD for the last two hours trying to get the case files released.

"No, goddammit, I will not hold," she says for the fifth time that morning. "At least tell me what the hell the problem is." She's been bounced around from department to department, and she hasn't been able to get a straight answer from anyone. The detective on the phone is the latest in a long line of irritating people.

"All our computers are jacked up," he says, his voice weary. "A bunch of our records are gone. They're saying it could take weeks to get it fixed. I know you think what you've got going on is important, but we're drowning over here. Do yourself a favor and let it go. Nobody can help you right now."

He hangs up on her.

"Dammit." It's one thing to deal with politics and stonewalling, but she can't abide incompetence. There's a knock on her door.

"You won't believe this," Carson says when she opens the door.

"Let me guess, computer problems and all the records are gone?"

"Yeah. But that's not the crazy part."

"Wait, seriously?" While she was trying to track down

the files from the LAPD, Carson was working on getting the autopsy report from the coroner. The LAPD should have it, but it was usually faster to get it straight from the source.

"Coroner's Office had some kind of system crash," he says. "Lost a bunch of records."

"LAPD had the same thing. Hell of a coincidence, don't you think?"

"You haven't heard the punchline yet," Carson says. "The pathologist who did the autopsy? She's dead. Car accident last night."

"Somebody's covering this up," she says, dialing her phone. "Call the local FBI field office, get a pathologist from them. I'm getting the rest of the team down here. I want another autopsy on that corpse and a full work-up before somebody makes it disappear, too."

Dearing drums his fingers on the steering wheel of his car and checks his watch for the sixth time in the last ten minutes. He's parked on the top floor of the USC Medical Center parking garage, looking down at the red brick building of the Coroner's Office on Mission Road near Interstate 5. He stole the car a couple hours ago from an impound lot on Figueroa with some bullshit paperwork and a fake badge number. The cameras are ridiculously easy to avoid. There's nothing to trace the car to him, so if things go south, he can abandon it without worry.

He's waiting for the office to change over to the night shift. The county doesn't like to pay employees overtime, so most of the staff clocks out at five on the dot, leaving only a small skeleton crew for body pick-up and check-in. The sun has already set, but he'll give it an hour, maybe two, and then head down. He knows the building, knows the layout, but he doesn't know where Gallegos' body is. There are at least three morgue rooms it could be in. He's hoping he can find it quickly.

He's been checking the police band with a handheld scanner, listening for any homicide or ambulance calls. So far it's been a quiet night.

An hour and a half later, he's out of the car and peering over the side of the parking structure. He's made bigger jumps. When he first discovered his powers, he didn't push himself, thinking that just because he had super-strength didn't mean he was invulnerable. It doesn't, but it does make him ridiculously tough. If all he had was muscle strength and the supporting bones and tendons weren't in sync with it, he would have torn his arms out of their sockets years ago.

He gives himself a running start and leaps from the top of the parking garage toward the roof of the coroner's building several stories below. He sails across the gap, a good twenty feet easy, and hits the sloping roof hard. Tiles scatter, falling behind him into the alley below. He scrambles up and to the back of the building, where there's a terrace for ventilation equipment and a maintenance entrance.

He ducks low behind the vents, waiting to see if anyone comes up to investigate the noise. Most of the work is done on the lower floors, with offices at the top. With the late shift on duty, no one should be in them right now, but it pays to be careful.

His plan, such as it is, is to get inside, find Gallegos' body, get him back to the roof and jump across to the parking structure again. From the coroner's building, he should be able to make it to one of the lower levels, and then he can run back up to where the car is parked.

Ten minutes go by, fifteen. He decides it's as safe as it's going to get and pulls on a pair of nitrile gloves. The last thing he needs is his fingerprints all over the place. He jimmies the maintenance door open. He inches his way down the stairs, listening for footsteps above the hum of the air conditioning and the buzz of fluorescent lights. The entire place smells strongly of bleach, with only a hint of something slightly off.

The County Coroner's Office is designed to hold about three hundred and fifty bodies, but they're not all kept in the same morgue room. He slips into the first one, the temperature noticeably colder and the stink of decay stronger. Rows upon rows of morgue drawers, each labeled with a number, but no indication of who might be inside them.

He starts pulling them open, wincing at the smell. The place is basically a freezer, and just like everywhere else in the building, it's been doused in a liberal amount of bleach, but a rotting corpse is a rotting corpse. He checks the identification tag on the outside of the black body bag. It's not Gallegos. Same with the next drawer and the next. He goes through all thirty drawers.

No Gallegos. Dammit.

Would they have put the body in some kind of hazmat containment area? A special room? Now that he thinks of it, he isn't sure what they do with dead Evos. He checks the computer on the desk in the corner of the room, but it wants a password. He goes through the desk drawers, looking for a logbook or anything that will show him where specific bodies are kept, but there's nothing.

He probably should have done that first, but his nerves have made him jumpy, and he's not thinking as clearly as he should be. Now is not the time to make mistakes. He forces his anxiety down. It's not like this is the first time he's broken into someplace he's not supposed to be. He's just never had so much on the line.

He slips out of the room and quickly crosses the hall to the second storage room. He checks the desk, but it's the same as before. Nothing for it, then. He starts sliding open drawers, hoping to find Gallegos in one of them.

"I don't care who the hell you are," Martinez says, glaring at Weller from his front door. "You're not getting anything until the morning." At just over five-feet-two with long, unkempt hair, the pathologist looks like an angry Pekingese.

"Doctor," Weller says, "I'm not here to ask permission." She shoves the court order to release Hugo Gallegos' body at him. He waves it away as if it were a mosquito.

She and Carson have tracked the doctor to his home in Echo Park to serve him the papers so they can go down and get started. They've been standing on his doorstep for the last twenty minutes.

"Yes, I got that. I don't care. You need two pathologists to sign him out before he can be moved. I'm one, another comes back tomorrow from vacation in the Maldives and the third one is currently cooling her heels in a drawer next to my office. So unless you can get a dead woman's signature, you're not moving him."

"I don't want to move him," Weller says. "I have an FBI pathologist with me who's going to do another autopsy. We just need to get access to the body."

Martinez frowns, grabs the paper from her hand and reads it over. "Ah. I see. And this can't wait until the morning? You do know he's not going anywhere, right? Because, you know, he's dead?"

Weller wants to scream at the man, but she manages to keep a straight face. "I am aware, yes."

"All right, then," Martinez says. "Let me get changed and I'll come with you."

"I said I've got my own pathologist."

"And it's my goddamn morgue. I'm not letting you people in there unsupervised. Wait here. I'll be out in five minutes." He slams the door in her face.

"That went better than I expected," Carson says.

Weller pinches the bridge of her nose. "I hate dealing with locals."

"Oh, come on," Carson says. "He's like some quaint country doctor. Gruff, but lovable."

"If he doesn't get a move on, that quaint country doctor's getting a boot up his ass."

"You really think whoever's behind this is going to go after the body tonight?"

"You mean Dearing," she says.

"No," Carson says. "I still don't think it's him. I think he's covering something up, but I don't know that he's involved in this. I get that he's a thug, sure. But hacking LAPD and county coroner records *and* arranging a car accident that kills the pathologist who did the autopsy? No. I don't know who's behind this or why, but it's not him."

Weller has to agree that the facts don't fit, but her gut tells her otherwise. Maybe it's just that she knows Dearing's hiding something. He's got something going on, something to do with this Evo that he isn't telling her. Or maybe it's just that she doesn't like him.

Whatever the answer is, she's certain she'll find it in that morgue.

* * *

Dearing's heard that if you spend enough time around the stink of corpses, your nose gets used to it and you don't notice it anymore. Horseshit. He's been in the morgue plenty of times, seen dead bodies, some in advanced stages of decay, but he's never had to stick his face into drawer after drawer for the better part of an hour. After seeing and smelling everything from gunshot wounds to stabbings to run-of-the-mill heart attacks, he'd like to find whoever told him that particular lie and beat him to death.

He's having trouble keeping his lunch down—the nausea is almost overwhelming. The last thing he needs right now is to throw up. He's halfway through the third morgue room and he still hasn't found Gallegos. Maybe they did put him in some kind of Evo containment drawer, though he doesn't know why they would. It's not like being an Evo is contagious. Hell, with all the homeless cases that come through here, they're in more danger of catching TB than suddenly coming down with superpowers.

He pulls another drawer and glances at the I.D. tag on the bag, and there he is, finally. Hugo Gallegos. Dearing unzips the bag and is assaulted with a stink like Satan's own butthole. Even with all the bleach and the near-freezing temperatures, Gallegos is ripe. It doesn't help that his skull is like a crushed melon and his torso is almost cut in half. Only shreds of meat and his spine are holding him in one piece.

"Well, hello, Hugo," Dearing says. "Fancy meeting you here." He zips the body bag back up and hauls Gallegos out of the drawer. Now, to get him back to the roof and then up to his car. He tosses Gallegos' body over his shoulder, and even with the body bag sealed, he gags from the stink so close to his head. When he's done with this mess, he's going to burn the clothes he's wearing.

He edges the door open and then halts. Footsteps around the corner, voices. He strains to hear. An argument. Martinez going on about jurisdiction or something. And then Dearing hears another voice and time stops.

"We just need a few hours with the body and then we'll be out of your hair," Weller says. "I don't know how to make it any more plain, Doctor. I have a court order. I have a pathologist. Why are you stonewalling?"

Dearing's mouth goes dry, his heart hammering. He holds his breath and listens. If they come in here, he's sunk. He clenches his fist. He won't go down without a fight.

"I don't like you, Agent Weller," Martinez says. Thank god for crotchety old farts. "And I'm not stonewalling. Before you're going back there, you're filling out paperwork. I hate paperwork. I think other people should hate paperwork, too."

"We signed in already," Weller says, irritation in her voice.

"Congratulations," Martinez says. "That wins you a dollar. Would you like to try for two? I'm talking about the county release. The office tracking forms. And anything else I think I need your signature on."

"Is it going to be like this the entire time I'm here?" Weller says.

"Probably," Martinez says. "Now, if you'll follow me."

The footsteps recede into the distance. Dearing figures he has a few minutes, possibly longer, depending on how annoyed Martinez is and how fast Weller can sign her name. He slips out the door, Gallegos' body slung over his shoulder. The bag sloshes as it shifts. As quietly as possible, he heads down the hall toward the back of the building. He goes up to the roof exit, his heart pounding in his chest, and tries to open the door. The knob doesn't budge. He must have done something to the lock when he picked it. He rattles it, but it doesn't give. He twists the knob, hoping to loosen it with a little extra strength, but instead it comes off in his hand.

This night just keeps getting better. He could kick the door open, but he's still hanging on to the hope that he can get out of this without drawing too much attention. He wants this to look like the body went missing, not that somebody actually came in here and stole it. And he really doesn't want anyone to think it was done by another Evo.

There's a side entrance downstairs next to the loading dock. It's more visible than he'd like, but right now he just needs to get the hell out of here. He heads downstairs past the morgue rooms and cuts down a hallway. He pushes open the big double doors leading to the loading dock and freezes.

That agent, what the hell was his name? Carson. He's standing outside on the loading dock smoking a cigarette and talking on his cell phone. Dearing ducks back into the hallway before he's spotted.

Well, shit. Now what? If he tangles with Carson, he's going to have to kill him, and that's just going to make things worse. His only option at this point is looking to be the roof again. Like it or not, he's going to have to break that door down.

"You're dead and you're just as much a pain in the ass as you were when you were alive, Gallegos," Dearing whispers to the corpse in the body bag. He looks through the window in the door and sees Carson crushing his cigarette butt with his heel and heading inside. He's still on his phone. Dearing moves fast down the hallway to get up to the roof.

"And don't think for a second you're using my

instruments," Martinez' voice echoes in the hall.

"He brought his own, Doctor," Weller says.

They're still around the corner but they're close, and Dearing's too far away from the stairs. If Weller doesn't spot him, Carson will. He ducks through the nearest door into one of the morgue rooms. He can hear them getting closer and closer until they stop right outside the door.

"Which room is he in?" Weller says. Dearing hears papers shuffling.

"Should be this one," Martinez says. "We're still digging out from under this computer glitch."

Dearing had wanted to be careful. Had wanted to do this low profile. In, out and no one the wiser. But that plan's out the window, and careful's a luxury he doesn't have time for. Dammit. He drops his head, grips Gallegos' body tighter against him and puts his arm out like a quarterback heading for the end zone. He runs full tilt at the outside wall of the room and rams into it with all the strength he can muster.

Dearing bursts through cement and brick, pipes and conduits, exploding out of the wall like the Kool-Aid Man from Hell. Dust and shards of brick blow out into the alley. Water gushes from burst pipes and wires spark. Dearing digs his feet in to stop before he hits the parking structure next door. He can't go up for the car—they'd catch him too easily. But if he can get some height, he can jump to one of the other nearby buildings.

He leaps three stories straight up to the top of the parking garage, grabbing the concrete rail that keeps cars from going over the side. He tosses Gallegos' body over the edge and follows it, going flat. He can hear shouts below. Weller and Carson are shouting at each other. He hazards a peek over the side and sees them splitting up. He's hoping it takes them a while to figure out that he went up, but he's not betting on it. He picks up Gallegos' corpse and runs across the parking structure. On the other side is the USC Women's and Children's Hospital.

It's a bigger gap than he thought. He's not sure he can make it, but he has to try. It's going to take them time to get more agents in to canvas the area. If he can jump across to the top of the hospital, he can get to one of the staff lots and steal a car.

"I take it back, Gallegos," Dearing says. "You're actually a bigger pain in the ass dead than alive."

He gets a running start and leaps. He barely clears the gap. His fingers hit the ledge and he digs in, crushing a furrow into the cement. But strength alone won't hold him up.

His fingers slip. He plummets, almost losing his grip on Gallegos' body. He catches the ledge of the floor below with his forearm and hangs on. He begins the slow, one-handed climb to the top of the building and to freedom.

"Which room is he in?" Weller says. She's ready to strangle Martinez.

"Should be this one," Martinez says. "We're still digging out from under this computer glitch." He leads her and the FBI pathologist, a man whose name she can't remember but who she's started thinking of as Comb-Over for his ridiculous attempts to hide his baldness, down the hall. Martinez had her sign five copies of the same damn form and three of another. She didn't know if this was procedure or if he was just marking his territory, but it was pissing her off.

Before he can open the door to the morgue, there's a tremendous crash inside the room. Weller draws her pistol, shoves Martinez out of the way and pushes her way into the room. She doesn't know what she's expecting. A car rammed into the side of the building. Maybe something larger, like a truck.

She's not expecting to see a hole blown out from the inside.

It wasn't a bomb, that much is obvious. Bombs don't detonate so precisely in one direction. Something tore through the wall, leaving an irregularly shaped hole twice as wide as a person and about as high. Sparks and water shoot from snapped wiring and ruptured pipes. Twisted rebar pokes out of the remaining hole like broken fingers. Brick and mortar, drywall dust and chunks of concrete litter the alley outside the building, scattered in a fan shape from whatever force blew them out of the wall.

An Evo did this. And unless it's one who has superspeed or can fly, too, they've got to be nearby. Carson bolts into the room, eyes wide in surprise as Weller steps through the hole. He recovers quickly, drawing his gun and following her.

There's no one outside. She looks up, but she can't see anyone. Maybe they *can* fly. Or maybe they can jump.

"Check around the side," she says. "I'll hit the parking structure." Carson nods and heads down the alley. Weller skips the ground floor. The walls have no gaps, so if the Evo went that way, there would be another big hole. She stops at the second floor, looking across the sea of cars. Visibility is terrible, and she can't be sure there's no one there. She listens for footsteps, but the traffic on the streets outside is too loud.

She heads up to the top floor. If someone did jump up here, staying on the second floor would have left them trapped. More maneuverability at the top, more visibility. And more places to go. She doesn't see anyone, but she checks between the cars anyway. It's less packed than the lower floors. She looks up at the only other building nearby, a hospital. Did the Evo jump across to it? She holsters her pistol. If anyone was up here, they're long gone now.

She meets Carson, Martinez and Comb-Over outside the coroner's building, her mind racing. It's obvious what the Evo came for. But did he get it?

"The body?" Weller says.

"Gone," Martinez says. "We've already called the police. They're sending people over now. Dammit. I hope they're quick about it. I'm going to have to get all those bodies moved."

Weller pulls Carson aside. "What do you think?" she says, her voice quiet. She has a hunch, but she doesn't want anyone else to hear it yet.

"Reminds me of the guy in Boise," he says. An Evo they took down in Boise about six months back had incredible strength and tore a wall through the local jail. Weller looks over the damage. He's right, it does look like Boise. Somebody punched their way through that wall.

"Okay, so someone with super-strength comes in to steal the body of an Evo who just happened to have super-strength."

"Or so Dearing told us," Carson says. "And don't forget the rock thing."

"Right. Two separate powers," Weller says. Something almost unheard of. "Told to us by the guy who killed him. I'm thinking the dead Evo only had one of those powers."

"And Dearing's got the other," Carson says. "It makes sense. All the other evidence goes missing. The only guy who benefits is Dearing."

"Something's not adding up, though," Weller says.

"How'd all the evidence go missing? Yeah, I still don't

think he could have pulled that off. He has help."

"Really good help." Dearing's the little fish here. She doesn't see how he could have made all those records disappear. Hack into multiple secured databases without leaving a trace, and then arrange an accident that kills the pathologist who did the autopsy in the first place. He isn't that smart. Or if he is, then he isn't the one who tore through the morgue. This break-in was sloppy; the hacks were much more subtle.

"So what do we do?" Carson says.

"First, we keep it to ourselves. The minute the LAPD gets wind that we're digging into one of their own as an Evo, they're either going to swoop in and take him or circle the wagons and protect him. Either way, we'll lose him. We need evidence."

"Get him to give us a DNA sample?"

She shakes her head. "That'd tip them off, and it'd take a court order. He'd get a union lawyer, and it would all work out the same way." She brightens and pulls out her cell phone. "We might not be able to compel a DNA test, but I think we can weed him out pretty quickly."

"The annual DNA test," Carson says. After the events of June 13th, Congress passed a law forcing law enforcement employees at any level to submit to annual DNA testing. All of the records are sent to the FBI. "But he's been a cop for years. His DNA tests would have to be spotless."

"We both know there are ways around that," Weller says.

Dearing tosses the shovel aside and wipes sweat from his forehead with the back of his hand. He's been digging for less than an hour and has managed a pit almost eight feet deep. One of the benefits of his particular power: he can dig faster and deeper than a normal man. A useful talent. If you're going to bury your sins, bury them deep.

He's buried a lot of sins.

He drags Gallegos' body out of the trunk of the Toyota he stole near the morgue and tosses it easily into the pit. He's been so focused on the task at hand, driving out to the desert outside Palmdale where he can dispose of Gallegos in peace, that he hasn't let himself reflect on what he's had to do. But now, as he shovels dirt over the dead gangster, he's got some time to think.

If Weller wasn't sure there was something wrong with his story already, she has to be now. Even if she didn't spot him busting out of the morgue, she's got to see how it just doesn't fit together. He's never been one to let somebody else handle his problems, so he's going to have to figure out what to do about her and Carson.

Dearing weighs his options. Take off? He's already outside L.A., he could just keep driving. But how long would that last? He'd never get past the border checkpoints into Canada. And even if he could, they'd just extradite him on suspicion of murdering Gallegos, and he'd be right back where he started. They might be more open to Evos up there, but they're not fans of murderers.

If Weller goes to the department with her suspicions, it'd take time and court orders, and he'd fight it tooth and nail, but his life would be over. All it would take is one DNA test he can't fake and he'd be sunk. He wonders if the man on the phone has a plan for that. Given how he had to deal with Gallegos' corpse himself, it could go either way.

The man got everything else—the records, the evidence. Why not the body? It's not like he doesn't already have Dearing over a barrel. It wouldn't have taken much to get the body lost in the system and conveniently disappeared.

The answer comes to him, and he feels like an idiot for not seeing it sooner.

It was a test. The man wanted to know how Dearing would handle it. Would he cave? Would he run? Or would he deal with it? He's not sure what pisses him off more, the fact that the guy thought he might just roll over and die, or knowing that he's being manipulated.

Dearing tosses the last pile of dirt onto Gallegos and walks over the grave, dragging his feet to scuff the area, blur the edges. He tosses around some rocks and branches from a dead Joshua tree. If anyone casually comes across the scene, it won't be easy to spot. His tire tracks are more of a problem, but that's easy to solve. He has a tarp in his trunk that he'll drag behind him, covering the tracks until he makes it out to the road.

Will Weller go to the LAPD? She might throw her weight around trying to gather evidence, but will she actually tell them what she's looking for and why? He doesn't think so. She'll want to handle it on her own. And given how the department has been about giving her access to Gallegos' case, keeping her out of the loop, hogging the glory, she probably doesn't trust them.

Maybe he can use that distrust to his advantage. If she's holding her cards that close to the vest, it will take a little while before she can get anything moving. That buys him time.

He just hopes it's enough.

In the Los Angeles FBI office, Weller is staring at Dearing's annual DNA tests, searching for something wrong. Though she's not a geneticist, in her line of work she's seen a lot of these test results. She knows what to look for. All Evos share a gene that's responsible for their powers. Find the genetic marker, find the Evo.

How it works is still somewhat of a mystery. Alleles, variations in the gene, indicate different powers. Through research, trial and error, sometimes just dumb luck, the more common powers have been catalogued and put into databases. People who can fly, have super-strength, can bend light—all of these have been mapped. One test can show if a person has the marker and if so, what their power might be. Provided it's in the database.

The problem with Dearing is that none of his reports show the gene.

Just like with drug testing, there are ways around the DNA tests. People can bribe the test administrators or they can buy clean DNA swabs taken from non-Evos on the black market. There's already a booming cottage industry on the Internet for swabs. This works well for one-offs, but doing it consistently is a challenge. The tests are usually performed unannounced and are handled by independent labs. For Dearing to fake it would require him to have a sample ready to swap at a moment's notice. It's doable, but is it feasible? If someone's life is on the line, Weller supposes that it is.

"How's your batch coming along?" Weller says. She stretches and hears her spine pop. She and Carson have been hunched over a table in one of the spare offices going over the reports for the last two hours.

"I got bupkes," Carson says.

They've checked and re-checked the lab results, looking for anything that might be out of the ordinary. Dearing has been with the LAPD for fifteen years, and in that time he's had more than just the usual annual tests. He was tested for the Academy, for entry into the LAPD, for every promotion and office change. He's been tested randomly, consistently, by multiple labs.

And none of them show him as an Evo.

"What are we doing wrong?" Weller says. "We know what he is."

"The evidence doesn't support it," Carson says.

Dammit. She knows Dearing's an Evo. There has to be something that can prove it.

"I need some air," Carson says. "And some coffee. You want any?" She shakes her head, still staring intently at the reports. Carson gets up and leaves the room.

Weller rubs her eyes. Between the mess at the morgue last night and coming in this morning to slog through paperwork, she hasn't slept. She tried. Even considered taking an Ambien, but her brain was buzzing too much. She knows something's here. She just can't see it.

And it's driving her crazy.

Is Carson right? Is there nothing here, and she's just being paranoid? She's seen her psych report at the Bureau. It doesn't come right out and say paranoid, but it comes pretty damn close.

Words like dogged, persistent, tenacious. Also suspicious, skeptical, cynical. Repeated so often that she's sure if she'd been anybody else, she'd be medicated and in heavy therapy.

She trusts Carson. Trusts his perspective. He's always been willing to call her on her shit. She knows she has a tendency to go off the reservation. He's good at roping her back in. If she didn't get good results, she wouldn't be in this job, and some of that success is directly due to Carson's level head.

A knock on the door. "Agent Weller?" She looks up from her stack of papers to see Assistant Director Bowder, head of the Los Angeles FBI office.

Bowder is in his fifties, with salt-and-pepper hair. Toes the line, does what he's told. A real company man. Technically he outranks her, but her team operates in a different part of the Department of Homeland Security that functions at a whole other level. And, like so many men in his position that she's had to deal with, he resents it.

"Assistant Director," she says. "What can I do for you?"

"I understand you ordered some records pulled through my office." She can hear the subtle emphasis on 'my'.

"No, I had them pulled through *my* office," she says. "And had them couriered here."

"It says you sealed the request."

"Checking up on me, Assistant Director?"

Weller knew something like this would happen. If she had been back at Pelican Bay, she wouldn't have had to lock down the details of the request. The fewer people who know what was pulled, the better. It was bad enough she had to deal with watching out for the LAPD, but here she had to watch out for her own people, too.

"It would be irresponsible for me to not know about everything that comes into or through my office. Agent."

"Don't swing your dick around with me, Walter. We both know you'll lose."

"I know why you're in my city, Tracy. What I don't know is why you're still here. You were supposed to pick up a body and go home. And now I have you sorting through, what are those, DNA results?"

Weller scoops up the two stacks as Bowder cranes his neck to see them. "They're part of an ongoing investigation."

"In Los Angeles. Which, as an Assistant Director and the agent in charge of this office, I'm entitled to see."

"No, Walter. You're not. And you know you're not. And

every time I'm down here, you pull this crap. What are you looking for? A promotion? A chance to knock me down a few pegs? Assistant Director not good enough for you? You want the sexy job of going after Evos?"

"I—"

"Let me stop you before you give me some bullshit answer," Weller says. "Mine is a job that doesn't just protect the national interest, but the world's. Things are changing. If we don't stay on top of it, everything's going to fall apart. You're not equipped to do this job. The less you know about it, the better. For both of us. So go away, leave me alone, and let me do my job."

Bowder stares at her, hate radiating from him like heat from a four-alarm fire. "I want you out of this office by this afternoon," he says.

"Happily."

He slams the door closed and stomps down the hall. Every time, every office, she has to deal with this. Her people get the same treatment just because her name's associated with them.

She doesn't know what bothers her more, that they all want her job or that they all hate her for having it.

She pushes it out of her mind. Bowder is a small-minded bureaucrat who isn't worth her time. She has more important things to do.

She grabs a report from the combined stack. She hasn't seen this one yet. One of Carson's. It shows the same thing all the others show. Dearing isn't an Evo.

But then her gaze is arrested by a detail. Most of the labs the LAPD uses just test for the Evo genetic marker. But a few test for more. Parts of the DNA that don't change. They're the same at fifteen years old as they are at seventy.

Carson comes into the room with a cup of coffee. "You find something?"

"These two reports?" she says. "They don't match." She digs through the stacks looking for others like them. She finds three a few years apart. They don't match, either.

If all anyone's looking for is the Evo gene, they won't find it, because it isn't there. But all of these results came from different people. Odds are good that none of them is Dearing.

"This doesn't prove anything," Carson says. "A good attorney can spin a story about lab incompetence. It's not like that hasn't happened before."

Carson's right. It happens more often than anyone wants to admit. Particularly in the early days before the mutation was well understood. After June 13th, everything changed. Paranoia was rampant and flawed DNA tests were common.

"Maybe not," Weller says. "But it's enough to compel a new test. And we can make damn sure he can't fake it."

"Do you think he knows?" Carson says. "That his results don't match?"

"If he did, he'd have tried to get rid of them a long time ago."

Weller marks each report's differences. Get it in front of a judge, get Dearing into the office to do a test where he can't mess with it. The minute she brings it to a judge, he'll lawyer up with a police union rep. She needs this to be ironclad. She'll strap Dearing to a gurney if that's what it takes.

"I've got you now, you son of a bitch."

Dearing wakes to the sound of his phone ringing. He glances at his alarm clock. He's only been home for a few hours, time spent washing up and putting his clothes, covered in dirt and stinking of Gallegos' corpse, into a trash bag. He'll take it to a junk yard he knows that'll burn anything he wants for a price, no questions asked.

Then he sacked out and was asleep in minutes. Looks like he was only asleep for minutes, too. Less than an hour. He grabs the phone. Murphy. This can't be good.

"Hey," he says. "What happened this time?" He can think of a good fifteen or twenty really bad things at the moment, any one of which Murphy could be calling him about. Whether it's as a warning or to throw him under the bus, he's not sure.

"You hear about the morgue?" Murphy says.

Dearing hasn't had a chance to see the news yet. Is he screwed? Do they know who he is? He could dig officially, but then he'd have to explain how he knows about it. He's been desperate for any information.

"No, what happened?" He tries to not sound too eager.

"Some Evo broke in and stole Gallegos' body."

"Jesus, they got any leads? A description?"

"Nobody saw, and that Fed was right there when it happened. That took balls. Man, woman, tall, short. No clue. And I'm okay with that," Murphy says. "Whoever it was did us a favor. That should put the Feds onto the Evo and off your back. The longer this guy stays in the wind, the better for us. And believe me, he's gonna stay in the wind. Evans and I got assigned to the case."

Talk about dumb luck. Or maybe it wasn't luck at all. "How'd you pull that off?"

"Don't know. Captain called us in last night. I figured our caseload was too full, but he cleared our slate to focus on it. We'll have this thing buried in no time." That wasn't an idle boast. Nobody buries evidence as well as Murphy does. Dearing wonders if a certain unnamed man on the phone knows that, too.

It's great that Murphy and Evans are on the case, but Dearing's still worried. Weller might not know it was him, but she's got to be suspecting. She's going to come gunning for him, that's a given. But will she bring the department into it, or will she try to take him down on her own? Dearing hopes her ambition outweighs her common sense.

"You round up anything on Gallegos?" Dearing says.

"Most of his crew scattered, but I found a couple still in town. They didn't know he was an Evo."

"You sure about that?"

There's a pause, and Dearing can almost hear his eyes rolling. "Yes, I'm sure."

Dearing knows the kind of man Murphy is. If he says he's sure, it's because he broke some kneecaps or shoved somebody's hand into a garbage disposal, and once he got what he needed, he made sure there wasn't anybody left to talk about it. That's one silver lining, at least.

"All right. I'm gonna do some digging myself. I want to make sure nothing can link us to Gallegos. If I'm scarce the next day or so, that's why."

"And if anybody asks?"

"I'll call in sick. You hear anything else, let me know."

"Likewise," Murphy says, his tone going dark. "One of us goes down, we all go down." The veiled threat hangs in the air. As if Dearing needed a reminder that he works with predators. He lets it slide. He knows Murphy's paranoia is doing the talking. Dearing doesn't need to prove he's the big dog. Not yet, at least.

"Yeah," Dearing says. "Watch your back out there."

"You too, man." The line goes dead.

And then the burner phone rings. Dearing grabs it off his nightstand. Still a blocked number, of course.

"Jim," the mystery man says when he answers. The

familiarity of his first name coming out of the man's mouth puts Dearing on edge. There's a sense of ownership there that makes his skin crawl. "We have a situation that requires your attention."

Dearing decides it's time to test the waters. "Yeah?" he says. "I need to hide another body? Need to break into the morgue again? You handled everything else, why not that?" He knows the answer, but he's curious to hear what the man's going to say.

"Jim, any assistance I've rendered has been entirely voluntary on my part. There's a saying about gift horses that might apply here. If you like, I can simply drop the whole affair, and let the chips fall where they may. Would you like that?"

"Are you threatening me?" Dearing says. "'Cause I'm kinda done with that for the day."

"I don't make threats. I either act, or I don't. You have a choice to make and a very short time to make it in. You can accept my aid, or you can let it go. It's entirely up to you."

He figured that would be the response. He's got Dearing by the balls and he knows it. And he wants to make sure Dearing knows it, too.

"Fine," he says.

"You'll let me help?"

"Yes," he says.

"I need to hear you ask."

Dearing says nothing for a long moment, then mutters through gritted teeth, "Will you help me?" The man's asserting control. If it didn't happen now, it would happen later. He knows this game. He's played it himself. Doesn't mean he likes being on the receiving end of it.

"Excellent. That's why I'm calling. Agents Weller and Carson have discovered a discrepancy in your DNA test results. Your use of black-market DNA was well thought out, but poorly executed. Much like last night's debacle."

Dearing feels gut-punched. What's wrong with his test results? "I had to improvise," he says, feeling defensive. "I'm sure the county can afford to replace a wall. What's wrong with my tests?"

"Be that as it may, it was still sloppy. As to your DNA tests, they were administered by different labs. Some were more thorough than others. Though they all show you're not powered, they don't match each other, either."

"Dammit," he says. What the hell does he do now? If Weller's figured that out, then they're going to come for him sooner rather than later. He's not about to give up, but he can't figure out what the hell to do. Running is looking better and better.

"I have a solution, if you'll hear me out," the man says.

Dearing wonders how much this favor is going to cost him. He's already deep in the hole to this man. Might as well go all in. "I'm listening."

"You're going to make a phone call," he says, and tells Dearing exactly what to do.

Weller and Carson enter the police station to give their official statement on what happened at the morgue. The newspapers are having a field day with the story but don't know exactly what to call it. Was it an attack? A theft? Is this the precursor to a new kind of Evo criminal? The police are keeping the few details they have to themselves, and Weller and Carson are doing the same. They haven't even filed reports to their own agencies. For now, they're keeping their suspicions about Dearing under wraps.

The station is still cleaning up the damage from the fire-casting Evo from the other day. Workmen are replacing ceiling tiles, blackened lighting fixtures, cracked flooring. Some of the desks have been cleared, their occupants taking temporary space on another floor. The rest are making do amid the noise of half a dozen floor fans trying to dry everything out.

Two detectives, Evans and Murphy, are leading the case. She'd spoken with them when the Evo first caught her attention. They're close to Dearing. She wonders how close.

"Detective Murphy?" Weller says, coming up to the man's desk. He looks up from his files.

"Agent Weller," he says. He stands and shakes her and Carson's hands. "I was going to be calling you two later today to get your statements on the morgue break-in... break-out. Whatever it was. I understand you saw the whole thing go down."

"Not as such, no," Weller says. "We were there, but we didn't see the Evo. He got away before we could get a look at him."

"He?" Murphy says. "You sure you didn't see anything?"

"Figure of speech," Weller says. Dammit. She doesn't want to give away that she thinks it was Dearing, especially not to someone who might be a friend of his. She hands him a file folder. Does Murphy know? Is Murphy an Evo, too? God, now she's seeing them all over the place. She liked it better when things were simple. An Evo robbing a bank was easy compared to this.

"Wanted to drop off our statements," Carson says. "Figure it might save you some time."

Murphy takes the folder and looks over the report inside. "Great. Thanks. Wish everybody was so helpful. That coroner, Martinez? He's a real piece of work."

Weller looks at Carson, who shrugs. "Yeah, really quaint

country doctor vibe with him. Hey, have you seen Detective Dearing around? I need to talk to him."

"No," Murphy says. "He's out today. Flu, maybe? Don't really know."

Weller's looked into Dearing's financials. He isn't living beyond his means in any big ways, but the little ones add up. He's got to be pulling down some extra cash from somewhere. So he's probably flush and can live below the radar for a while. But will he run? If he stole Gallegos' body, it was to cover his tracks. Go to all that trouble and still run? No, he's coming back. She and Carson haven't told anyone about his DNA tests. And until they know where he is, they're not going to.

"We'll catch him another time, then," she says. "Hey, how'd you get the coroner case?"

Murphy shrugs. "Luck of the draw," he says. "Case like this, nobody wants to touch it. Evos who can tear through walls? Me and Evans drew the short straw. You sure you two don't want this?"

"Oh, we do," Weller says. "But we'll let you do the legwork for us before we swoop in and steal it out from under you." Murphy laughs uneasily, like he's not sure whether she's joking or not. Weller just smiles.

"We'll, uh, we'll keep you posted," Murphy says.

"Appreciate it, Detective," Weller says. "We'll be in touch."

"You buy that thing about Dearing being out sick?" Carson says once they've gotten outside the station.

Weller shakes her head. "Not a bit. He's up to something, but I don't think he's doing a runner. Probably trying to clean up some other evidence before he shows himself. Something we don't know about yet."

"How about Murphy? You think he's in on this?"

"If he's friends with Dearing, I think he's dirty, but that's a far cry from covering up an Evo. No, I don't think so."

"So what do we do now? I can get Judge Horner on the phone. We've got enough for a warrant."

"Yeah, I think it's time we—" Weller's phone rings. A number she doesn't recognize. Local. She answers it.

"Weller," she says.

"It's me. Dearing." Weller freezes mid-step. She nods at Carson's questioning face. "I can't do this anymore, Agent Weller. I just… I just need to stop." Dearing sounds like hell. Like he's three days into a bender, voice like ground glass.

"All right," Weller says. He sounds like a jumper. Fragile, like if she says the wrong thing, this moment will shatter, and he'll be lost to her. If it were that simple, she'd let him jump. But when Evos get suicidal, they tend to take a lot of other people out with them. "What can't you do, Detective? Can you tell me?" If she can get him to say it, to admit what he is, she might be able to talk him off that proverbial ledge.

"You know what, Weller. You know." Whatever's going on with him, he still doesn't want to admit what he is. She can work with that.

"Okay," she says. "Do you want to meet? Talk?"

"Yeah," he says, his words slurring. She wonders if he's drunk. "Talk. Let's talk."

"Great," she says. "Come into the station. Better yet, meet me at the FBI field office. We can—"

"What, do you think I'm crazy?"

Was kind of hoping, yeah, Weller thinks. "No," she says instead. "Not crazy at all. Just a guy who wants to get something off his chest. Isn't that right? How about we meet…" She searches for a place. Any place that's out of the way, clear of people. Someplace she can take him into custody easily, quietly. The man tore through a goddamn wall like it was a wet Kleenex. She doesn't want to imagine the kind of damage he could do in a crowd.

"Grand Central Market," Dearing says before she can finish her sentence. "Downtown."

Dammit. "I don't know where that is," she lies. She doesn't know much about Los Angeles, but she knows her way around the criminal courts downtown. She's spent plenty of lunch hours there while cases were being tried at the Stanley Mosk Courthouse or the U.S. District Court. The market is packed with lunch counters, food stalls, produce marts. Day or night, the place is a zoo.

"Third and Broadway. I'll meet you there in an hour." He hangs up. For a second there at the end, he wasn't slurring and sounded suddenly more lucid.

"That was him?"

"Yeah," she says, punching an FBI number into her phone. "Get on the horn to the field office. I want as many men as we can get downtown in less than an hour. Quietly."

"That's going to take some doing. Do I tell them who we're going after?"

"No. Just say we've got a potential Evo situation and I need men. Have them meet us at the Justice building on Alameda. I'll brief them when we get there. I don't want Dearing's name getting around. The last thing we need is the LAPD involved. He'd spot them in a hot minute and run."

An FBI operator comes on the line, and Weller gives him her name and ID number. "I need an immediate trace on a phone that was used to call this number a few minutes ago."

"One moment," the operator says, and puts her on hold. It won't take long. In the digital age, it all happens at lightning speed. They can backtrace the call, get a location. Maybe they can avoid this whole mess and take Dearing in before he can represent a danger to civilians.

The operator comes back on the line. "You sure you got a call, Agent Weller?" he says.

"What are you talking about? Of course I got a call."

"We're not finding anything in the system."

"Look harder," she says. "I need to know where the call came from. Now."

"Ma'am, there's no call in the system. I'm looking at five different screens."

Weller punches up her call history. Right there on the screen. A fifteen-second call. Blocked number. "And I'm seeing the call on my screen. So you've got a problem and you need to fix it right the hell now. Call me back when you have a location." She hangs up.

The Bureau's got direct access to every call that comes into one of their phones and standing agreements with most of the service providers enabling them to pinpoint a phone's location, whether it's actively making a call or not. It just needs to be on.

So how the hell can they not find it?

"Got Assistant Director Bowder," Carson says, handing her his phone. "He wants to talk to you. The 'It's an Evo problem' isn't flying."

She snatches the phone from his hand. "Assistant Director Bowder. What's the problem?"

"I don't know, Agent Weller. Why don't you tell me?"

"We've got a developing Evo situation in downtown L.A., and I need a tactical team here in less than an hour. I'd use my own people, but they're not here."

"Then call local law enforcement," he says. "Why aren't you involving the LAPD in this?"

"You know I don't need to tell you a goddamn thing, Walter. My taskforce—"

"Is going to get people killed," he says, interrupting her. "You want me to send a tactical team into downtown Los Angeles, teeming with civilians, without involving the police and without telling me what they're getting themselves into?"

"Do I need to remind you of my job, Walter? Of how dangerous these things are that I go after? Do I have to explain who put me in this job? Who I report to? If I want to commandeer each and every one of your people I can, and you know it. Or do I need to quote the Patriot Act amendment that makes you my bitch? Now, get me a goddamn team, do it fast and do it quietly."

She hands the phone back to Carson. "Assistant Director?" he says. "Yes, sir. I understand, sir. Excellent. We'll meet them at the DOJ office downtown. That would be perfect. Thank you very much, sir." He hangs up.

"I hate that man," Weller says. It amazes her that even now, after the June 13th attack in Odessa, after so many dead, people like him still don't get that there's a war on. It's humanity versus Evos, and humanity's on a losing streak.

"I'd say the feeling's mutual. We're meeting them in twenty."

"That won't give us much time to get them in place."

"Maybe we should just shoot Dearing when we see him," Carson says.

"I'm considering it."

Weller sits at a table in the back of the Grand Central Market, surrounded by the crush of the lunch crowd and the scents of a dozen different cuisines. She scans the throng for any sign of Dearing, but she doesn't see him. She has a sniper on the roof of a nearby building watching the building and a three-man tactical team waiting in a van on Broadway. Carson is doing a slow circuit of the market. If Dearing's already here, she or Carson will spot him, and if he isn't, the sniper will see him on the way in.

She had been serious when she told Carson she was considering having the tac-team gun Dearing down. If he's an Evo and he decides to go ballistic in here, a lot of people are going to get hurt, possibly die. But if she shoots him and turns out to be wrong about him, everything she's worked for, everything she's tried to build would come crashing down. Her career would be over. She'd probably go to prison for a very long time.

Dammit. She knew at some point something like this was going to happen. She'd run into an Evo who was higher up on the food chain than a lowlife bank robber. She's just glad it's some pissant police detective and not, say, a senator.

And she knows Dearing is an Evo. Can feel it in her bones. But without a DNA test or at least an eyewitness display of what he can do, she's on rocky ground.

"Target spotted," one of the snipers says over the radio. "Coming down Broadway from Third."

"I have him," Carson says. "He's inside. He's…"

"What?" Weller says. "What's he doing?" She tenses. Does she call in the tac-team? Does she clear out the building? Dammit, what was Dearing doing?

"He's buying a latté."

"Say again?"

"He's buying a latté at a coffee joint near the entrance. How did you say he sounded when he called you?"

"Broken," she says. "Like he was about to jump off a bridge."

"He doesn't look it. Shit. He's spotted me."

"Tac-team, get ready to move." Weller stands up, craning her neck to peer over the sea of people. She spots Dearing and Carson talking. He's right. Dearing doesn't look like a man teetering on the edge. Carson glances over his shoulder, and Dearing follows his gaze.

He waves.

What the hell is going on? A minute later, a very confused Carson is leading Dearing over to Weller. Dearing looks relaxed, a little annoyed, but he's clearly not about to snap.

"Agent Weller," he says. "I'm here. What's this all about?"

"You tell me," she says. Her hand is hovering near her pistol. She can feel the weight of all these people in here with them. If he moves, can she take him out fast enough? Can she keep these people safe?

"The hell are you talking about?" Dearing says. "You called me. Said you had something important to tell me about the Evo I took down."

"No," Weller says. "You called me."

He frowns. "No, I didn't."

"That's impossible," Weller says. Is it? But doubt creeps in around the edges. Scenarios unspool in her mind. The phone call that wasn't in the system. The non-matching DNA results. The missing evidence. Was all that a ruse to set Dearing up? Or to set her up? But why? There are always whispers of conspiracy. Some of them are even true. Terrorist cells, Evo organizations intending to eradicate humans, human organizations eradicating Evos. No one caring who gets in their way.

"These days, the impossible happens hourly. What exactly did you think I said?"

"That you—"

Gunshots ring out, forcing them to the floor. Short bursts

of automatic weapon fire. Weller's radio is a cacophony of confusion. Yells, multiple voices all going at the same time. The people in the market are adding to the noise, their screams as they scatter mixing with the screams in her earpiece, making it impossible to determine what's going on. Half the crowd is hunkering down, the other half running over each other trying to get away.

The radios go silent, the gunfire stops.

"Who the hell is shooting?" Weller yells. "Somebody talk to me, goddammit."

"This is Sniper One. I have visual. Somebody got into the tac-team's van. He's coming out. He's got one of tac-team members by the arm. White male, bald, red goatee. I'm taking a shot." A gunshot rings through the streets, echoing off the buildings. "Holy shit."

"What?" Weller says. "What the hell is going on?"

"The bullet went right through him. And then he turned into smoke," the sniper says. "He just turned into green smoke. The smoke's flowing into—Holy shit, he just exploded our man's head. What the hell is this guy?"

Green smoke. Gas. Oh, no.

She looks at Carson, his wide-eyed look confirming her fears. It's the Evo she locked up in Pelican Bay less than a week ago. The one they used the new nasal shunt on. Who murdered five police officers, wounded three agents. Who they only took down when he was foolish enough to hide in the bank vault he was robbing and they managed to electrify it, turning him solid.

"Barton," Weller says, remembering his name. "How the hell did he get out?"

"He shouldn't have been able to," Carson says. "He had the nasal shunt. We had an incinerator installed outside his door."

"Who the hell is Barton?" Dearing says. "What's going on? Tell me or give me a radio."

"He's an Evo who can turn into toxic gas and will try to get into your lungs. But instead of just poisoning you to death, he likes to go solid and explode you from the inside."

"That sounds bad," Dearing says, pulling his phone out and punching in a number.

"What the hell are you doing?" Weller says.

"Calling this in. We've got an Evo out there who can turn into poison gas, and he's crawling into people's bodies and blowing them up? I don't even want to know what the hell he does after that happens. We need backup."

She wants to bat the phone out of his hand, but she knows he's right. They can't handle this on their own. And what's the point in hiding anything from him now? A minute ago, she had been sure she knew what was going on. Sure that Dearing was an Evo hiding in plain sight. Now she has no idea. Somebody's playing them all for fools. Dammit, how did she not see any of this? How did everything go to hell so fast?

"Tell them they need shock batons," she says. "Hitting him with voltage will make him go solid for a short while. It might keep him solid enough where they can take him out. And tell them to wear gas masks. Better yet, hazmat suits. Treat it like a chemical spill."

Dearing nods. He gives his name and badge number when the dispatcher comes on the line, starts rattling off details.

"Sniper One. Do you still have eyes on him?" Weller says into her radio.

"Negative."

"Can anyone see him?" A chorus of negatives answers her.

"He's here for us," Weller says. "We need to get out there."

"With respect, ma'am," Sniper One says, "I just watched

him pop a skull like he was dynamiting a zit. I think that's a really bad—" His words are cut off by a choking cry. There's a sound like a rushing of air, and then a thick, wet pop.

Weller bolts for the door. If she can draw Barton off, get him to focus on her, maybe she can distract him long enough that… She's not sure what, really. She doesn't have a plan. Get out there. Draw him off. Maybe the police can take him out.

Most of the civilians have gotten out of the market, but there are plenty of stragglers, people hunkered down in food stalls, behind walls. They're afraid, and they should be. They can ignore what the world is turning into until it comes in and smacks them in the face. If it wasn't for people like Weller, they'd all just let the world roll over them.

"What the hell are you going to do?" Dearing says, close behind her. Carson has moved on ahead, his own weapon out. "The man can turn into smoke. Can bullets even hurt him?"

"He knows Carson and me. Definitely wants to kill us. We had him locked up in a high-security cell after catching him robbing a bank. He murdered five police officers and wounded three agents."

"And me? How the hell do I figure into all this?"

Weller doesn't know. She thought she knew what was going on, but now, with Barton out of his cell, she doesn't know what to think. If he escaped, why wasn't she contacted? Why wasn't there an alert posted? She had thought Dearing was behind all this. But, and she hates to admit it, now she's thinking he's innocent. If someone can get a dangerous Evo released from a high-security prison without setting off any alarms, doctoring some DNA test results would be child's play.

So was their plan to kill Weller and throw the blame

onto Dearing? Why him? Because he killed another Evo? God, how deep did this rabbit hole go?

"No idea," she says. "When we're done with this nightmare, we'll figure it out. But right now we need to take Barton down."

"SWATs are on their way," Dearing says. "They're scrambling with an Evo Containment Unit. Squad cars are holding back. They're not equipped to deal with somebody like this."

ECUs have been part of SWAT teams ever since the June 13th attack in Odessa. Created with the same amendments to the Patriot Act that spawned Weller's department, they had better funding than most police forces, better armor, better weapons. Even with all that money, it was a never-ending race to stay one step ahead. New powers were showing up all the time. They just couldn't keep up.

It was the same thing that plagued Weller's team. None of the police departments could rival what she could bring to the table. They didn't have the power of the federal government behind them. If she'd just had a little warning, she would have gotten her own team down here to deal with this themselves. But everything was happening too fast.

She had expected this trip to be in and out. Grab a dead Evo for study and go on home. She's landed in the middle of something, something big, but she has no idea what. Whoever is behind it has resources and connections she can't even guess at.

"You told them he can turn into poison gas?"

"Yeah," Dearing says. "That's why they're sending the ECU. They can handle themselves. I'm worried about us and the people out there."

She still doesn't trust Dearing, not as a cop at any rate, but he's in the shit along with her right now, and they're going to need all the help they can get.

"Barton'll take hostages," Carson says. "That's what he did in Des Moines. He ended up killing three of them before we got the rest out."

"How'd you catch him?" Dearing says.

"He was holed up in a bank vault. We electrified the whole thing. The shock disrupted his powers long enough for us to get him sedated and locked up."

"If he was unconscious and solid, why didn't you just shoot him?" Dearing says.

It's a good question, and after seeing the victims' photos, Weller had asked it herself. The greater good demanded he be kept alive and studied. She thought it was the right call then. She's re-thinking that now.

"Agent Weller!" A yell from out on the street. "I know you're in there. I got a nice young man here who would desperately like you to come on out and have a chat with me."

"Told ya," Carson says. Weller glares at him, but he just shrugs.

"You do that, he'll kill you," Dearing says.

"I don't think he's going to kill the hostage," Weller says.

"Let the cops do their jobs," Dearing says. "They'll be here in a few minutes."

"If I don't see you out that door in ten seconds, Agent Weller," Barton yells, "Bryce here is gonna have himself an awful headache."

Shit. "I'm coming out," Weller yells back. Then, quietly, "I'll try to get him to release the hostage and stall him long enough for the ECU to get here."

"How close was your tactical team to the entrance?" Dearing asks.

"Just outside."

"Okay," Dearing says. "They had shock batons, right?"

"And twelve-gauge shock rounds," Weller says. They loaded just like typical shotgun shells, but instead of shot, they fired a multi-barbed projectile that punctured the skin and delivered twenty seconds of high voltage. Against most Evos, it was a perfect deterrent. The shock disrupted their muscle control, their ability to control their powers.

But against Barton, they'd be useless. The rounds would just go right through him like any other bullet.

"You draw his attention," Dearing says. "We might be able to get hold of them and get the drop on him."

Weller considers it. Is this a trap? Is Dearing on the level? Her paranoia is saying no, but she doesn't see how she has much choice.

"Clock's ticking, Agent Weller," Barton yells.

"This is insane," Carson says. "We need backup. That hostage won't be the only one dead if we go outside."

"Fine," Weller says. "I'll try to get him away from the entrance. Grab those batons. Make it count."

Pat Barton isn't looking so good. One eye is a deep red from busted capillaries. The last two fingers on his left hand are taped together with duct tape and pointed stiffly away from the others. His nose is a big, purple bruise, one nostril torn and caked with blood. The shunts, even the new ones, are designed to go in deep and stay there. Extracting them requires either a doctor or a pair of pliers and a lot of determination. She's pretty sure he didn't find a doctor.

Barton stands behind the hostage, one arm around his neck. He's little more than a kid, early twenties, wearing a suit that's just a tad too big for him. Maybe an intern in one of the nearby law offices, or at one of the financial firms.

Lot of big corporations down here. He's sweating, shaking, eyes wide in terror.

What's worse are the corpses. The three men of the tactical team are lying in pools of their own blood, their heads so much pulped meat. She looks up at the sniper's location. His headless body is hanging limp over the ledge where he'd been perched, blood running in long streaks down the side of the building.

"Agent Weller," Barton says, his voice thick and nasal. "It's really good to see you."

"Barton," she says. "I'm here now. You can let the hostage go." She slowly begins to circle him. Barton keeps his attention on her, pivoting to keep facing her.

"No, I don't think so," he says. "I'll hang onto him. We're getting to be best buddies. Maybe I'll explode his head like that comedian who sledgehammers watermelons. That would be pretty funny." He shakes the kid. "Don't you think that would be funny?"

"Y—yes?" the kid stammers. Scared, confused. Doesn't know what to do or say. Just wants to go home and forget this ever happened.

"I'll get you out of this," Weller says. "You know the police are coming, right, Barton? They've got the equipment to take you down. You're not going to walk away from this."

"I was thinking more that I'd float." He waves his free hand lazily in front of himself, the two broken fingers jutting out and ruining the effect.

"What happened to your hand?" she says.

"One of your oh-so-friendly guards decided I wasn't walking fast enough," he says. "Decided to, uh, motivate me."

Even with all this going on, Weller finds herself wondering how Barton's powers work. It's not just him who turns into gas. It's his clothes, his shoes, the items in his pockets, the tape around his fingers. He can turn into a toxic gas and back at will, and yet when he goes solid, everything is as it was before. He's still got a torn-up nose, a blown-out eye, busted fingers.

"Yeah? That sounds awful," she says, still circling ever so slowly. She doesn't want him to figure out what she's doing. "I'll be sure to have a talk with him when I get back."

"Oh, he's dead," Barton says matter-of-factly. "So are all the other guards in that wing. And your people in those offices outside the cells? I tore through them like a fat man at a buffet table. They're all gone. Every last one of them."

Weller goes cold, the blood draining from her face. "That's not true," she says. It can't be true. "I'd have been notified the minute it happened."

"Really?" he says. "Huh. I wonder if your phone's working right. It hasn't been doing anything strange today, has it?"

"You son of a bitch." All thought of her safety, the hostage, Carson and Dearing flies away from her like a panicked bird. "You're not doing this alone. You can't be. Who are you working for? Is it another country? Other Evos? Terrorists? Tell me what the hell is happening, Barton."

"That would be a spoiler," he says.

Blind rage fills her. She wants to kill him. Tear him apart piece by piece. Make him suffer. She closes her eyes. Probably not a good strategic move, but right now she doesn't care. She collects her thoughts. Counts to five. When she opens her eyes, her anger is tamped down hard and tight, compressed into a diamond, lodged deep inside her. She'll let it out soon enough, and when she does, Barton is going to pay for everything he's done.

But right now she has other concerns. She keeps walking,

slowly, casually. Barton keeps pace, never takes his eyes off her, or his hand from the kid's neck. Finally she gets his back to the market entrance. Now she just needs to keep it there.

"How does that work, exactly?" she says. "The gas. How come you don't choke on it? If you can rearrange yourself into smoke, shouldn't you be able to fix something as minor as a couple broken fingers when you turn back? Is it that you can't? Or that you don't know how?"

"Oh, I'll show you," Barton says. "Just you wait."

Behind him, Dearing and Carson creep out of the building toward the van. Its doors are thrown wide open. Carson steps up into it, wincing as he makes an almost imperceptible sound. Weller keeps her eyes on Barton, her breathing even. She can't flinch. Can't give any sign of what's going on. She hears the van creak under Carson's weight, but if Barton can hear it, he gives no sign.

"I think you don't know what you can do. What your limits are. How to control yourself. Great, you can turn into poison. Whoop-de-fucking-do. There's a guy who can make earthquakes. A woman who can make you see and think anything she wants. You're nobody, Barton. You're a two-bit thug who got the golden ticket and doesn't even know what to do with it. Rob banks? Was that it? Was that your big goal in life?"

"Lady," the hostage says. Tears streak his face. Long rivulets that remind her of the sniper's blood staining the building. "I think you're making him mad."

She doesn't want this kid to die, but she needs to keep Barton's focus. Give Carson and Dearing some time to get behind him. She can see them out of the corner of her eye, slowly creeping up on him, shock batons at the ready.

"Oh, you're making me mad, all right," he says. "And let me show you what happens when I get mad."

"Barton, no!" But it's too late. He coalesces into a Barton-shaped cloud of green gas that condenses into a thin rope and envelopes the kid's head. It flows into his mouth, his nose, his ears, through the corners of his eyes.

The kid—God, what was his name, she can't remember his name—clutches at his face, his throat. Claws at himself, trying to get the smoke out. He's choking, can't make a sound, his skin goes blue as the poison takes hold. His chest expands, his eyes bug out. He falls to his knees, choking, digging into the sidewalk like he's tearing a hole all the way to China.

And then he explodes, his body tearing apart at the seams, green gas flowing out of him.

The gas wavers, takes on a shape, solidifies. And there's Barton, standing right in front of her. Not a speck on him. A sick, feral grin on his face. He's proud of what he's done. Ecstatic. She was wrong about him. He's not a two-bit thug—he's a monster.

"I'm going to kill you," she says, her voice barely more than a whisper.

"You gotta catch me first," Barton says.

"I think I can help with that part," Carson says behind him, swinging the shock baton at his mid-section. Weller can't look. Can't tear her eyes from the intern's destroyed body. It looks like it's gone through a combine thresher. She wonders how they're going to identify him. She hears the contact, the loud, bee-sting whine of the shock baton. Can see the sparks dancing in the corner of her vision.

She's going to relish this. She's going to take Barton apart piece by piece. She'll have the doctors dissect him and pull every little genetic secret out of this abomination. And when they can't get any more from him, when he's nothing but a hollowed-out shell, then she'll throw him into a deep, dark hole where he can be forgotten.

She looks up, a slow smile playing at the corners of her mouth. And freezes.

Barton's still standing, a shit-eating grin on his face. Carson is on the ground, unconscious, twitching. Smoke drifting lazily from his body.

And Dearing's holding the shock baton.

"You son of a bitch," Weller says. "You were part of this the whole time. You're the Evo who was at the morgue."

"I didn't plan this," he says, as though it's some kind of an excuse. But not an apology. An explanation. "Everything just sort of fell apart. If you hadn't come here, Weller. If you hadn't dug. We wouldn't be here right now."

She looks down at Carson's body. If he's alive, he won't be for long. They can't let him live. They can't let her live, either. She pulls her gun from her holster. She might not be able to put a bullet into Barton, but she can sure as hell put one into Dearing.

Green gas erupts into her face, and her shot goes high. She doesn't know if she hit Dearing, if she hit anything. The gas is all around her, blinding her, choking her. Its acidic stink fills her nose. She bats at it, knowing full well that it won't do any good. She tries not to breathe, but it doesn't matter. It forces its way into her nose, her ears, her eyes. It burns on its way down her throat.

There's nothing but mounting pressure and pain. She falls to her knees. Through rheumy eyes and a green haze, she can see Dearing standing there, watching her. His face flat, empty, like there's no one home. She wonders if there ever was.

She raises her pistol again, her hands shaking like a final-stage Parkinson's patient. She won't die without taking at least one of these bastards with her. Dearing steps in front of the gun, lines up her shot for her. She tightens her finger on the trigger.

And then she's gone.

"You're Dearing," Barton says. He's taken care of Carson's body. It was really just a formality. Dearing beat him to death with the shock baton. Between the voltage and a super-powered swing, the Fed didn't stand a chance. Barton's job is just to make it look like Barton did it.

"Yes, I'm Dearing."

"I'm not supposed to kill you."

"That's what I hear."

The man looks at the shock baton in Dearing's hand and raises a questioning eyebrow.

"It's just for show now," Dearing says. "Hell, from what I saw, if I swung this, it'd just go right through you, right?"

"Just like the bullets, yeah." Dearing and Barton look over at the bodies. In the distance he can hear sirens.

"If I kill you," Barton says, "they say they'll lock me back up. Someplace they say I won't get out. I don't even know who they are. Do you?"

Dearing shakes his head. "No idea. They told me what to do, what to say. I'm just following orders." Are they orders, or are they puppet strings? He's traded one bad situation for another, no doubt about that. But how bad will it get?

"How do you think they'd do it?" Barton says.

"Do what?"

"Catch me. Lock me up."

"How'd these guys get you? Something about a bank vault?"

"Yeah. I holed up there. Wasn't sure what I was going to do. Kind of freaked out. Wasn't coming out. They weren't coming in. So they electrified the vault. Knocked me right out."

"Maybe don't stand in any more vaults," Dearing says.

Barton laughs. "Yeah, I think that'd be a good idea. So what now?"

Dearing feels for Barton. He really does. He's in a similar bind. Shit options, poor decisions. He wonders what led him to this point. What choices did he make that ended with him standing on a sidewalk with the blood of half a dozen people on his hands? What would he have been if he hadn't been born different? Would being normal have saved him? Or was he doomed no matter what he did?

"There's just one more thing," Dearing says. He points to the street corner. "We need to lock in the evidence. Go there, face across the street."

Barton narrows his eyes in suspicion. "Why?"

"Because there's an ATM on the opposite corner that's got a camera with a clear shot, and the police need a good picture of you. After that, you take off, go to your rendezvous point and our mutual benefactors will get you out of the city."

"They're never gonna let me go, are they?" Barton says.

"No," Dearing says, sprinkling a little truth into the lies that come pouring out of his mouth. That's the trick of a good liar. Always mix in some truth. He's a very good liar. "But they'll treat you right. And they'll take care of you. It's just a job. Like any other. They just need something for the news and the cops, and then you get the hell out of here."

Barton considers it. The police sirens are getting close. He nods. "All right." He walks to the corner, wisps of green gas blowing off him in the breeze. Dearing notices that his feet hover an inch above the sidewalk. He hadn't noticed that before. He wonders how Barton fares in a stiff wind.

Barton faces the ATM across the street. "Here?"

"Yep. Now, don't look at me. Keep staring at that camera."

"For how long?"

Dearing steps behind him, the shock baton tight in his fist. He really hopes this works. "Just a second," he says. He holds his breath, hopes he doesn't get a face full of Barton, and plunges the shock baton into his back. It passes into the man's smoky body with just a little resistance, like air pushing back at him.

"The hell?" Barton says, looking at the shock baton protruding out of his chest.

Dearing thumbs the trigger on the baton, sending fifty thousand volts through it. Barton goes solid as the voltage hits him, his screams choked off as his heart solidifies around the baton, exploding from the sudden displacement due to plastic and steel. His body convulses, jerking on the end of the baton like a fish on a line.

He keeps the voltage going until he's sure Barton's dead. He releases the trigger and Barton falls, pulling the baton out of Dearing's hand. His body hits the pavement, twitching.

Sirens nearby. Everything looks perfect. Crazed Evo, kills a bunch of federal agents and a hostage. Dearing the only one left standing, another Evo kill to notch on his belt. It's all picture perfect. He's scot-free.

Until his new keepers decide he shouldn't be. He looks at Barton's smoking corpse and wonders how long it's going to be before they do the same to him.

Du-Par's diner in the Valley at four in the morning. Too early for the breakfast crowd, too late for the last-call barflies. The diner smells of pancakes and bacon, coffee left too long on a burner. The staples of late-night dining.

An African-American man with a thin goatee in a black suit and tie sits at the back of the restaurant, a chipped cup of coffee in front of him. He sees Dearing and nods. Besides a cook and a waitress who looks like she's been working there since the fifties, the place is empty. Dearing slides into the booth across from the man.

"Glad you could make it, Jim," the man says. "You should try the pancakes."

"Thanks, I'm not hungry." His stomach has been a roiling mess since he got the call that afternoon. Three weeks and not a peep. He knew the man wouldn't leave him alone. Whoever he worked for had spent too much money, invested too much time for that to ever be a possibility. But as long as Dearing didn't hear anything, and as long as he wasn't in jail, he could pretend that they had forgotten about him.

In the weeks since Barton killed Weller and her people, Dearing's gotten a commendation, a story on the evening news. Everything pointed to a conspiracy of Evos that he had managed to foil. They were still out there, went the story, but this brave police detective had saved the day. He didn't like the scrutiny, but it hadn't lasted long. A Kardashian went and put another selfie of her naked ass on the Internet, and everybody moved on.

"Pity," the man says. "They're divine. So how are you doing? How's work?" As if they're old friends catching up.

"Job's all right," Dearing says. "They're putting me up for a promotion. Probably make Captain this year. But you knew that."

"I did. But it's not like it isn't well deserved. You have a lot of untapped potential. Moving up in the world."

"And I suppose you want to tap it?"

The man grins, sips his coffee. "I don't know. You're a little rough for my tastes." Dearing gives him a scowl in return, and the man laughs. "The company thinks you can do great things. You've already shown yourself to be a quick thinker, good in a crisis. You take orders well."

"What company is this?" Dearing says. "And for that matter, who are you?"

"You can call me Harris. The company is a little firm called Renautas. A forward-thinking sort of business. Tech, energy, genetics, bio-engineering. We've got our fingers in a lot of pies. But one area we're particularly interested in is enhanced people like yourself."

"You want to study Evos. There a good profit margin in that?"

"Not really, no," Harris says with unexpected candor. "Oh, sure, there are powers that can give us a business edge, but we're trying to change the world. Make it better. Make it the sort of place that's good for people, all people, to live in."

"That include letting an Evo rampage through downtown L.A. and kill a bunch of federal agents?"

"It also includes destroying and doctoring evidence to keep a powered police detective hidden from the eyes of those who wouldn't understand."

"Touché. So how far down does this hole go? You have eyes and ears in the federal government?"

"Hands, too. We arranged to cut communication at the detention facility and then let the enhanced loose. Barton was the one we wanted, but there were so many there we could have had our pick. They rampaged through the place like a wildfire."

"You let a bunch of Evos out of a maximum-security prison?"

"Oh, god, no," Harris says. "We're not stupid. We put them in our own."

Dearing stares at Harris, realization slowly dawning on him. "The Feds were competition. You have your own facilities, your own prisons. Let me guess, you have a federal contract now and some congressman who's just itching to move all the troublesome Evos over to you. And then you, what, experiment on them? Control them? Blackmail them into working for you?"

"Do you think what we've done is blackmail you, Jim?" Harris says. "You don't have to work for us. We're not forcing you to do anything. Hell, I haven't even made you an offer. We don't have the evidence that shows you're enhanced. That's all been shredded. Your DNA test records are squeaky clean. And you're not due for another test for, what, eight months? Nine?"

"I can just walk away?"

"You can just walk away."

Dearing knows that's not true. Maybe Harris is telling the truth about the evidence, but with a group like this, a group with that much power, he wouldn't get very far. They'd find some way to screw him over. Maybe they'd frame him. Maybe they'd just expose the things he's already been doing. That would be easy.

"I'm not walking away," he says. "So what's the deal?"

"I'm glad to hear you say that. Renautas believes much the way the federal government does. Some enhanced people are dangerous. Some need to be put away for a long time in facilities that can actually hold them. There's a lot we still don't know. How powers work. Who gets them. Who doesn't. But governments are slow. They can't turn on a dime. Things are moving too fast for them to react to it, and when they do, the response is too much, too little or completely wrong."

"And Renautas will save us all?"

"We're trying. I think we're doing a pretty good job. But

we need help. We need people like you. People with powers who can do what needs to be done."

"And what exactly is that?"

"There are enhanced people, dangerous people, trying to slip through the cracks on an Underground Railroad of sorts. They're trying to get across the border to Canada, forge new identities. But we have an opportunity to get to them before they can do that. You know the tricks. You know how they think. It makes you the perfect person to hunt them down."

Dearing could have told Harris to save the sales pitch, but the man is just so into it that Dearing doesn't want to interrupt. Dearing doesn't much care if other Evos get across the border, end up in a cell, or wind up dead. Dearing cares about himself.

In this arrangement, he'll be a dog on a leash. But at least he'll be alive and outside a prison cell. Harris will be directing the action, calling the shots. Dearing's not crazy about that, but this is early days. One never knows what opportunities might present themselves. And in the meantime, he can play their game, do their dirty work. Smile and eat the shit sandwich that's just been handed to him.

"What about funding?" he says. "I mean, it's a job, right? I'll incur expenses."

Harris smiles. "I'm sure we can work something out. Is that a yes?"

"That's a yes." Even as he says it, he wants to throw up. But he plasters a smile on his face that he hopes looks genuine.

"Glad to hear it. Welcome to the team. You've made the right choice."

Dearing doesn't feel like he had much of a choice at all.

ABOUT THE AUTHORS

David Bishop ("Brave New World') is a comic book, crime, science fiction, horror and fantasy writer. He is the former editor of the UK comic, 2000 AD. He has published twenty novels, including tie-in novels set in the worlds of *Judge Dredd*, *Doctor Who*, and *A Nightmare On Elm Street*.

Timothy Zahn ("A Matter of Trust") is the *New York Times*-bestselling author best known for his eight *Star Wars* novels. He is also the author of the Quadrail series, the Cobra series, and the young-adult Dragonback series. Recent books include *Terminator Salvation: Trial by Fire*, a sequel to the movie, and *Cobra Guardian*, the second of the Cobra War Trilogy.

Stephen Blackmoore ("Dirty Deeds") is the author of the urban fantasy thriller, *City of The Lost*, as well as the Eric Carter *Necromancer* series. He is also the author of a *Wasteland* video game tie-in novella, a *Gods & Monsters* tie-in novel, and *Khan of Mars*.